But this time the gate had a guardian.

I felt her before I saw her, that same surge of power I'd felt from Jürgen, but more elemental, more penetrating. Both Matteo and I stopped abruptly. His grip on me tightened.

She took form from the shadows that clung to the structure where the light couldn't penetrate the fog. The delicate lines of her face took shape first, upward sloping eyes, cheeks, and jaw. Her skin had the same pale hue as the clouds around her and her eyes were a ghostly blue, narrowed coyly. She stepped forward and Matteo went completely still beneath my hands. Her long, long silvery hair danced around her face and her glittering gown flowed in the same mysterious storm. My whole body screamed a warning at a mind that had long since gone numb.

Then she laughed, a light airy sound, completely at odds with the seductive threat I felt coming off her.

"Ah, Matteo, are you going to hide her from Hadria? Keep her for yourself?"

Matteo jerked into motion.

"Get lost, Cirena."

Again the tinkling laugh. She tossed her head back, her hands clasped in merriment. Matteo's arm turned to steel as he held me against him and pushed his way around her. She floated easily aside, her glee never faltering as she watched us.

"Oh, little Matteo, but what if I want her for myself?"

Praise for Tonya Macalino's
Previous Novel

Spectre of Intention

Amazon Reader Reviews:

"'Spectre of Intention' is a cross-genre triumph. Tonya Macalino spins a story webbed with threads of romance, science fiction, mystery and thrill—all cocooned into one gripping ride."

"Both the read and the ride are fast, furiously addictive, and fantastically executed. Overall, a damn fine read!"

"If you like reading character-driven fiction with a strong protagonist and a deft narrative style that never interferes with an old-fashioned ripping good yarn, then Spectre of Intention should be your next read."

"Tonya Macalino – remember this name. You'll be seeing a lot of it in the years to come."

"The villains are bad, the heroes are good, and yet they all manage to rise above stereotypes and cardboard cutouts to become real people with real motivations that the reader can truly care about. All in all, a fabulous first novel, and one that I'm sure will build a fanbase eager for more of Macalino's work."

"I highly recommend it for anyone who likes their romance with a lot of mystery, history, sci fi and paranormal aspects all rolled into one!"

Media Reviews:

"Spectre of Intention had me from the beginning... I couldn't read it fast enough!!... I look forward to reading more from Tonya Macalino! I recommend this book to others and purchase it as a gift. Put it on your TBR list!!"
— *Keeping Up With The Rheinlanders*

"Spectre of Intention is a fantastic read . . . a novel that puts a very sci-fi spin on what initially seems to be a traditional caper, but quickly becomes something more....This is a very dark, very edgy, very creepy story, but there are some moments of romance and humour. It's a very tense read, and one that almost demands your full attention, so the brief mood changes are definitely welcome. Fast-paced, with well-written dialogue, and a mystery that teases you from chapter to chapter, this was definitely a fun read."
— *Bibrary Book Lust*

"The author skillfully winds us in future-tech woven with psi-abilities and explores every person's right to privacy. Action-packed, *Spectre of Intention* is ripe with physical vocabulary designed to keep you attuned to Kaitlin's fear and longing. An intelligent, well-researched scifi is always good to find, and I learned a ton about space elevators. The human story in this book balances the physical science for the technically impaired, mixed in with spicy scenes of passion between the heroine and Cam Glaswell (fans self)."
— Kelly McCrady, author of *The Empire's Edge*

"Tonya Macalino is definitely a writer to watch! SPECTRE OF INTENTION is a fresh, intriguing novel with a captivating heroine."
— Donna Fletcher Crow, author of *A Very Private Grave*

stand alone titles from Tonya Macalino

Spectre of Intention

The Shades of Venice Series

Episode One: Faces in the Water

don't miss
The Shades of Venice: Episode Two
Stealing Lucifer's Dreams

coming Summer 2012.

CRYSTAL
MOSAIC
BOOKS

This is a work of fiction. All of the characters, organizations, and events portrayed in this novel are either products of the author's imagination or are used fictitiously, and any resemblance to actual persons, living or dead, business establishments or events is entirely coincidental.

FACES IN THE WATER

Text:
Copyright © 2011 by Tonya Macalino
Excerpt from STEALING LUCIFER'S DREAMS Copyright © 2011 by Tonya Macalino

Cover:
Photograph Copyright © Shutterstock
Cover design Copyright © Lisa Holmes

All rights reserved.

For information, address Crystal Mosaic Books, PO Box 1276 Hillsboro, OR 97123

ISBN: 978-0-9836303-3-3

Printed in the United States of America

Author's Note

Perhaps it has happened once to you. Perhaps you sat once amongst the stones in solitude and felt something, a wavering sense of the ancient, a feeling that something significant had happened right here where you were sitting. What if, as you were lost in that feeling, a spry old woman invited herself to sit down beside you? What if she leaned in and whispered, "Once upon a time, right where you are sitting, a youth lifted up his bow and his quiver and set off to become a man...."

And suddenly you no longer sat in a tumble of stones, but in a vibrant, living place where the soil and the forgotten foundations remembered their stories to you in resonant voices. Just sitting, absorbing those stories, brought your soul to life in ways you hadn't felt in years, in ways that would stay in your memory for always.

This is the way Alyse explores the ruins of Venice. You won't be able to use her tale to map a tour of the ancient lagoon city. But as Alyse weaves her own myth, Venice and her stones will share their endless legend with you as well.

I consulted a mountain of sources in pulling together the threads of this story. There are a few specific people I would like to thank for their help in accumulating and interpreting that mountain:

Doreen Harper and Gil Jordan at the Northwest Montana Historical Society for compiling a list of resources on historical Kalispell and its local folklore. I've never had so much fun doing long distance research!

Melissa Sladek, the Interpretive Ranger for Lone Pine Park, for bringing the landscape to life with the story of the park's Lone Pine.

Alberto Toso Fei, author of "Venetian Legends and Ghost Stories," for clarifying some gaps in my understanding of the Venetian mythos. He has several other books available at www.elzeviro.com.

Susan Lied, my ex-pat informant, a wonderful, kind woman who performed little acts of translation (Vittorio's gondolier song) and answered all my local questions about Venice with enthusiasm and amazing punctuality.
I would also like to thank my readers Raymond Macalino, Trixy Buttcane, Jack Buttcane, Rob Richards, Tom Cutts, Margaret Hammitt-McDonald, and Teri Watanabe for wading through my rougher drafts with determination and insight. A writer could never ask for a more dedicated and thoughtful support team!

The haunting image of Alyse and her Venice on the cover is the work of Lisa Holmes with the support of John Vincent. I will forever be in awe of these two talented people. Thank you so much...

With that I would close with the typical disclaimer: What errors I've made are my own.

May they serve the story well.

To my husband, Ray,
who, though he put no words to paper,
dreamed this dream at my side.

Chapter 1

People say you have to be suicidal to be in my line of work. Do I believe them? Depends on the day.

Some days being one of only six sensory immersion artists in the world means nothing more than listening. Like today. I listened to my naked feet complain about the lines of sharp cold pressing into them from the diamond-pattern catwalk; I listened to the tiny hairs on my legs, belly, arms, and face bask in the gentle flow of thick aquarium air...and I listened to my heart trip as the dark blue dorsal fin broke the water's surface in the isolation tank just a half meter below me.

Mo, my onboard AI recorded each of these sensations directly from my brain and sent them back to our library at Lone Pine Pictures.

This promised to be a hell of an enactment.

The only thing missing was the easy sibling-like banter I usually shared with the three other members of my team. Instead, we each occupied our own isolated section of the same two meter strip of catwalk over the brightly lit isolation tank. The blame was mine. They didn't want to be here. I wasn't changing my mind.

End of discussion.

I gave Tamsin Leonides, our field producer and my best friend, the nod. The two aquarists and the marine biologist charged with the care of Ike, that juvenile blue shark pacing the water below me, had sensed the tension in my team. The biologist's thick, gloved fingers rapped on the railing, sending small vibrations through the bones of my elbows on the same hollow metal bar. I didn't want those boys going logical on me and balking.

Tamsin wandered casually in their direction.

I knew what the three men were thinking: Ike was a national treasure, rescued from the toxic soup formerly known as the Atlantic Ocean. I was a billion-dollar piece of movie-making equipment. The orderly parts of their scientific minds would see the combination and extrapolate the most likely outcome—a very public disaster and the end of their distinguished careers.

Fortunately for the livelihood of my team, Tamsin was the most innocent of con artists. She easily pinned the trio on the ladder platform. Out of the corner of my eye, I watched her block their mental retreat with an arsenal that was one part professionalism, one part enthusiasm, and two parts well-built, blue-eyed blonde. People tell me I'm intimidating. Not Tamsin. She's approachably pretty. Then she opens her mouth and people fall in love.

"Oh, no, not at all. She's brilliant with animals. In all the years we've been doing this, we've never had a serious animal accident. In fact, you should have been there, Jessie. You would have loved it. You remember *Spirit Guide*, that wolf movie? Well, when we were doing the enactment for that scene where..."

Behind me I heard Ben Norris-Stevenson, our stunt coordinator and my bodyguard, make a choking sound barely audible above the filtration system. Even I cracked a smile. I suppose Tamsin's claim depended on your definition of "serious." Possibly your average urbanized citizen would consider having her tibia cracked by grizzly bear fangs "serious." Or maybe getting a few ribs shattered by a pissed off buffalo would fit the bill.

But Tamsin's little exaggeration was safe. When the shark boys looked over at me, all they saw were long expanses of unmarred skin courtesy of my onboard medic, Margie. Gotta love Margie.

Satisfied that the progress of the enactment was in good hands, I squatted down next to Ryan Gunner, our swarm operator. It was time to integrate with the swarm cameras and get this show on the road.

Even in a crouch Ryan was at least a head shorter than me with sleek short brown hair, a slightly Hispanic cast to his features—as opposed to my hint of the Orient—and a timeless baby face he had finally stopped trying to hide with that ridiculous beard. He gave me one quick glance and then kept his gaze studiously averted. It wasn't because he had issues with the bikini, either. He'd seen me in less.

Grief makes some people uncomfortable. My way of dealing with grief—with this off-schedule enactment—made my people *very* uncomfortable.

I watched him work for a minute as he dragged icons across the clipboard, logging a selection of cameras into the library I use to create sensory tracks for Lone Pine's full-immersion films. It wasn't my way to play other people's games. The awkward silence was theirs, not mine. I didn't feel the need to honor it.

Especially when there were things I genuinely wanted to know.

"How was Haylee? Did she like that Rumpelstiltskin book?"

"Yeah, it was a good pick. Monitor showed all kinds of spikes. So, um, thanks for letting me take the detour."

Haylee is Ryan's six-year-old niece. She's six years old today. She was six years old ten years ago. Haylee is one of the victims of Sleeper's Syndrome, a disease that put thousands of kids sixteen and under into a stasis-like coma. She "sleeps" in the Children's Castle down in Vermont.

Haylee was the sweet, sad reason Tamsin and I picked the aquarium in Portland, Maine, instead of something a little closer to Montana where we're based.

"I'm sorry I wasn't able go with you this time," I murmured.

Ryan still wasn't meeting my gaze, but his fingers stopped sliding over the camera settings on his clipboard. "No big deal. You had your own stuff to deal with."

I just nodded. The conversation was started. That was good enough. I reached past him and pulled the sheet of camera focus dots from his gear box.

"How many?" I asked.

"Nine little water birds." Ryan finally looked up at me, his soft eyes wary. I could see him gathering up his courage to cross the line. He wasn't heeding my mental "no." Maybe I needed to work harder on my telepathy.

"But, Alyse—"

I stood up and turned away. Not enough to say "fuck off," just enough to say "not now." Ryan wasn't a personal issues kind of guy. He dropped it.

So instead I got Ben.

Great.

How hard could it be to understand I just needed to get this over with?

Ben stepped forward from the rail, his normally cheerful face grim. I shot him a pointed look. I wasn't going to break my concentration by talking about why I was here or even thinking about it. My heart was already beginning to race despite the calm concentration I'd spent the last hour building up. My eyes strayed to the shadow image of the predator drifting around the edges of the small pool below us.

Ben reached out his hand. I turned over the sheet of focus dots. His elegant black fingers precisely placed the first dot between my eyebrows, applying an even pressure without brushing my skin. Ben respected how much I hated being touched skin to skin. If only he respected how much I was done talking about this.

"Alyse, we're here for you, baby, but—"

"Ben," I warned. Subtle body language did not work with this man.

The only member of our team taller than me, he stared me down for a long moment. For such a goofy guy, he could do intimidating really well with that bald head, trim moustache and goatee, and chiseled face. Unfortunately for both of us, I was used to it. Finally, he let his hand drop.

"Alright. What do you look for?" he asked, peeling off the next transparent dot and pressing it between my breasts. He let his gaze linger on what my tiny pale blue bikini top revealed before he moved on to my shoulders.

That's Ben for you. The prince of subtlety.

"Arched back, cocked tail, lowered pectoral fins, shaking head…Ben, he's barely a meter long. He's just a baby."

"Alyse, that baby got teeth on its *skin* can rip you open. Forget about the ones in its mouth."

"We've done worse."

"Yeah, but not when your head was cut off from your common sense."

Behind Ben, I saw Ryan jerk his gaze away. I carefully breathed out my retort. I wasn't going to let them rattle me. That wasn't something I could afford during an enactment. Not only did it taint the sensory data, but most predators had built-in fear detectors and I had no wish to introduce myself as potential prey.

One dot went between my shoulder blades. Then Ben hooked my bikini bottoms with his pinky finger and tugged them down a centimeter. His knuckle accidentally brushed my spine. I shuddered.

"Sorry."

"Trying to make Steffi jealous?"

"Not if I want this dick the same length when I wake up tomorrow morning."

Ben gave me a second to settle out before he placed one dot just above my tailbone and one just below my navel. I pulled my rice-stick-straight black hair into a knot and he attached a dot to the crown of my head and one to the sole of each foot. Despite his best efforts, by the time he was done, my whole body was humming. And not in a good way.

I stretched, then let my muscles fall loose, shook it off as best as I could.

"This is going to be a beautiful enactment, Ben. Make you millions of dollars. Now stop wringing your hands like an old lady and let's get to work."

Ben stepped back. "Look at me," he demanded. I obliged, if just to get it over with. "Me and Steffi are still expecting you to come out to the track with us on Friday. You fuck up here and miss that, Steffi's gonna kill me. She's got Monique all greased up and ready for you."

Another retort to choke on. Steffi hates me and I'm not sure I feel much better about her.

But I appreciated his intent and valued his friendship even more. Okay, and maybe I really liked gunning Monique, his vintage 1998 Corvette convertible, through the defensive driving course at the Kalispell Antique Auto Course. You caught me.

"Understood." I gave him my warmest smile while he stood there with his arms weirdly at his sides. It frustrates Ben to no end that I don't do hugs—like he has something important to say, but somebody cut out his tongue. Finally, he brushed a hand over my hair and finally, finally let it drop.

It was time.

Steady, so steady, I turned back to Ryan. "Think we're ready to get started here."

Ryan opened the case and released the swarm. Each tiny camera rose into the air about a half a meter away from my body and fixed on its target dot. It used to distract me the way each video-camouflaged little globe would mimic my every move, zipping in and out, dodging obstacles, but always staying in line with its focus dot on my body. After nine years I rarely noticed it any more.

What I did notice was the little blue fin, and the smaller tail that followed it, still drawing rippled V's in the water beneath my feet. I knelt down and peered out between the blue horizontal bars of the railing. Ike rose close to the surface. He peered back up at me with his flat dark eye. Black to black our gazes held.

My dad had been a volunteer nature reserve keeper in Fiji. He used to tell a story about the shark god Dakuwaqa. He said that the shark god lost a fight against the octopus god that guards the island of Kadavu and, to save his own life, Dakuwaqa promised never to harm anyone from Kadavu whenever they went out to fish or to swim.

I reached my hand out over the water. The young shark seemed to hover. My heart, my soul hovered with him.

My dad, he *wasn't* from Kadavu....

"Alyse, don't."

A rough, powerful hand closed over my arm.

I jumped, snatching my hand back to catch myself on the railing. I jerked around. Apparently, Ryan had summoned up the courage to cross that line after all. He looked up at me with those sweet, serious eyes. In that moment he just might have broken my resolve—if he hadn't touched me. With his hand pressed to the flesh of my upper arm, all I could feel was that horrible grating sensation of skin on skin.

"Please let go of my arm."

"Alyse."

"Please let go, Ryan."

He let his hand fall away. The relief was instant, but so was the regret. The one time he reaches out to me and I smack him away. Instead of trying to formulate a complicated apology, I snagged my goggles and my gill from the catwalk and walked away.

Tamsin hadn't been able to keep the shark boys from noticing that last exchange, no matter how quiet we'd kept it. I didn't give them a chance to react.

"Dr. Brown." I reached out and shook the marine biologist's gloved hand, while I gave his two team members each a nod. "Let's get started." I gestured them toward the ladder. They went. There are advantages to being half a head taller, less than half dressed, and half again more confident than the men you are dealing with.

Ike gave the three scientists a wide berth as they settled into the chest-deep water. After a short wait, they moved out in a ring and made a space for me to descend. I wasn't convinced that threatening the young fish with four adult humans was the best strategy for this enactment, but bureaucracy had tied my hands on that score. Unlike the shark boys, Lone Pine Pictures wasn't ignorant of my past exploits.

Tamsin sent me off with a smile and nod. She'd learned back in college not to argue with me when I got like this. And I liked to think at least she understood why I had to do it.

I lowered myself down the ladder face forward, disturbing the water as little as possible with my entry. The water was an expected shock. Of course Ike couldn't have been recovered off the coast of Mexico. He just had to pick northern Maine. I indulged in a momentary envy of the scientists in their insulated wet suits. Then I gave my goggles a quick rinse in the chill water and pulled them on. I snapped the gill over my teeth and gave Dr. Brown a thumbs up. The four of us lowered into the water.

࿓

He was beautiful.

In the aquarium lights, his long fins gleamed a brilliant blue, his underbelly a pure white. The sleek ribbon of his body rippled through the patterned glow.

I gave my body a moment to adjust to the liquid atmosphere. I had a thousand files of the feel of water against my skin, but I had Mo focus on every detail of the brush of this circulated solution as it slid over me like weighted velvet. This file would not be like the others, a trespasser flirting with a lethal environment that would never be hers.

Curling my legs, I drew my feet away from the rough textured floor, flexing my toes until the memory of the sharp edges faded. I felt the living water smooth over the soles of my feet. After only a moment's hesitation, I pulled off the goggles. The sting of the salt water faded quickly. I pulled the knot from my hair and let the soft billow of it surround me, caressing my skin. My senses unfurled into the water, detecting the gentle rocking motion of my companions, the fluid glide of my guide.

My guide?

I watched him pacing the water, knew his urgency, his tension. I lifted my hand to my lips. If my lungs had been just a little stronger, I would have spit out the gill between my teeth. I wanted nothing interrupting the pure sensations in this file. This was different. This time I wasn't the interloper.

I belonged here.

I knew the moment the shark saw me. His streamlined head swiveled in my direction, his dark, deep gaze fixed on mine. I drifted forward. A subtle shift in that single eye, a surprised widening, the half-circle mouth opening as if to speak, revealing the small rows of razors within. A warning. A warning I should understand.

Understand. Understand.

What should I understand little fish? What should I hear in this rushing silence? Your power? Your connection to that darkness where creation has its beginning and death has its ending?

He swirled again.

Understand.

Reality jarred my body. My shoulder bumped the biologist. I had floated so far forward? A surprised panic electrified my skin.

Dr. Brown turned, shook his head at me. I hesitated.

Then Dr. Brown reached out...and pressed me back.

I looked down at the gloved hand on my chest. I looked up at the shark shooting forward. He was not beautiful. He was terrible. He was not young and small. He was huge and very, very old.

I fought against the inertia of the water to raise my arm in front of my face. He hit me. I didn't feel the teeth pierce the flesh of my arm. I felt my shoulder jerk. Hard. My back hit the concrete pool wall. My head hit next. I struck out with my feet, freed myself from the water. I struck out with my captured arm, rapped against the wall. I heard a sickening snap. The impossible weight fell away.

I looked down into the pink, churning water. A beautiful, small young fish drifted lifeless toward the pool floor. I opened my mouth and my gill dropped to the water. I don't know what I wanted to say—to protest the horrible loss somehow. I'd had the chance to understand. Now it was gone. Destroyed.

Understand what?

Fucking losing my mind.

A stocky shoulder caught me across the stomach; one of the aquarists hefted me up the ladder. For a moment I lost the world to a haze of gray.

When clarity returned, Ben had me propped up on his lap and Tamsin knelt at my side, rifling through her pink shoulder bag. My lips were numb, my body loose, my left arm slowly lighting on fire. I glanced down distractedly.

Oh good, I thought. *It's still there.*

A familiar tingle started in my left rib. Slowly, forcefully it started up the path of my spine.

"Tamsin, Margie is kicking in now."

"I know, I know. I'm looking!" Tamsin's chin-length, wavy blonde hair obscured her face as she dug deeper in her bag. "Got it!" Her hand emerged with two vitamin-mineral poppers. She popped me with one just under my left rib and the other on my shoulder. Close enough.

Ben pulled the web of wet hair back from my face.

"How you doin' in there, baby? You don't look too good."

I peered down at my arm again. In the mess of scrapes and cuts, three large triangular gashes rode high on my bicep. A matching pair bisected my lower arm. I assumed the damage was mirrored on the other side.

"Thing's got a fucking big mouth." God, the words were hard to form.

Tamsin set to work irrigating the gashes with antibacterial solution. The first squirt and I grayed out just enough to hear a disembodied shout.

"Geezus woman, shouldn't you maybe give her something first?!"

"Calm down, mother hen. She got her head smacked against a concrete wall. Her vagus nerve is just a little overloaded. 'Lyse, honey, just as soon as I get you taped up, we'll take you home to Dr. Keith. Make sure all your gear is okay."

I nodded, preferring to keep my eyes closed as a swell of nausea rose and fell in the deepest pit of my stomach. Between the tug and snap of Tamsin's tape and the progress of Margie's little repair bots struggling their way toward the damage, the pain was becoming very real.

"How is she?" That was Dr. Brown. I wasn't opening my eyes for Dr. Brown.

"You want to tell me how the fuck that tiny little fish tossed her half way out of the water?" Ben demanded.

"She was staring it down—"

"Sir, maybe you'd like to think real carefully before you go shootin' off there. She outweighs your little guard dog by 25 kilos at least. You want to tell me what I'm supposed to put in my report to the director tonight? Look at the size of those fucking bite marks! Somethin' you maybe didn't think to tell us here?"

Silence.

I heard feet shuffle somewhere behind me. "Ben, look at his suit. He didn't see what happened. My cameras show him being knocked clear. Alyse, here's your robe."

"Thank you." I love Ryan. He has such a clear, linear mind. The girl is freezing to death. Here, let's cover her up. My kind of guy.

The soft cloth settled around me, but Ben wasn't done yet. "Knocked clear?! Knocked clear by that oversized trout down there? You take pictures of the sleeve of his suit. I want pictures of that for my goddamn report. I wanna know how a ten-centimeter-thick trout went an' scraped a Jaws-sized stretch out of his goddamn suit there."

More silence.

Ten-centimeter-thick trout. A ten-centimeter-thick trout couldn't body-slam you with his snout. Could have so easily taken me apart. Instead he only nipped my arm. Nipped, oh, god!

"Hold still!" Tamsin chided, yanking my arm back over. Whoops. Guess I flinched.

One last tug and snap on the back of my bicep.

"You want something for the pain, 'Lyse, honey?"

Now she asks.

"In a minute. Thanks."

I opened my eyes. The camouflaged cameras still bobbed around me. Ryan climbed over Tamsin in the narrow space on the catwalk. He still had his clipboard in his hand. He learned on his very first shoot not to shut down until I gave the word. Sometimes you caught the best material after the official enactment was over.

"Cut?"

The two aquarists had just emerged from the tank. The one named Robert cradled Ike's body in his arms.

"Not yet."

I pushed the robe to the side and rose to my feet, remarkably steady for all that very professional swooning I'd performed over the last few minutes. On standing, I discovered a headache to accompany a long strip of road rash running over most of my upper back. I blinked for a moment while the sensation crescendoed and then leveled out.

Robert and I approached each other. I ran my hand down the length of Ike's fragile little body, then reversed the stroke to feel the dentricles scrape at the frail flesh on the back of my hand. Tenderly, I lifted the young fish's head and looked into that mesmerizing eye, searching for...something. But he was gone.

Then so was I.

"Alyse!"

Chapter 2

"Alyse Kate Bryant, your Grandpa Don would have skinned me alive for this." Emory Ranger, the Director of Sensory Immersion Services for Lone Pine Pictures, pushed his chair back from his glass-top desk. He ran his hands through his thick white hair, then smoothed it out again. Emory was still good-looking for his age; he wasn't a worrier. I had him worried.

"It's not like I climbed in the tank with a full-grown great white."

Emory glanced over at me. "You look like you did."

He was probably referring to the bright red and purple bruise across the side of my forehead from this morning. Apparently, I'm not a graceful fainter. I'd pitched straight forward...into the steel railing. My knees were now also similarly hued from breaking the rest of my fall. Margie's little bots would have it all cleaned up by tomorrow night, but right now I hurt, I was exhausted, and I was in no mood to defend myself to anyone.

"I didn't and wouldn't. Have some faith."

Emory sighed. "I'm trying." He pushed his gym-honed body up out of the chair. After tapping at his desk for a few bars, he wandered to the floor-to-ceiling window overlooking the city lights of Kalispell, Montana. "Your mother is still here?"

"Yes. She'll be staying at my condo for a few weeks."

"Why don't you take some time off? Spend some time with her. It's only been a week since your dad's funeral."

Do. Not. Think.

Instead I jumped on the easier alarm. Take time off? My shooting schedule didn't have another hole in it until next year. I sat up straighter and spoke to his back. "Emory, you know I can't. *Russo's Watch* needs—"

"No." He turned to me. "No one needs anything more than you need your health."

"Emory, I'm fine. I'll just go home and sleep—"

Emory strode over to me, put his hands on the arms of my chair, and lowered his head until we were eye level. "No—you—are—not. And I'm not going to sit here and watch you kill yourself."

I was the first to back down. I was too tired to fight back the prick of tears threatening to betray me. I turned my head to the side. "Are we done here? I have a full schedule tomorrow."

"Yes, you do. You'll be spending the next three to five days doing documentary work in Venice."

"What?!" Venice? Venice was the flooded ruins where the carriers of Sleeper's Syndrome were quarantined, the people who had put all those children to sleep a decade ago. If the exhaustion hadn't already had me trembling, the anger would now. "Are you out of your ever-loving mind, Emory? I'm *not* taking my people to Venice."

Emory straightened. "You don't have a choice."

I straightened to match. "You wouldn't."

"This time, I *would*." He would what? He would spring the steel trap in my contract: Rejection of reasonable assignment equals one month in solitary confinement—a minor inconvenience for Lone Pine, an excruciating torture for me. And Emory knew it.

As long as this tech was in my head, they owned me. The crude reminder churned my stomach. How could he even consider talking to me like this? Except for a few pesky scraps of DNA, the man was practically my uncle!

"*Reasonable* assignment, Emory. Sending me and my people to Venice does not qualify as reasonable!"

"Quite the contrary. The invitation came across my desk last month." He began a slow circle through the thick steel gray carpet back to his chair, his expression implacable. "The camp has been declared safe for visitors twenty-five years and older. The carriers are taking bids for a big project—they want to create a full sensory immersion tour of the ruins."

He tossed the card at me—textured wood pulp with gilt edges that shadowed and glinted as it whirled toward my face. I reached up and caught it. The second my fingertips pressed into the rough paper, it felt like someone had snapped a steel-toothed bear trap over my arm. My shark bite. I muffled a scream, crumpled over my right arm.

The card dropped to the carpet.

The pain fell away with it.

Understand.

Understand.

Emory ran to my side, grabbed me by the shoulders. "Alyse?"

Gritting my teeth, I lifted my head. The pain might have fled, but Emory was close enough to see the sheen of sweat on my face and clammy pallor of my skin. I pushed myself back up in the chair.

"Are you alright?" he asked, suddenly every bit the uncle.

"Yeah, I'm fine."

"Your medic should have that thing mostly healed by now."

Cautiously, I closed the fingers of my left hand. Nothing. I tried again, a little faster, a little harder. Still nothing. I stared past Emory to the invitation lying in the thick plush of Emory's carpet. A memory of the pain shuddered through my body.

"I must have twisted my arm wrong or something." I tried twisting it again, but still couldn't replicate the moment.

Emory backed off, followed my line of sight to the card on the floor, and snatched it up. He waved the thing in my face. I couldn't help it: I shrank back. One warning was enough.

"That is it, Alyse Kate. The argument is over. You are going." He pushed off the chair and rose to his feet.

"This is ridiculous, Emory! Who on earth would possibly go to this thing? It's called a quarantine camp for a reason."

"You can't catch it, Alyse. You're what, thirty-five?"

"Thirty-two," I growled.

Emory leaned back against his spotless glass top desk and folded his arms across his chest. "And you never had the gene therapy for Brighton's disease, so you can't become a carrier, right? You are going. Consider it a paid vacation. It says right here on the invitation you'll have a luxury suite at the palace with full amenities. You can paddle around in a boat and build up your library at their expense. And come home without a broken bone."

"Emory...." I couldn't finish what I wanted to say I was so pissed. I put a hand over my eyes and tried to get myself back together. Why do people always assume they know what's best for you? Of all the stupid—.

"And maybe you could even take some time to grieve."

I stood up and walked out.

֍

Ben, Ryan, and Tamsin were waiting for me among the chairs and potted plants in the brown on brown hall cum lobby outside Emory's office. Ryan and Tamsin were nursing coffees. Ben, the quintessential health nut, had his hands wrapped around a cup of tea. They stopped murmuring when they saw my face.

Tamsin let out a hiss. "It went bad."

I had to take a couple tries at clearing my throat. "On the contrary, he is sending us on a little 'paid vacation.' To Venice."

Ben and Tamsin stared at me. Ryan turned a nasty shade of pale.

"You don't have to go," I quickly assured Ryan. He didn't even blink. A horrible thought occurred to me. "I never asked. The woman who infected Haylee...."

"Carol Patterson. Haylee's first grade teacher."

"Would she...?"

"She was murdered three days after the announcement was made."

"God." Just what I needed: to go to a place where people had more emotional baggage than I did. I paused as Mo, my AI, announced that Emory had forwarded tomorrow's itinerary. I gave her the go ahead to open it. Ryan, the only other member of my team with an AI—his military issued—also turned his head to face a blank wall, so he could read the message.

Mo adjusted the font color to better contrast against the dark brown paint in the corridor. I skimmed the schedule.

"Looks like you all have until ten tomorrow to think about it. Just leave a message with Mo—whatever you decide."

Tamsin tapped the lid to her coffee cup. "Venice. Good Lord. I mean we've done a lot of crazy stuff before, but it was a specific definition of crazy."

"Yeah, the freakin' non-infectious definition," Ben agreed.

Tamsin's frenetic energy ratcheted up another notch. "Is this Emory's idea of an early retirement party or something? I don't know about this. I don't like this one little bit. What are we going to enact in a quarantine camp? I mean I don't think we need to actually contract Sleeper's Syndrome to put a file together for it. What could Emory possibly be—?"

"You can't catch it, Tamsin," Ryan interjected, throwing a brick wall in front of her.

I added a few more bricks. "Emory said they want to build an immersion tour of the ruins. He's sending us to bid. You know: dress up, drinks, listen to the spiel. Your part of the business." I touched my fingertip to my forehead. "He specifically said that my role was to come home without a broken arm."

"Yeah, I'll bet he did," Ben murmured, giving the wall a dirty look meant for me.

"Is it an indy?" Tamsin asked.

"I don't know. I doubt it. The invitation went to Emory. Look. Take some time. Think about it. I'm not holding any of you to it. Just let me know early enough that I can pack my backup gear if I need to."

I took a deep breath, then turned to Ben. "I'm going to have to stop back by Dr. Keith's for a couple travel kits. He said three to five days."

Ben reached back behind him and pulled a second cup of tea from the arm of the waiting bench. He handed it to me. "Well, I guess let's get goin' then."

We said our good nights, then Ben and I headed back down the hall. Two doors down led us back into the lab of my "mechanic," Dr. Keith Marshall. The poor doctor was just switching out the lights when we walked in.

"Hey, Doc."

Dr. Keith jumped and squealed. It was times like those I was positive the doctor was a girl—just never positive enough to use a pronoun around him/her. Dr. Keith was short and boxy with brown hair clipped close and a mouth on constant rapid fire.

Sometimes I got the feeling it was Dr. Keith's way of keeping people at arm's length.

The doctor pressed a hand to a square chest. "You absolutely scared me to death," the doctor proclaimed. "Travel kits I presume? How many will it be this time?"

"Five day minimum."

"Ah, you and Bryce are going out on an enactment together, then. I always did like the work you did together the best. I finished looking over your tests, dear, and everything looks perfectly fine. None of that wetware was dislodged and your medic did a right fine job as usual. Now let's see." Dr. Keith unlocked the cabinet behind his/her spotless lab table. No creative chaos anywhere in this room—as long as you discounted the space in the good doctor's head. "Five day minimum. Ten kits should do it. Your tests did show signs of severe fatigue, though, my dear. So you go on and get that girl home, Ben. Make sure she gets some rest. And you, too, for that matter. I know how hard she works the bunch of you. She went through three bodyguards before she found you. She doesn't know how lucky she is to have you, you sweet boy, you. Now you two run along. I've got to log the supplies out of the inventory, then I'm going home, too. Little Chester can't feed himself, you know. Good night now!"

Ben and I found ourselves standing back out in the hallway, me with a bag full of travel kits in one hand, a cup of tea still in the other.

I took a swig of tea.

My mechanic could out whirlwind Tamsin any day of the week. Every time I went near her, I left with my head spinning. I clung to one bit of data: my wetware was fine. Between the shark and the invitation, I sure as hell didn't feel like my wetware was fine....

The tea burned going down. I coughed a bit, then sighed contentedly.

"Tamsin thought you'd be needin' something 'lil stronger than chamomile, if you were gonna get any sleep tonight."

"God bless, Tamsin." Chamomile flavored whiskey wasn't going to make it to my list of favorite mixed drinks, but it would do the trick for right now. I took another swig.

Ben and I spent the ride down the elevator and across town through the chute in companionable silence. Ben and I spend a lot of time together. Companionable silences are very necessary.

I'm not sure if it was the whiskey or the downtime, but by the time we reached our building I was ready to talk again.

"Have you had a chance to check in with Steffi?"

"Are you kidding, man? You gonna send me out to do a five-day *doc-u-men-tary*? I'm gettin' my ass laid tonight. Besides we're gonna take a look at this sweet 1955 Corvette. It's got this crazy windshield washer you run by pushin' this foot pedal. It's crazy, man! Can you imagine? You're driving along, goin' ch-ch-ch with your foot. Unbelievable. So how 'bout you? You gonna stay up and play strip poker with your mama?"

Now that was an image I had to laugh about. Although, if she'd married my dad, maybe my mother had been the strip poker playing type sometime in the distant past. How one thought led to another in my exhausted mind I could never be sure, but halfway down the hall to our adjoined condos I froze and looked down at the bag in my hand.

"Bryce is going to be there?"

Ben laughed. "Hello people! A record-breaking delayed reaction here from Miss Alyse Kate Bryant!"

"Ben, I think I don't like you very much right now."

Ben threw up his hands as we resumed walking. "Hey man, it's not me you're gonna have to be worryin' about."

"Yeah, I know."

Once, about five years ago, I broke a very sacred rule: Never date a co-worker. Especially if that co-worker is contracted to be your co-worker for the rest of your technologically viable lives. Especially when every element of that relationship, right down to the most intimate sexual encounter, will become very, very public. The relationship had been the most amazing, insane, and hellish year of my life.

And Tamsin absolutely can't understand why I walked away from it. She tries to fix this "mistake" of mine every chance she gets. Fortunately, those chances are few and far between. And this half of Lone Pine's sensory immersion male/female pair tries to keep it that way. You'd be amazed at the ways I've learned to reprocess old sensory files. So what were the odds that Emory "Tight Wad" Ranger had arranged separate shuttles for our two teams? Zero. Tamsin and Emory were on the same side in this little battle. *Shit.*

Ben was yucking it up about tomorrow's upcoming entertainment right until he slid the keycard through the lock on my condo door. Then he was all business. There had been two attempts on my life since I started this job nine years ago—both nut jobs from the Flaming Sword of God, remnants of the same group that turned Old Hollywood into a big crater lake in the middle of L.A. Only one of the attempts had been on Ben's watch and that had been two years ago. The freak had been waiting right behind the door in my bedroom. God, it still gives me the creeps to think about it.

Over Ben's shoulder I could see my mother with her back to us at the far end of the living room. She didn't turn as he led the way in.

"Good evening, Mrs. Bryant."

"Good evening, Ben."

I walked in behind him and closed the door. Even with my mom inside, Ben still checked all the nooks and crannies. Not only does he take his job seriously, but he loves to put on a good show for my mom. While Ben disappeared down the side hall to bang closet and cupboard doors officiously, I dropped the bag of travel kits on the kitchen counter and passed through my tiny dining area to the living room where my mother was standing in front of the wall of sliding glass doors.

"Looks good, Alyse."

I turned back. "Thanks, Ben. Say hi to Steffi for me."

"Will do. Get some rest, ya hear? And don't forget to do those stretches I gave you and try a hot shower. It's gonna help the beat up some."

The connecting door to his condo was through my dining room. We exchanged a two-fingered wave as he closed the door behind him.

And then it was over.

All the movement, all the distance, all the noise that had buffered me from this moment, it was gone. My mother, Simone Arlington Bryant, turned to face me. Her small, pale face was splotched with red. Tear tracks striped her cheeks.

"Kate, how could you be so selfish?" she whispered.

※

I closed my eyes. I was too far beyond my threshold to erect my usual defenses. I whispered back.

"I had to know, Mom."

A little over two weeks ago at the Aquatic Nature Reserve in Fiji, in the last moments of his life, my father had faced down the maw of a three-and-a-half-meter bull shark. Carlton Bryant's end had been violent and slow. He'd had no living will. It took him three days to die in his half-eaten body. Sometimes I hate technology.

"Let me see."

I set down my cup of tea and obeyed, pulling my thin, black sweater over my head. The pieces of medical tape on my arm had turned neon "good to go" green. I peeled back the first one. Beneath it was a thin pink line three centimeters long. While she watched, I peeled away each of the other nine strips.

My mother, in her impeccable brown sheath dress and matching cardigan, stepped forward to get a closer look. "I don't understand. Emory said the shark was a two-week-old blue."

I looked again at the pattern of lines on my arm. I tried bending my elbow. The tooth marks didn't line up. Of course, neither did the images of the shark in my memory: small, sleek, and blue became black, crushing, all-consuming. I shook my head.

"I don't know. The thing rushed me head on. It seemed so huge, like its mouth was bigger than my head. It was barely a meter long."

I gritted my teeth as my mother reached out to brush her fingers over the marks. I do my best to hide my aversion to touch from my family. But of course they know. She kept it brief.

"A two-week-old. Born when your father died," my mother murmured and chuckled under her breath. "How ironic. I wonder what he was trying to tell you."

To hide my surprise, I pulled my sweater off the couch and pulled it over my head. "What do you mean?" I asked as I pulled my long hair free. I was so tired. I just wanted to spend some time on my balcony, take a shower, and crawl into bed. But this I had to hear.

"On the islands they tell a story of a great chief who haunted the waters as a shark. There was a boat full of people. Twenty-two, I think the old man said. They saw a mullet, but when one of them tried to catch the fish, just as the pole struck it, it transformed into a shark. It was the great chief, Ratu Golea. He told them he had just died and his people had buried him without his wives, the wives who would secure him safe passage to Bulu, the afterlife. He overturned the boat and all of the people fell into the water and were at his mercy. Twenty of the people he ate to replace the wives who had not been strangled to join him. Two, a husband and a wife, he left alive, but he bit out a chunk of each of their calves, so they would have proof when they went out to tell his story."

My mother has a velvet smooth storytelling voice. She can put even the most squirmy three-year-old in thrall. I blinked myself awake and ran a hand over the achy "proof" I'd been left with. I remembered that inexorable draw I'd felt to that fish, the powerful sense that there was something I was supposed to understand. What would Dad have been trying to tell me? I shook my head.

"I don't know. Maybe he was just sending me home. And for that I killed him a second time." I pressed my hands to my face for a moment. Then I picked up my cup of tea and tried another swallow. It wasn't soothing anymore. I put it back down.

"Emory said he's sending you out again tomorrow...on a long one, a documentary."

I nodded, felt a flare of anger, then the required guilt. Not much of a comfort visit for the new widow, if the one doing the comforting was never around.

"Will you be here when I get back?" I asked.

Mom watched me for a minute, then nodded. "I will. Emory has invited me hiking and I would like to spend some time with Ian and Michelle before I go. I was actually thinking about checking in at the old house to see how the renters are doing."

I was picking up some loud subtext. She was thinking about moving back stateside. I didn't know how I felt about that. Retiring in Fiji had been Dad's dream. Part of me didn't want that to be put away and him with it.

"I need to call it a night. You need anything?"

Mom shook her head, her glossy, chin-length brown hair swinging. Looking at her china-doll perfection, I realized anew how little I looked like my mother. When I was a kid, people used to think she was my nanny. And they thought Dad had borrowed me from the neighbors to use for picking up women. Dad would just laugh. He always said kids helped cut down on the loneliness of adulthood, gave grownups a safe subject to use to break the wary silence. Loneliness. That I would remember him speaking of that when what I remembered most was his laughter....

Seeing my mother lost in her own thoughts, I drew her in and gave her the hug I knew she needed, careful to keep my hair between us. That loneliness was hers now and I could see it growing in her, the realization that her constant companion of thirty plus years had gone. Forever. I should have been the one trying to help her fill it.

Right now I just couldn't.

I excused myself and retreated into the sanctuary of my room.

It was a battle of will against the unbearable weight of exhaustion, but I forced myself to strip down, pull on a robe, and slip out onto the balcony. I was instantly glad I did. The crisp September air lifted my hair from my neck. I breathed it in deep, then sighed it out again. Finally, finally home. The woods beyond my balcony welcomed me with their tangy, rich winds and for a brief second I relived that moment in the water where I had known I was someplace I belonged perfectly.

For those woods alone I would dance.

Ben had choreographed me a slow, simple routine of stretches to help me let go of days like today. I stepped to the left of my tiny grassy knoll with its miniature Japanese maple and began. With my knees bent, I released my body forward. The silk robe slid across my skin the way I imagined a caress ought to feel. The front of my robe gapped open. The autumn mountain wind slipped inside, drawing my nipples erect, coaxing my nerves to awareness. I spread my feet and released all the way down until my hands and my hair reached the stone-tiled floor. The breeze billowed the skirts of my robe, sliding its cool fingers up my inner thighs. I dropped to a crouch, cut off the seductive advance, then rolled up to standing. Back and forth, the wind and I slipped and stretched, pressing our advantages while the woods and night shimmered around us.

Like floating through the water.

When I finally finished the routine, I walked out to the cast iron scrollwork of the balcony railing. My condo overlooked the woods, my woods, Lone Pine Park—a dimly lit threshold of spindly pines and brush that darkened into waves of hills and valleys beyond the reach of light. I pulled in a deep breath of life. The wind still called to me and I ached to go wandering beneath the trees. I drew a muslin pouch from my pocket—my woods away from home. I usually refilled it on my brief return visits. There would be no chance this time.

I looked back out into the hidden hills. The lone pine was long dead, the marker guiding pioneers northward to Canada, but sometimes in the moonlit dark, on a night like tonight, I felt the pull of that old windswept tree. "This way, this way, this way home."

Wouldn't that be nice? "Just come here, to my secret place, and you will be content." I smiled softly and slowly turned away.

On my way back through my Spartan room, I stopped at my small dresser. Out of the framed collection on its dark walnut surface, I picked up a picture, a photo of Dad and me on a hike in the park. I moved it to my nightstand next to my platform bed. I lit the sandalwood candle I'd picked up at the bonfire last month and brought it with me to the bathroom.

With the cozy chill still kissing my skin, I opted for a bath, instead of a shower. I let the oversized claw-foot tub fill as I washed my face, brushed my teeth, and pulled out a black silk-cotton blend camisole and short set for bed. The rumble of the water comforted me and I moved half-asleep through my evening ritual.

When the water had reached just below the overflow drain, I turned it off and stirred in my favorite lavender salts. Then I reached over and switched out the lights, leaving only the flickering candle glow to see by. I slid into the tub.

It was perfect.

I sank in just until my breasts were covered, as far as I could go with my lanky frame and still keep most of my legs submerged. I spread my hair over the side. All the aches still left over after the stretching slipped slowly away. It was late; I couldn't stay in long. But I took a moment and let the hot water rock over me, let the steam dampen my face, let the provincial scent of the lavender flood my senses. The water crept up my neck, stroke by lapping stroke. My head lolled to the side on the cool enamel.

He came for me.

His huge powerful body burst through the water straight at me. I had enough time to see the black rot of old carrion, the red blood of fresh kills on his row after row of serrated teeth. He hit me straight in the face. My scream was choked with water.

I flailed. My elbow hit the wall of the tub. The pain opened my eyes. I scrambled from the tub in the near dark. I jerked the towel down and clutched it around me as I collapsed to my knees on the bath mat. I coughed and gasped and shivered so hard. There was a knock at the bathroom door. The door squeaked open.

"Kate? Kate!"

Soft arms wrapped around me and for once it wasn't more awful than right. I burrowed closer. "Mom," my voice hitched with the first sob. "Mommy, he died—." A huge, terrible pain in my chest cut me off, but I had to tell her. She was the only one who would understand. "He died so awful, so scared. My daddy! I can't...I can't....I can't!" I pounded a useless fist against the tile as I screamed.

She held me, rocked me as if I weren't twice her size.

"I know, baby. I know."

Chapter 3

I took the shuttle's only gurney and slept from Kalispell, through sub-orbit, right through the landing in Milan. Mo beeped me awake as Ryan finished parking the shuttle in international long-term. I sat up. For an emotion-based phenomenon, grief has a way of hollowing the bone and muscle out of your limbs, of emptying the pit of your stomach and the contents of your skull until you're not sure if the husk of you is just going to blow away on the next stiff wind.

Or maybe it will simply collapse in on itself as you sit there trying to remember how to move.

I blinked a few times, working to get my brain to engage. This was no state of mind for wooing potential clients. I do occasionally fancy myself a professional.

Mercifully, Tamsin pressed a cup of coffee into my hand.

"Rise and shine! Aiieeee!" Tamsin squeaked as Ryan dropped the hatch directly behind her, blowing a gust of rain-soaked air up the back of her cranes-and-cherry-blossoms baby doll top. I chuckled into my coffee. Now who was shining? Nothing like a nice snug black turtleneck and jeans to make a girl feel superior.

With his pack already shouldered, Cael Jones, Bryce's bodyguard/stunt coordinator, headed out into the dim sunlight to scan the largely empty parking structure. Cael was new and this was my team's first time out with the stocky, cleft-chinned Caucasian. I'd have to get Ben's take on him once we got to the hotel.

A few paces behind Cael, Ryan rumbled down the shuttle steps. Bryce's swarm operator, Johanna Emmett, an athletic redhead with her corkscrew curls habitually tied back in a stubby, spiky ponytail, was right behind him. Johanna has a competitive streak wide enough for an entire platoon. Poor Ryan. Our hapless cameraman does his very best not to play. Johanna grabbed the hatch frame and swung down.

"Oh, yeah, well, guess what I just read? Your Mr. Fleming also wrote kiddie books. *Chitty Chitty Bang Bang* wasn't about a Russian spy. It was about a flying car full of snot-nosed brats!"

Tamsin and I just looked at each other and shook our heads. If Johanna thought she was going to beat out Ryan on James Bond trivia, she had serious reality issues. I pointedly looked away as Bryce and his field producer, Tomaas Ende, followed the pair out the hatch. When I was sure they were clear, I jumped down from the cot and swung my own mobile apartment onto my back—a long, black pack full of enactment gear, clothes, medical necessities, and travel food. With a groan, I jogged the straps and frame into place.

"That's one way to go avoidin' it."

I looked from Ben's smirk to Bryce's retreating figure and back to Ben again. I just wiggled my eyebrows sagely. That was about as much linguistic tango as I was up for until the coffee hit my brain.

"What? What are you guys talking about in your little code this time?" Tamsin demanded. I gave her a nudge toward the door. "No, no, cough it up. I'm the best friend, remember? College roommate, remember? I resent you letting this yahoo horn in on my role." Ben grabbed her hand and spun her out in a pretty little twirl, then snapped her back to him until she was wrapped in his arms.

"Yahoo? Where do you get these weird-ass phrases from, *ex*-best friend?"

Tamsin went from mock swoon to affront.

"Ex?!" she sputtered. Ben started hustling her toward the door. "I'll have you know... Alyse, just you wait and see what I picked up on my last shopping trip to Aladdin's!"

Ben threw up his hands. "This boy can't compete with no silk and leather. I surrender!"

Somehow my little Fred Astaire/Ginger Rogers duo made it down the stairs, very cleverly leaving me doing the one-legged lurch with Tamsin's enormous backpack. Why the thing even has shoulder straps, I have no idea. She never ends up carrying the damn thing.

Fortunately for my spine, Milan had a coupler car transit system. By the time Ben and I got Tamsin's bag across the seventh floor of the open air parking garage, down the elevator, and to the station, Cael had a car waiting. We hustled inside. The gear went on the floor in the middle of the car, the humans on the bench seats along the windowed walls. Tomaas and Tamsin had a few words, then ordered up the route to the central train station. The car rolled forward. The chain of cars on the road opened up and ours slid into the gap with only the slightest bump signaling the connection.

I took in the water-warped view out the window as I sipped at my coffee. If you have to be in the urban jungle, there is nothing like an old European city in a slow, somber rain. The water streaks old stone and stucco, hiding the grime of occupation and age. The sheeting of water and highlighting of shadow gives an eerie spark of life to the demons and angels, the heroes and villains, ornamenting the secret places. The occasional bundled pedestrian huddled beneath an umbrella was the only distraction from the melancholy magic.

Speaking of melancholy, I turned from the window to face Ryan. "You sure about this? You can always skip the party if you want. We'll let you know if we land the job."

"Cream cheese and mushroom turnovers, pomegranate seeds in champagne, crab with herbed butter, and you want me to stay up in my room?"

"You found the menu?"

"How 'bout chocolate ganache-filled strawberries and sugared grapes? Or would you prefer the honey-almond, slow-roasted chicken?"

"How did you get the menu?"

"We're not the only ones who were invited tonight. They're having some kind of big shot open house—artists, historians, architects. Here." The full, public announcement popped up in my vision. I turned my gaze toward the ceiling, but it was covered with an ad for an international house of fashion, so instead I closed my eyes to glance over the event description. According to the schedule, after being wined and dined, we would be taken on a tour in the morning, followed by a presentation, and then have the afternoon to prepare our bid.

Mo switched off the image and I opened my eyes. Mistake. Bryce was watching me. He was draped over the facing seat as easily as if it were the overstuffed couch in his own living room. My mouth went dry. God, how many more years would I have to wait until those blue eyes stopped tying me up in knots? I didn't even acknowledge his gaze. I just turned back to Ryan.

"Doesn't really answer my question."

Ryan shrugged. "I'll live. Not like any of 'em put those kids to sleep on purpose."

"No, I don't suppose they did."

"Fact is, they thought they were helping people. They volunteered for the study. Can you even imagine? They tried to help stop an epidemic of blindness and this is what they get for it. Locked up on an island for the rest of their lives."

"Shouldn'ta been messing with those freakin' dead guys' DNA anyway."

I looked up to see Johanna dangling over us. Ryan so did not need this right now. I straightened.

"And I suppose you're going to tell us that the Sleepers were some sort of demonic clan from before the dark ages and that the Brighton's Disease patients are now infected with demon DNA?"

"Just sayin' it was stupid to mess with them in the first place. There they were sleeping in that tomb for how many centuries, we go patching people up with their DNA, and now we got kids sleeping in castles for almost a decade. Stupid."

I stole a quick glance at Ryan. He'd sunk back into his seat.

"At least in the war, most of the casualties were real casualties. They died. You could have a funeral and move on after a couple of years," he mumbled.

If I could have killed Johanna right then, I would have. She took one look at my face and knew it, too. Then she surprised the hell out of me. She dropped into the seat next to Ryan and draped an arm over his shoulders.

"Sorry, man."

"Yeah."

She gave him a quick squeeze and moved on to the back of the car. We both watched her go. Finally, I leaned back into my own seat.

"If we get there and it gets too real, if you need a break, just tell me."

"Now who's being the old lady?"

I chuckled and let it drop. If he thought he could handle it, I had to believe him. No choice. I demanded the same from him almost every day.

༄

Tomaas and Tamsin had timed us a seamless transition from coupler car to train. In a tangle of straps and limbs all eight of us managed to get our gear stored in the overhead bins. It had been years since we'd traveled as a complete caravan. I'd forgotten how big everything could get when that many people were doing anything together. I settled with my daypack into a window seat and dragged Tamsin down with me.

"This is your seat. Stay in it."

Tamsin looked at me like I'd grown a third eye. "Alrighty?"

I opened up my pack and offered her a chocolate-covered bribe. For myself, I pulled out my little loosely woven cotton sachet. I untied the green ribbons and worked it open with my pinky finger. I stared inside in surprise.

"Mom did it."

"She refilled your moss and pine needles baggie?"

I breathed in the earthy scent. My missed ritual, refilling my sachet with whatever caught my eye in my woods, Mom had done it for me. She'd known I wouldn't have time.

I leaned my head back against the seat and closed my eyes. Mom.

What the fuck was I doing leaving her alone right now? She didn't have a sachet that needed filled, but I could have taken her to the storytelling at the Tuesday night bonfire. The comforting flow of history, that sense of belonging summoned through sharing words by firelight, she would have loved that. It would have meant everything to her. God.

Tamsin rustled around beside me. When I opened my eyes, she was gone. Traitor. I scowled at the hideous red and purple striped upholstery in her absence, then turned my head toward the window. The huge, ancient buildings were piling into each other in a faster and faster blur.

I knew the second Bryce slid into the seat beside me. I resigned myself to it. He didn't say a word, just began tracing the veins and tendons of my wrist with the whisper soft touch of his fingertip. A tingle raced over my skin; my lungs constricted. I watched him perform his delicate seduction on my flesh. I didn't pull away. I drank it up, this little sip that I allowed us. Why with him? Why only with him was touch intoxicating? It wasn't right. It wasn't fair.

I rolled my head to the side to look at him. Bryce Deacon was beautiful—if you were into the tall, brooding romantic with unkempt blond hair spilling into hooded cobalt blue eyes. And I was. God, I was. Of course, I wasn't the only one. People tripped over themselves to get his attention. It wasn't that he was a snob. His charisma didn't come from self-absorption. It came from intensity. From the outside, it felt like the intensity of him could light up your whole world, if you could just be a part of it. And it could. And then it would wash you out, blind you, burn you away. I closed my hand into a fist and withdrew my arm.

Bryce took over the arm rest, leaned in close to point out the window.

"We're headed to Padua."

I nodded, trying to remember I cared. I followed his gesture to look out the window. To do any different would have brought my face far too near his.

"You haven't started your research, have you?" he murmured.

"Been busy. Mom's in town."

"So I heard. Alyse, I know I'm the wrong one to say it, but...that was a damn stupid thing to do."

"You're right. You're the wrong one."

"Doesn't mean I don't care what happens to you." His breath pressed hot against my neck. My brain threatened to abandon me to fate.

I felt his intention before he even moved. *Don't. Don't. Don't.* He reached out. He spread his long fingers across my inner wrist. He wrapped his hand around my now naked forearm. My heart slammed against my chest. Fiercely ignoring the hormones buzzing in my ears, I shook him off.

"So, what's the story with Padua?"

"It's the beginning of the story, Alyse, the city founded by Antenor, the traitor, when he fled Troy with his followers, the Veneti."

Veneti. Mythical ancestors of the Venetians, Mo supplied.

Thank you, Mo. Mo's expanding library of the relationship between my vital signs and conversational cues allows these handy little interjections. Well, sometimes handy. Sometimes ridiculously off base. This time handy. I do so hate looking stupid. Especially when Bryce knows what kind of compulsive legend collector I am.

"It seems to me Antenor's treachery depends on your source. Can you really blame him for being a Greek sympathizer? Who wants to lose their sons and daughters over an adulteress?"

"Ah, but he opened Troy for slaughter. Dante named the level of hell reserved for traitors after him."

I arched an eyebrow at him. "In the original stories, he was the wise counselor. It's only later that he gets set up as the one who opens the horse for the Greeks, the terrible traitor whose house is spared by the mark of the panther's skin. Not really a very likely scenario, you know. When a city like that burns, the whole thing burns. Having a panther skin on your door isn't going to do damn thing."

Bryce's smile was slow and sly. "You want the story or not?"

I shot him a glare promising physical damage. He just chuckled at me. What good did it do, I had to wonder, to have the stigma of being intimidating, if you could never use it when you needed it?

"Alright. This legendary Trojan and his refugees founded Pavatium in 1183 B.C. More than two thousand years later, the people of Padua found his remains in a triple sarcophagus—one of marble, one of lead, one of cypress. Ecstatic to have their mythic origins confirmed, they moved the sarcophagus to a church to honor it. Then in the mid-thirteen hundreds they reopened the coffin and the ruler of Padua took the proud warrior's sword for himself. As if in payment for that slight, Antenor began to slowly withdraw his mythic splendor from the city. First, the church was demolished, leaving the sarcophagus and its housing standing alone on a street corner. Then the scientists got hold of the skeleton and turned great Antenor into a nameless barbarian warrior born centuries too late to have inspired Homer."

"Science always did know how to ruin a good myth."

Bryce straightened with a laugh. "I thought you would enjoy that one."

Somehow I had ended up facing him, smiling and easy. I didn't even see it coming. He reached up and stroked a hand down my cheek, those vivid, glittering eyes fixed on mine.

"Take care of yourself, Alyse. None of us wants to lose you."

I was too stunned to move. He rose and disappeared down the aisle. The warmth of him faded from the air around me. It had been four years since he had touched me like that, since he had looked at me like that. Four years.

※

Our arrival at the Quarantine Processing and Visitation Facility in the swampy remains of Pavatium quickly turned into a little family reunion. *All* of the other sensory immersion teams were crammed in the gray institutional waiting room. It seemed that the other two movie houses had gotten word that we'd had a last minute change of heart on the invitation. In other words, all six of us immersion artists, plus our respective teams, were getting a ruler across the knuckles because I got in trouble with the boss.

Good thing I'm good with the poker face. I couldn't decide whether it was funny or just damn embarrassing.

"...shark."

"You are shitting me."

I saw my two counterparts, Diedre and Kelsie, pause and glance in my direction. I nodded and turned away.

They knew. Everyone knew everything about everyone in this business. There were no secrets. Sometimes...sometimes it just got old.

Thankfully, the crowd didn't start milling toward me. If anything, they had the decency to give me space. No, this evening I wasn't the star of the show. This time it would be

Kelsie Jasinski's new partner, Lex Cusso, from Atleiter Productions.

From the edge of the lobby I stepped around Ben and Cael discussing security protocols and moved in for a better look. Lex sat perched on his gear bag chatting with a couple of the Enchanted Mirror people. Seeing that fresh, young face left me with a twist of anxiety in the center of my gut. I knew, in this, I was not alone.

The last time the teams had all come together was a little less than a year ago. For a funeral. Carl Loren's death had been a shock and a warning for all of us. Carl had died of "grafting." To put it simply, Carl's wetware, the part of his AI implant that interacted with his central nervous system, had penetrated his brain. Slowly, over time, his faulty gear had disrupted his perception of reality and then ultimately his bodily functions until one day, during an enactment, he hadcollapsed into convulsions at Kelsie's feet.

Unfortunately, once the wetware has begun grafting, there isn't much they can do without damaging the brain. And that little hidden product feature scared the crap out of all of us. Every little daydream, every little sense of "otherness" became suspect. I thought back to the shark, to those sensations in the water. How would you ever know when the sensations were no longer your own? How would you ever know when the machine had taken over and it was simply your turn to go?

And there sat Lex: the newer, younger model. I personally couldn't help wondering if the kid was really in his right mind. At least we original immersion artists hadn't known about the possibility before we signed on to have our brains tampered with. I watched him push off his pack and head in our direction. With his cocky stride, Greek nose, and tight black curls he ricocheted off me with a very formal hello, wound through the cluster of guys, and zeroed straight in on Bryce. Predictable.

"He's kinda cute, huh?" Tamsin had reappeared at my elbow as a voice came over the loud speaker informing us that the boat would be departing for the Doge's Palace momentarily if we could just make our way out to the pier.

I lifted my pack onto the back of one of the bolted down chairs and slipped into it.

"He is," I granted. "I wonder how Kelsie feels working with someone seven years her junior."

Tamsin laughed. "Oh, I'd say she likes it just fine."

I glanced discreetly over at Kelsie. Yep, she was watching her young partner from across the room with an expression decidedly more spicy than simple professional interest. So much for the sacred rule. But then who was I to say? Bryce and I had ended badly, but Sam and Deidre from Enchanted Mirror had married and always seemed happy enough.

"I wish her luck then."

"I'll bet you do. Shall I get out of your way and let you scream at her to come to her senses?"

"That's okay. I'll try to restrain myself."

We jostled along with the rest of the crowd, but I could tell my friend was about ready to explode with something. I gave it a few steps, then raised an eyebrow at her. That was all the prompting she needed.

"I've decided there needs to be a really great looking, witty guy at this party. I'm so bored, Alyse!"

"Excuse me?"

"I need to be swept away in a flurry of romance."

"And this will cure you of the deep melancholy that's been dragging you under for so long."

"Absolutely."

"Glad we got that cleared up."

I shook my head at her as all twenty-four of us trouped through the white tiled hall toward a set of double doors. I suspected that the reason for Tamsin's itchy feet had more to do with her career than her romantic life. I'd been guessing for a while that she was ready to move on from being a mere field producer to directing her own films. But how would she ever broach the subject with me? She'd gotten me into this contract. I was stuck until I was outmoded. Did that mean she should be too? I knew if I'd been anybody else, Tamsin would have been long gone by now—she was more famous for her cut-and-run routine than for her undying loyalty. While I was touched and grateful, it didn't give me the right to take advantage of her by putting off that talk as long as I already had.

Soon. Sometime soon.

The seal on the flood doors broke as we approached and the doors swung open to reveal a paved runway raised up over the swamp. The black strip disappeared only a few meters out into a thick fog. The voice overhead informed us we would find our boat at the end of the runway.

"Is it just me," I asked, "or did that voice carry a distinct tone of 'ominous warning'?"

"What I want to know is how we are supposed to film anything in that pea soup?" Tomaas demanded, falling in step with Tamsin and me. That sent a murmur through the group.

The fog got cold fast. I felt bad for Tamsin in her leather pants and filmy little top, but there was nowhere to stop and pull out a sweater for her. The group, in a moment of hive mind, stepped a few paces out into the fog, then settled to a stop.

"Oh, we gotta get that," Ryan whispered.

Raw footage. Perfect raw footage. I knew what Ryan and the other swarm operators saw: a thick mist, so dense with secrets, it simply couldn't be recreated in a studio. As for myself and the other immersion artists, we felt the feather light brush of ghostly fingers across our faces, down our throats—both sensual and just a little bit frightening. I was already calculating how many different ways I could use a clip like this, which upcoming project I might be able to use the sensory footage on, to whom we might be able to sell the video track.

And for once Tamsin wasn't calling Ryan and I compulsive library builders.

But then, I should have realized why.

Bryce stepped out of the crowd. "May I suggest one pair gets it and shares the file, so we don't all end up missing the boat?"

Like anyone was going to say no. And like there was any question as to which pair that pair would be. I kept my flinch hidden behind a wall of professionalism. I wanted this footage the way Tamsin coveted chocolate. If that meant doing an enactment with Bryce, then...oh god.

I joined Bryce in silent acquiescence.

"Tamsin, I'm going to need to borrow your shirt. Did anybody bring a skirt?" I asked. So much for feeling superior in my turtle neck and jeans, but this enactment needed clothes that could whirl and brush like the fog.

Deidre tossed me a swirl of dark green silk. Tamsin got to open her pack after all. She pulled out a thick fleece sweatshirt. She switched shirts in a clever move that only revealed a quick glimpse of creamy white skin. I, on the other hand, was not nearly so discreet. Not much point to it by now. I shucked my boots, socks, jeans, and sweater in exchange for the skirt and blouse. Bryce kept his loose slacks, but added a long sleeve rayon shirt.

"Sandals or bare feet?" I asked since we were sharing the file.

"Bare feet, definitely bare feet," Kelsie and Deidre, my female counterparts concurred.

Bryce pulled off his shiny black shoes and his socks as well. Ben and Cael positioned a basic array of focus dots on our bodies, heads, and faces. Johanna and Ryan released their swarm cameras. Both Bryce and I laid a finger over the recording indicators behind our right ears and gave the physical confirmation to turn on our AIs' recording features. Our friends and competitors receded silently into the fog beyond.

"Any of you need the tell light? It's messing up the shot," Ryan shouted. The tell light is a red glow a little below and to the rear of my right ear required by law to let Joe Public know he is on film. Immersion artists and their cameramen find them annoying. A chorus of no's came back as the reply. I told Mo to switch it off.

I turned to Bryce then. Those cobalt eyes held mine. We stood alone in a perfect pocket of unreality, crisp black below us, hazy white all around us. I swallowed a sharp flash of nerves. How many years had it been since we'd done an enactment together? Three years? Four years? Just how badly was I going to regret this in the morning?

I saw something flash in those eyes—pain, hunger, something more. I waited with him until it settled inside of him. Everyone might know everything in this business, but it didn't make it their business. We could at least feign privacy.

But the boat was waiting.

"You or me?" I asked finally.

"Your choice."

"You then."

We retraced our steps to the door. Then I nodded him forward. Two steps, three. He was gone. Fog was wonder and a secretive mystery, longing and an imposed blindness. Fog was madness and a primitive, rising, desperate fear. Everything, all of that, all at once in one body. And that was what I would capture.

At first I wandered out into the earthly clouds with a sway, floating my body forward, just capturing the otherworldly brush of the heavens across my skin, between my fingers, my toes.

Beautiful.

I did a turn, let my hair float out, then around me. As I settled, I shook the strands back from my face, savored the quiet anonymity, the freedom. Then I caught a glimpse of the flutter of blue rayon. Then I heard the near-silent pad of bare feet against the asphalt. Then I caught the musky scent of sweat and subtle aftershave.

That look in his eyes: the pain, the hunger, the something else.

The something else.

And all of a sudden, the mist transformed from shimmering organza anonymity to cold, almost angry need. My fists clenched at my sides. Startled, I felt that something else flash in my own eyes. Then I savored it.

Fog was madness and a primitive, rising, desperate fear.
The hunt.

I crept forward, step, after step, after step. Bryce reappeared, released from the mist. I reached out and barely teased my fingers upward through the back of his thick, silky blond hair. As he began to turn, I darted away, back into the veil of water. I heard the hush of his pivot, the long pause, then the turn back.

I waited a beat.

Slowly, I slipped up on him, snaked a hand over his shoulder and under the caress of his loose shirt. He looked down, reached for my hand. I snatched it back and fled.

Tiny rock chips pressed almost to cutting into the sensitized flesh of my feet. The fog penetrated deep into my lungs. My mind was clear and electric. I crept forward again. Two steps, three, four. He wasn't there.

Had I gotten myself turned around in the mist?

I froze, all too aware of the steep drop from the runway into the swamp below.

Then suddenly he had me. He caught me from behind, running his big hands up over my breasts, then down over my belly, then spreading my legs so I straddled his thigh. His erection pressed into my ass. I gasped, cried out. He pinned me against him with his right arm, used his left to pull my head to the side. His breath beat short and fast against my pulse.

The threat transformed me into a frenzy of fear and need. I twisted and jerked and broke free and ran. The fog and the dark path led to nowhere, off the edge of the world. He tackled me. We lifted free of the earth, then hit, hard. He rolled me, pressing my hands above my head and into the biting surface of the path.

"Cut!" Tamsin shouted. "The driver says he can't wait any more."

Bryce didn't move. He stared down at me, his eyes still wild, his breath still ragged. My own eyes were wilder still. I strained toward him; he pressed his cheek to mine.

His voice sounded wrong as he whispered in my ear. "Careful, Alyse. You have to be careful here."

Confusion and reality slowly drew back the veil as our teams began to materialize around us. I stared up at him as he lifted his head, nearly fell back into the frenzy I still saw in that face.

Then abruptly Bryce jumped to his feet. He offered me a hand up. I hesitated, unable to follow the quick transition. He reached out and took my hand. I swept Deidre's skirt to the side and pushed myself to standing. Together yet separately we limped over to Johanna and Ryan. They were seating the cameras in their cases. Johanna looked up with a grin.

"I'm going to need a cold shower after that one!"

Ryan and I exchanged a silent look. Bryce and I avoided looking at each other at all.

I switched off my recorder and groped for normalcy. "Well, I am going to need a hot one. And a solid right block when Tamsin sees what we did to the back of this shirt."

"I heard that! I should darn well know better than to loan you my clothes! I loved that shirt!"

We were only a few paces away from the boat, but Bryce and I were both shivering by the time we climbed on board. The boat was large, but flat-bottomed, black with intricate gold trim on the sides. Its canopy offered about as much protection as the powerful winged lion perched on its prow. The driver, an ancient old man, bustled around us until he was satisfied with our arrangement and how his boat sat in the water. Then he took a long pole and pushed off.

I sank back into the padded bench. Mo had finished melding the video and sensory files. I forwarded the material to Deidre and Kelsie. It was a short clip, but hopefully it had something useful in it for them. Now that I was coming down off of it, I never wanted to do another one like it for as long as I lived.

Bryce sat down next to me. I closed my eyes, leaned my head back, and felt the sharp tingle as Margie sent out a couple of her fix-it bots to repair the abrasions on my back and shoulder.

"Oh, my God. You guys are good." Deidre's smoky voice came from the back of the boat.

"Wow. I mean I'd heard, but I never felt the raw stuff before. Wow."

That was Lex. I couldn't help myself; I looked over at Bryce. We shared a cocky grin. Take that, cute new kid.

The driver must have been navigating by tracking map alone, although I never saw the old man reference one. As the group settled into silence, the boat ride became eerily peaceful, our vessel alone, gliding over the black water, through the loosening veil of clouds. But as we moved further out to sea, the water grew choppier and I grew more restless.

Then my shark-bitten arm began to twinge.

I pulled back the sleeve on Tamsin's shirt and glanced at my limb. Just the lines of the larger tooth marks, no inflammation, no redness. I replaced the thin fabric and wrapped my hand around my forearm where the pain was the worst. Looking out over the dark water, I forced myself to relax against the pain. Then I stiffened. The water alongside the boat grew darker, thicker. Then I saw what I knew was the ripple of a dorsal fin. The bones in my arm screamed.

And suddenly I knew: *I should not be here.*

I whipped around, forgetting Bryce and not one of my team sat next to me. Bryce was watching me, worrying the bone pendant on the cord around his neck. He didn't say anything, just tucked the pendant back into his shirt and closed his hand over mine. His touch felt so real, so warm; I twined my fingers through his, trying to bring the sensation closer. Slowly, the pain began to recede and the foreign panic faded. I sank back into my seat, but I couldn't keep my gaze from sliding to the dark water below. Bryce gave my hand a squeeze.

"We'll be careful," he murmured.

Again with the whispers of caution. I didn't know what that meant, but I nodded. He drew his hand away.

Sitting up straighter in my seat, I ignored the part of me that protested the loss of his comfort, the part that wanted to burrow into him. Instead, I peered purposely up ahead, trying to make out any landmarks, any interruption at all in the fogscape. This boat ride was already far longer than advertised.

And I wanted off.

As if sensing my thoughts, Tamsin twisted her curly blonde head around and looked over her seatback at me.

"We're going to be late." She drummed her fingers on the rain resistant seat cover. "This is just going to mess *everything* up. I mean, I need time to scout—."

A rusty old voice cut her off. "You'll arrive when you're meant to arrive."

I heard the echo that meant Mo was translating for me. I looked up over Tamsin's head and saw the driver looking back at us. Then I looked further up and I saw it, a crystal staircase that rose out of the green, lapping water. A golden glow radiated from the shrouded portal at the top. I hated not knowing what I was looking at. Determined to erase any remnants of my previous panic attack from both our minds, I leaned over to Bryce, gesturing up at the stairs.

"Help me out here."

"About fifty years ago, around 2143, the Venice Archeological Society paid to have the Doge's Palace encased in aquarium glass. They could only afford to have the first floor done. In the end, it didn't matter. The water still comes up through the foundation. The carriers have turned the top two floors into a luxury hotel. They created a new entrance to the palace with a floating dock and a staircase that comes out on the second floor."

"Thank you." God, I hated being unprepared.

A pair of doormen in tuxedos descended out of the low cloud cover and crossed the clear dock to help the driver pull the boat in snug. Ben and Cael were the first to disembark. They each pulled out their handhelds and did a quick scan.

"Nothing."

"Me either. All right, come on up."

Unfortunately, at an event like this we had more than just some leftover psychos from the Flaming Sword of God to worry about. We also had the Seers to look out for. The reason there is such a high-level defense system around Venice isn't because people are worried about the Sleeper's Syndrome carriers trying to escape. The carriers volunteered for quarantine—so would you if every child under sixteen you came in contact with fell "asleep" and never woke up again. No, the security was to keep the Seers from trying to break *in*. The Seers believed that if they either killed or blinded all of the carriers, the children would wake up again. They've tried to enact this "cure" several times. They managed at one point to blow up part of St. Mark's Basilica, the church attached to the Doge's Palace. It wasn't far from any of our minds that right now the defense system was down and people of unconfirmed ideological leanings were wandering in and out of the camp.

I followed Tamsin onto the dock. The transfer wasn't as easy as it looked and I spared a worry for the more elderly members of tonight's guest list. The second Ryan stepped off the boat, though, Tamsin the Tyrant went into full schedule recovery mode. Part of Bryce's crew was still waiting in line and she was already driving the four of us up the stairs by force of impatience alone.

"Hold on, Tamsin. I want to get this shot," Ryan said.

"Later. Let's go!"

"It won't be here later." Then he struck on the perfect bargaining tactic. "Alyse and I can put together a local short for your bid. Make it more personal."

Tamsin turned. "Oh, fine! Make it quick."

I still wore my array, so I just passed Ben my pack and Ryan tossed up a handful of cameras. Ben, Tamsin, and Ryan scrambled up the stairs to get out of the shot. I turned on my recorder.

I took a few breaths to slow myself down. Then I began to follow.

It was strange, but I felt so light ascending that crystal staircase alone through the mist. It was like walking into a dream—everything was indistinct, not quite tangible. The glow that drew me forward condensed into shapes, four-petaled flowers, the curves and cones of Arabian rooftops. The new entryway built into the original palace façade began to solidify. Shaped like the ornate stems of ancient keys, the columns on either side of the stairs became real marble I could reach out and smooth my palm over.

I passed between them.

Ahead I heard voices rising and falling in exclamation. My feet stopped on the rough stone of a terrace, the space between the clouds and the broken promise of magic before me. It was a hotel, not the ancient throne of the masters of the sea. A sorrow washed over me. I let it.

Then I stepped forward.

"Cut. Okay, let's go, go, go!"

I switched off my recorder and the cameras flew back to their keeper. Between that piece and the fog bit, Ryan and I could put together a wicked tour introduction sequence. Might as well at least pretend we were here to work.

I took my pack from Ben and he helped me struggle back into it. The disappointment that lay beyond the golden light wasn't complete. The transformation had been tastefully done. Old wood had been used wherever possible. The marble of the small check-in counter was pitted and uneven, obviously pulled whole from a staircase somewhere in the flooded ruins.

"Welcome! Tamsin Leonides, Alyse Bryant, Ben Norris-Stevenson, and Ryan Gunner. Your suite has been keyed to your IDs. Here is a map to your room. This evening's ball will begin in fifteen minutes. I will let the mayor and his chief of staff know you've arrived."

I hate it when people read my name from the DNA dog tag embedded between my shoulder blades. Call me old-fashioned, but I still think people should have to ask for the privilege of using your name. The woman behind the counter didn't really look like she was ready for a discussion of modern manners, though. She had the dazed expression of someone who had been forced to beam all day for no apparent reason.

"Thanks ever so much!" Tamsin handed out the maps and muttered under her breath. "Fifteen minutes. I can't believe Emory would do this to me! How am I supposed to—?"

Ben threw an arm over her shoulder. "Slow down there, girl! He was lettin' us all crash long enough—"

"—to be late! Up those stairs double-time you silver-tongued co-conspirator." She whacked Ryan with her map. "Can I just get this one shot, please, please, please? This is the biggest project we've ever bid for and it's only 30% in-house. That means the other 70% is independent. Clarissa will be your little love slave forever if we land this thing."

"Didn't hear you say no."

"That's beside the point. Step lively army boy." Tamsin chased him up the stairs with her map.

"I was NOT in the army."

"I was just trying to let the Anti-Terrorist Force save face."

"Very funny."

While they bantered, Ben and I blinked at each other as we trotted behind them up two flights of dimly lit stone stairs. 70% independent? Apparently we'd both missed that section of the project outline. We make a very minimal salary off of in-house projects, but we take full profit off of independents for one simple reason: I own my library, not Lone Pine—though they have free use of it. We are the only team with that privilege. Mine was the first contract and my grandfather had been a very wily negotiator. I'm sure Emory has been kicking himself ever since.

Our staircase opened out onto a landing, then turned right and funneled us up into a wide corridor. According to the little red dot we were following on the map, our suite lay at the end of the hall. The security system recognized our approach and admitted us into the suite's small parlor. The wall paper was richly colored with a deep turquoise background and a pattern of shapes like gold peacock tails. Centered on the far wall huddled a false fireplace with a couple of Victorian-style spindly chairs and a deep white loveseat with artfully arranged brick red throw pillows. While Ben checked everything over, the other three of us pulled off our packs. Tamsin didn't even give Ryan and I time to roll out our shoulders.

"Into the showers. Now! Let's go."

I popped open my pack and pulled out my overnight bag where I'd stuffed all my arrival essentials, including what Tamsin had dubbed my evening battle armor. People had the annoying habit of touching you at these things, so I took the required fashion precautions. Tamsin saw the bag and grabbed it away from me.

"No, I got you something. Hold on. It's from Aladdin's. I promise you'll like it. Hold on." She dived into her bag, emerging with a fairly large and battered box with the Aladdin's logo scripted across the top. She shoved it into my hands as I headed toward the sleeping room to the left of the fireplace. Ryan had already disappeared into the one to the right.

I made short work of the shower. As soon as I stepped out, Tamsin stepped in. I hurried with drying my hair. I wanted to try on the outfit before she got out. I'm good at putting myself together, but Tamsin has that special flair. I rarely argue when she decides to use it on me.

I opened the box. If only I got presents this nice every time I screwed up an enactment. I lifted the dress from the box. The short-sleeved bodice was one part stiff black satin with a wraparound mandarin collar, one part draping maroon silk below that collar, revealing just a hint of temptation. The skirt was a sleek fall of yet more silk. I opened the side zipper and the jewel clasp on the collar and slipped inside. Aladdin's has my profile. It fit perfectly. I looked in the full length mirror at the foot of my small bed.

"Wow."

I hadn't had the chance to play dress up in ages. Living under Ben's thumb all this time had been worth it. I looked amazing. I turned back to the box. There was more. A pair of long black gloves attached to the dress sleeves with cute little garters. Black satin leggings went under the skirt as I discovered the skirt fell open in the middle when I sat down. A pair of clear acrylic heels with hammered gold trim were my glass slippers.

Tamsin poked her head out of the steamy shower.

"You like it?"

"Tamsin, it is amazing. What did I do to deserve this?" I picked up a handful of the skirt and let it slither through my gloved fingers. What a beautiful sound.

Tamsin snagged a towel and started putting herself together. She talked to me via the vanity mirror as she worked. "I thought you could use a little pick me up. That's all. Gave me a chance to bicker with Simon for a couple of days. And you do know how I like to get his spiky little tail feathers in a bunch. So you really like it?"

"I love it," I promised her. I displayed one glass slipper through the slit in the skirt. "I feel like Cinderella. I'm going to the ball."

Tamsin giggled as she pulled on a pink, layered little number that made her look like a tiny, little fairy. My fairy godmother. She grinned over at me as she grabbed a little jeweled handbag.

"Do you think Prince Charming will be there?"

Bryce threatened to rise up in my mind. I flicked him away.

"God, I hope so."

Chapter 4

If this was Cinderella's ball, the king and queen who greeted us at the door were magnificent. The man, a tall Asian mix with a sweep of rich black hair, radiated power. I wasn't surprised when he introduced himself as Jürgen Phan Mai, the mayor of the new "city" of Venice. I remembered reading somewhere that he still acted as president of his multibillion dollar company, Off World Technology. The woman next to him, Dr. Suzi Rosenbaum, inclined her head regally. Her short, dark brown hair only served to make her petite profile that much more elegant. She, Mo told me after prompting, was formerly the Executive Director of the Australia Museum of Natural History. The mayor presented her as his chief of staff.

Tamsin made our introductions. She and Ben each received a gracious welcome. I stepped forward, offered a gloved hand. Our palms connected and Mayor Phan Mai snapped out of his polite stupor. A mixed expression flickered over his face—

confusion, surprise, fascination. He glanced at his chief of staff, but she only returned a puzzled look.

"Alyse Bryant," he repeated.

"Yes," I confirmed, resisting the urge to tug my hand back. I watched his eyes, trying to guess what about me had caught his attention. It was attention I was increasingly sure I didn't want. Up close his aura was more than imposing; it sent a thick spiral of unease through my chest.

"Thank you for accepting our invitation. I admire your work. I've always felt it showed a deep empathy for the characters as unique individuals."

"Thank you, and thank you for inviting us. We're looking forward to hearing the stories your ruins have to tell."

"And we look forward to sharing them with someone who can appreciate them." He finally unclasped my hand, but I in no way felt released from him. His smile seemed almost predatory. That strange wild feeling from the mist threatened to resurface and I quickly, frantically quelled it. He gestured toward the portal to the ballroom. "I hope you enjoy the party. Maybe we will have a chance to discuss the city's rich folk history in more depth later this evening."

"I look forward to it." *With as much enthusiasm as I look forward to being attacked by...well...say, a shark, for example.*

His attention turned to Ryan and I was finally unleashed. I exhaled quietly and stepped down the receiving line to Dr. Rosenbaum.

"Welcome, Ms. Bryant." As our hands clasped, her eyes narrowed almost imperceptibly. This time, I pulled my hand away. Manners be damned. She just smiled ever so slightly. "Enjoy the party, Ms. Bryant."

"Thank you."

As soon as all four of us had entered the ballroom and stepped out of earshot, I leaned over to Tamsin. "That was very...."

"Cool! Did you see the way he was looking at you? We've got this one in the bag."

"I don't think men who make business decisions with their dicks get as far as the Jürgen Phan Mai's of the world. And I don't think that was exactly carnal desire lighting his eyes."

"Are you kidding?! Sweetie, he's still staring at you. I bet all you'd have to do is grab him by his shiny black lapels and drag him over into that dark stairwell we just came out of and he would take care of all your years of sexual frustration before you could even show him where the zipper is on that little ol' dress."

"I'm not hearing this!" Ryan interjected.

"That's okay," I assured him while I pointedly refrained from glancing back over my shoulder. "I'm not either. Tamsin, let's just focus on finding you an archeologist with a nice tan."

"I was thinking more about a cultural historian with soulful eyes."

"Soulful eyes. Check," Ben said. He and I surveyed the crowd. I'm not sure what I was expecting, but it was certainly not a crowd this big or this polished. Crisp black tuxes moved through a sea of colorful dresses that ranged from flowing to barely there. Maybe Tamsin's chances at a whirlwind romance weren't that bad after all.

"I'm still not hearing this," Ryan grumbled.

I just chuckled as Ryan and Tamsin launched into an argument regarding the responsibility of an all-but-married friend to help his single friend in the eternal search for Mr. Right. Ben and I both caught sight of the buffet along the left wall. We didn't try to interrupt Tamsin in the middle of her diatribe, but simply led the way to some long overdue nourishment.

The room was long and my plate was full before we even made it halfway down the display. At the far end a quartet played Vivaldi. The dance floor in front of them lay empty, but the dinner tables beyond that were packed. The four of us found a relatively empty corner and stood with our plates to take in the lay of the land.

"We're gonna need to split up," Tamsin decided. "Talk to as many people as you can."

"A whole room full of subject experts," I realized aloud. The idea of it buoyed up the professional in me, even while a general sense of disquiet pressed me down. Despite the money, despite Tamsin's enthusiasm, I wasn't convinced I wanted this project. And it wasn't just because I was pissed at Emory anymore. I glanced in the direction of the door. The mist, the boat, and now this. I could admit that last night's little breakdown hadn't quite worn off, but this distracting sense of wrongness didn't seem to emanate from my own emotional turbulence. Or maybe it did.

Maybe it did.

Either way, time to get to work.

Screw you, anyway, Emory Ranger.

As was traditional, Ben and I paired off together. Once we finished our plates, we wedged our way into the crowd, listening for a conversation to interject ourselves into. Ben discreetly checked his weapons scanner every few meters. I took this and his unusual quiet as a sign. He was more nervous than he was letting on. That didn't help.

"...one of the first democracies..."

"I was reading this morning that the city was originally founded by refugees fleeing the Goths. Ironic, huh?"

"...all under water now. I don't see how they are going to pull this off."

"...in this very room, the Sala del Maggior Consiglio." I paused to listen more closely. "The original works were lost, but the Italians were able to copy the major works like Tintoretto's *Paradise* which covered the entire far wall where you came in. That was—at the time—one of the largest paintings in the world and done by a seventy-year-old man no less." I turned to look where the balding art historian pointed. All I saw was a high, wide wall covered with tastefully striped wall paper in burgundies and golds. "Along these side walls were the portraits of a little more than half the doges, including the black curtain where Marin Falier's portrait should have been."

"Marin Falier?" I could have asked Mo, but I suspected this man's explanation would be more entertaining.

He turned to me and the sparkle in his eye told me I was right. "The Venetians guarded their political freedoms...aggressively. Falier conspired to make himself into a dictator. They lopped his head off. And made sure no one ever forgot it."

Now that sparked my curiosity. I gave Ben the signal to stay put and keep listening as I backed away. I found a small pocket of space near the wall, apart from the crowd.

Mo, historical overlay: Sala del Maggior Consiglio.

It took her a few moments, but layer by layer reality gave way to the ghost. Thick gold moldings grew out of the smooth surface, became the ornate frames for enormous paintings covering the entire ceiling and all four walls. The lower portions of the walls displayed wood paneling and benches, their colors and lines rich with age. Where the wall joined the ceiling was a series of smaller, molding-framed portraits, the doges.

"He was right there. *Hic fuit locus ser Marini Faletri decapitati pro crimine proditionis.* In this place would have been Marin Falier, decapitated for the crime of treason," a voice behind me murmured.

I jumped, spun around. Jürgen Phan Mai caught my arm. I grabbed his other sleeve before I fell into him. We stayed locked like that for an eternal second. The solidity of him shocked me. Why, I'm not sure. Maybe because he didn't look quite real. The lines of his face looked painted—by the thick brush of a Japanese master. His eyes held an almost cruel mirth. I stepped quickly back.

Unfazed, he handed me a flute of pomegranate seeds floating in champagne.

"Think if they could see what you are seeing. The intoxicating juxtaposition between past and present. Think if they could absorb the stories we come from into their psyches as easily as if they had lived them themselves—the fairies, the witches, the ghosts, the devils, the traitorous doges. Are you running from me...Alyse?"

I gripped the champagne glass with both hands and caught myself before I took a third step back. My tripping heart held me silent.

He nodded toward my glass. "You should drink that. When the ice melts, only magic will draw those pomegranate seeds out."

Obediently, I raised the glass to my lips. The tingle of champagne filled my mouth, the icy seeds slid over my tongue. I bit down. The tiny jewels burst in an explosion of tart sweetness. The mixture slid down my throat, warming me, opening me. Suddenly, I felt terrifyingly vulnerable standing there before him. The look in his deep eyes said he knew it, enjoyed it.

I found my voice.

"Thank you for the champagne, Mr. Mayor."

"Jürgen."

"Jürgen."

I raised my glass in salute, then turned, and fled.

൪

I didn't run through the forest of bodies. I slipped between, skirted around, darted through. Back and forth and back and forth until I was lost amid the swirl of garish sparkle and shrill laughter. The crash of warring conversations beat down on me as I came to a stop. Disorientation overwhelmed my mind as the crowd pulsed around me. In the huge ballroom I had managed to cut myself off from my team. I wasn't at all sure I had cut myself off from our haunting host. I couldn't understand my reaction to that man. I don't intimidate easily. My team seemed to find him charming.

I couldn't get those hard, hunting eyes out of my mind.

I tossed back another mouthful of champagne-laced pomegranate seeds. The heat in me grew. Behind me, the crowd roared with laughter. Carefully, I turned.

I stood on the edge of the audience where Bryce was holding court. His rich voice retold the story about a tangle with a frightened octopus. I cracked a small smile, the sight of a familiar face enough to take the edge off my strange fear. I stepped through the crowd. Bryce turned toward me. His cobalt eyes passed over me, looked through me. I stopped. There it was again. Like every time. When we were alone his attention engulfed me; when we were in the world...I didn't exist for him. The times when we were alone made it so easy to forget that. So pathetically easy.

I turned away, shaking off a hurt that should have long been over. Mature, responsible adults knew better than to seek comfort from their exes. That was me. The epitome of the mature, responsible adult. Embarrassed, I pulled free of the cluster of bodies.

Mo still held the image of the original hall of the Great Council in place. My gaze lit on the far wall, the wall covered in the layers of the painting the art historian had called *Paradise*. Tier after tier of saints and angels rose up the wall to an apex of golden heavenly light emanating from a red-robed Jesus. Even Mary bowed down to him in his glory. Bryce and his adoring admirers. Except this disciple had spent years extracting herself from that overpopulated painting. Perhaps I'd just needed that harsh little reminder of why.

I swallowed the last of the champagne and studied the few stray seeds that clung to the sides of the glass. *Lonely made stupid.* How many times had Tamsin and I said that to each other, to ourselves? I shook my head at myself. Maybe Tamsin wasn't the only one in need of a little whirlwind romance.

Now I had an empty champagne glass to off-load. I pressed back toward the buffet. I could discard the glass, circle back around the way I'd come, and hopefully find Ben in the process. With his height and my heels, I ought to be able to spot him.

I found the discard tray at the end of the fruit table. I reached out to set my glass down at the same time as another guest and had to catch the fragile flute before it toppled to the floor. I glanced over to apologize and found my gaze caught.

Finally, a Venetian in Venice.

My Venetian smiled back at me with dark eyes fringed with long lashes. His wavy black hair fell nearly to the shoulders of his trim tuxedo jacket. High cheekbones mirrored the lines of beautifully chiseled lips. Now there was a true work of art. And if I was going to keep staring, I was going to have to come up with something to say.

He beat me to it.

"Alyse? Alyse Bryant from Flathead High School?"

Caught off guard, I straightened, looked again at my Venetian. And came up with nothing. "I apologize. You're going to have to help me."

His smile broadened and he held out his hand.

"Matteo Ranier. I was a senior when you came back to Kalispell. I don't blame you if you don't remember me. If memory serves, you'd come back to help with your grandmother. You probably didn't pay much attention to upperclassmen mooning over you from the back row of Mr. Ricks' drama class."

Mo, hurry up with that damn picture!

Finally, she pulled it up. *Wow.* It just goes to show what a few kilos of muscle and whole lot of confidence can do for a gawky teenager with good bone structure. I had a vague memory of him in a bit part in Macbeth. He was right, that had been a very distracted time for me. Didn't mean I couldn't play a fragment of a memory for all it was worth, though.

"Got you. The years have treated you very well, Matteo Ranier."

"I'd say the same for you. Would you care for another glass?"

Alcohol and I had a cautious relationship, but as I drowned in those soft brown eyes, my common sense lost the battle.

"Absolutely, I would love one."

He didn't look away as he flagged down a waiter. The fresh flute of glittering red gems rolled from his bare fingertips to my gloved ones. He reached over and took a second glass for himself. A gray-haired matron tried to slip past us to deposit her half-empty dish. Matteo turned and with a gentle hand at the small of my back drew me back out into the clusters of socializers around us. Smooth and chivalrous. I hid a smile behind the rim of my glass. Perhaps the evening could take a pleasant turn after all. He guided us through the noise to the edge of the empty dance floor.

I kept my sip small, then turned to my new companion.

"What brings you to the ball?"

His smile dimmed for just a millisecond, but I saw it and he knew it.

"I live here."

I lowered my head. Of course. He was a carrier. The sparkly little glow around us flickered with my disappointment. Which was, of course, ridiculous. I was going to be here a maximum of five days. It's not like the circumstance had ever offered the possibility of a long-term relationship. I tossed my disappointment aside and raised my head with a sheepish look.

"I walked into that one, didn't I? My apologies. But all two hundred thirty-eight of you aren't here tonight, so what did you do to get lucky—besides look sexy in a tuxedo?"

His laugh was genuine and so was my relief. After playing flesh and fire with Bryce and then predator and prey with Jürgen, I wasn't willing to give up the chance for a simple, lighthearted flirtation with an old school chum. A gorgeous, old school chum with whom I had absolutely no baggage.

"I'm the Employment Secretary. I work for Jürgen. I create viable jobs for the citizens who are able to work. A lot of what we're doing tonight and tomorrow is about creating a more active economy for the city. Jürgen has insisted...." He stopped and it was his turn to grin sheepishly. "Sorry. Boring."

"No, fascinating. I'll admit, I hadn't spent a lot of time thinking about it, but there's still living to be done, isn't there?"

Matteo nodded and a lock of that thick, dark hair fell forward. I reached out, stroked it back for him, wished I dared take off the satin gloves and really feel it. He watched my fingers as I drew them back. We were standing a little closer than was polite. If I concentrated, I could feel his breath against my face, smell the pomegranate on his breath.

"Yes. Yes, there is still living to be done."

We stood like that, watching each other. I know I wasn't the only one wishing in that moment, so I grinned and grabbed his arm.

"You know how to dance to this stuff?" I asked.

"Not a clue."

"Good. You know what Mr. Ricks always used to say—"

"—grin and fake it," we finished together.

"I'm not sure I'm drunk enough for this," he said, stumbling to a halt part way onto the dance floor. We looked down at our half-empty champagne glasses. I shrugged my eyebrows at him.

"Bottoms up!"

We tossed back the last of the spiked fruit. I tried not to laugh as I crunched down on the seeds. Spraying champagne out the nose would not be terribly romantic. We set the glasses down at an occupied table, ignoring the startled commentary of the occupants. Then my Prince Charming seized my hand and we ran out onto the dance floor.

And he made my Cinderella skirt swirl the way the girl in me always dreamed it would: in lightness and laughter.

Chapter 5

The crowd thinned. The lights dimmed. The music slowed. The dance floor filled.

And I had my head nestled against Prince Charming's shoulder. His warm arms were wrapped around me; his chin rested on my head. We ignored the music and swayed.

So, of course, my team found me.

"Alyse?" I flickered back to reality at the rumble of Matteo's voice. "Those friends of yours?"

I glanced in the direction he gestured, knew the second I made eye contact with Tamsin, I was going to be skinned alive. Ben and Ryan weren't looking too friendly, either.

"Yes," I answered finally. "They're my co-workers. Come on over and meet them. I promise they aren't as dangerous as they look."

"In other words, you intend to use me as a human shield."

"It's not just your feet that are quick." Inwardly, I winced at the sound of my voice. Apparently, I'd drunk enough to dance—and then some.

I took Matteo's large hand in mine and led him off the dance floor, cursing myself every step of the way. Definitely, definitely drunk. Ryan kept his expression under wraps, but Tamsin and Ben both stared at me in surprise.

"Well, I guess there's gotta be a first time for everything," Tamsin said when we got in range.

"Alyse, baby, you gone and got yourself smashed," Ben announced for anybody who had missed the obvious. He'd gone from angry to worried.

I ignored them and tucked myself under Matteo's arm. "Team, this is Matteo Ranier from Mr. Ricks' drama class. Matteo, this is Ryan, our swarm operator; Ben, our stunt coordinator; and Tamsin, our field producer."

Tamsin gave him a nod. Ben and Ryan each accorded him a very manly handshake. Weird. Something was definitely going on.

"Nice to meet you, Matteo. Can we borrow your dancing partner right quick? Just a quick business consult. We'll have her back to you in a jiffy." Tamsin shot him a cheerful grin.

Matteo returned the smile. "I need to check in with my boss as well." My prince pulled free and with a nod that only half hid his smirk, turned, and wandered into the waning crowd. I watched him go. As soon as those beautiful square shoulders disappeared from sight, all three of them pounced at once.

"Alyse, are you out of your mind? He's a carrier!"

"Are you okay, baby? I've never seen you like this. This ain't the place to be lettin' your hair down."

"What's Mr. Ricks' drama class?"

I felt a wave of affection for those three confused faces. A slow smile spread across my face as I turned to Tamsin.

"You're right. Soulful eyes are better than a good tan."

I turned to trail after my Venetian. But Ben caught my arm, pulled me back. Wobbly as I was I stumbled against his chest. He lowered his head to my ear.

"You scared us to death, Alyse. I don't like this place. I got a really bad feeling about it. That Phan Mai freak at the door, I don't care if he's rich as God, something's freaked about him."

That stopped me. I'd thought I was the only one who'd noticed.

"Rich as God, dark as the Devil," I agreed. I looked up at my protector. His goofy face was gone. He wore his kick-ass scowl. "I'll stay away from him. I promise. Here, I'll turn on my tracker."

"No. The Seers got handhelds, too. Damn it, Alyse." He sighed. "If we was anywhere else, I'd say, go nail your high school sweetheart to the wall. You need it. But not here. Let's just get this job done and get out of here. Even better: fuck the job. Check out with Golden Boy and let's go home."

"Can't do that."

"Won't do that. Alyse." He slid his bare hand across the naked flesh of my neck. My nerves screeched in protest. "Is it really worth it?"

I hissed and jerked away. "Asshole!"

The joyful floating feeling was gone. I rubbed at my neck where the grinding ache just would not go away. I glared at my friend and tears nearly came to my eyes. I hate alcohol.

"Do you think I could possibly forget? God, you can be a shit sometimes!" I dropped my hand. "And it's *can't*. Not *won't*. The security system has been reengaged. Nobody's going anywhere until six o'clock day after tomorrow. Try reading sometimes. It's *your* job to know that."

Ben wasn't done. I was. I'd already said more than I would have without the overpriced rotten grape juice lubricating my jaw—and I knew it. My low outburst had gotten us a wide radius of attention. I backed away. Tamsin and Ryan closed in.

"Honey," Tamsin whispered. "We're just asking that you be careful. He's infected and you're a little vulner—"

"It's not contagious and I'm embarrassed that we're even having this conversation." That was a little hypocritical given my initial reaction to Emory's announcement. I took a step back, bowed my head, touched a finger to my temple. "I'm sorry. I—"

"—need a break. That's why we're really here, isn't it? Not to film a documentary."

I raised my eyes, saw Ryan looking up at me, knew I didn't have to answer him.

"Go on. Just be careful. We'll watch your six."

I laughed. What else could I do? But I also didn't stay long enough to be recaptured by their collective concern. I crossed an empty corner of the dance floor and folded myself into layer after layer of crowd. The romantic rush was over. I looked around myself surrounded as I was by strangers and felt suddenly tired. Matteo was nowhere to be seen. I thought of trying to collect more stories, but my heart wasn't in it. I thought of the false fireplace in our suite upstairs, but my heart wasn't in that either. Then I remembered the terrace at the front of the palace. Maybe it was time for a walk in the clouds.

And if Ben got an ulcer because I got out of his line-of-sight, the asshole deserved it. I took another rub at my neck.

Getting past the tangle of chairs, tables, and lingerers required a good number of winning smiles. One of those smiles hooked me a winning admirer. A tall, well-muscled Norwegian stopped me with a hand to my arm. His voice came through as an echoey translation.

"You are Alyse Bryant? You did the body work for *The Ones We Love*." His giant voice shook with a knowing laugh. "My girlfriend, she loves that movie."

I snapped my professional face in place before my annoyance could show through. The words "body work" always sent up a big red flag: here comes a cretin. The cretin gave me a wink.

"Rika has all your work, but we use that one at least once a week."

Through long practice alone, I refrained from replying, "Your Rika must be a real sadomasochist to need that movie to get her rocks off." Instead, like the good PR machine I am, I smiled graciously and thanked him and his Rika for supporting the art form. Or something along those lines. My mouth goes on autopilot at times like that.

I managed to extricate myself from his massive grasp and got a little more aggressive about burrowing my way out of the social heap. I couldn't complain. I'd only been recognized once tonight and he'd at least closed with a little flattery, claiming I should have been in front of the camera instead of in the editing room. At least I was choosing to take the comment as flattery, anyway.

I pulled my skirt out from between the last of the chair legs and I was free.

Then I spotted him.

He sat slouched down in a chair, tie pulled free, spoon twirling between his fingers. I only wavered for a moment before I made my decision. I walked up to the table, rested my hands on the back of an empty chair.

"Hey."

Matteo looked up.

He wasn't quite fast enough to mask the pain in those liquid eyes. He knew what had been said. Guilt tugged at me.

"You finish checking in with your boss?" I asked.

"Your friends finish warning you off?"

I leaned out over the table, propped myself up on my elbows. His gaze dropped to the loose silk that now barely contained my breasts.

"You ready to blow this masquerade?" I asked.

He raised his gaze to my face. He set the spoon down with a little click.

"I thought you'd never ask."

⚘

Matteo tucked his tie in his pocket and offered me his arm. The minute I wrapped my hand around his bicep, I felt my smile return.

"You like hot chocolate?" he asked.

"I indulge occasionally."

"Let's go up on the roof." He grinned at my skepticism. "It's always foggy this time of year."

"And cold," I reminded him.

He looked over my satin and silk dress. I let my heel hit the floor extra hard. The bounce of my breasts got his undivided attention. The hungry expression on his face got mine. A slow, sweet spiral of heat settled deep in my belly. I savored it.

"Gracie's has...heat lamps."

"I'm sure it does," I replied with a wicked grin.

He wrapped his free hand around mine, laughing and shaking his head. "My eighteen-year-old self wouldn't have known what to do with you."

"And your thirty-year-old self?"

"Is getting more ideas than I can fit into one night. Come on."

He led me out the tall doors, down the corridor, and back up the stone staircase. After that I was deliciously lost. He took us through a doorway off the stairs I would never have seen in the shadows. In the near dark, we navigated a series of closets and corridors. Then it was up a narrow metal ladder. Not an easy feat in a dress and heels, but they don't pay me the big bucks for nothing.

No Ben. No message to get my ass back there right now. He had let me go.

A sense of exposure, vulnerability made me hesitate near the top of that ladder.

Then a hand lowered in front of me. I looked up, saw those gentle, playful eyes and felt that hesitation melt away. Matteo took me by the arm and half lifted me onto the roof.

I let out a breath as the jolt of the night breeze hit me. He shrugged out of his jacket and pulled it over my shoulders. As the heat and the rich earthy scent of him wrapped around me, I felt every muscle in my body go lax. I caught myself swaying toward him.

"You alright there?" His hands squeezed my upper arms; his face was far too near mine. His lips parted with a murmur. "Keep looking at me like that and you're not going to get your chocolate."

I pulled back, my heart racing in alarm and surprise. I had to lick my lips to answer him.

"Couldn't...couldn't have that."

The rapt intensity on his face said I would have to be the one to break the spell. I turned to face the thick fog.

"So, which way to Gracie's?"

He let go of my arms and took my hand. A disciplined man. I rose up on my toes as he led me out across a muddy patch of browning grass. I would have to explain my touch restrictions before things went too much further. Some guys could deal with it. Most couldn't. I hadn't meant for things to slip this far before I confessed. And now the rejection would hurt both of us. I pushed the ugly thought aside. I was here to share a cup of cocoa and a flirt with a gorgeous man. If that's as far as it went, that was fine.

As we walked, I stole a glance at that finely sculpted profile, dark against the white backdrop of mist. Matteo had turned somber. We couldn't have that.

"So, has there always been a football field on the roof of the palace?"

Matteo's smile was small and knowing, but he accepted my lead.

"It's a small park. And no, we built it. The café is in the center, provided we don't miss it and walk right off the side."

"Comforting."

"And you got lucky this time. Here it is."

The tiny booth materialized with pretty little wrought iron tables and delicate scrollwork chairs all seated on a small, circular island of colorful mosaic. Several of the tables were already occupied. Apparently this was where the on-duty locals came to escape the invaders for a spell. Matteo brought us right up to the order window.

"Two sipping chocolates and a dessert."

Gracie, a thin, pinched crone with overlarge teeth and an incredible smile, gave him a familiar pat on the arm. "Mix up your cultures a bit: have the *Bayersiche Dampfnudeln mit Vanillesauce.*"

Matteo sought my approval with the raise of an eyebrow. I replied with a slight nod. As Gracie ladled up the chocolate and plated the *Dampfnudel,* Matteo and I turned and looked around us. He gestured toward the mosaic at our feet.

"Gracie has been working on this since Jürgen set her up with this place. It's a copy of the Genesis Cupola from the Basilica."

"A rough copy," Gracie interjected over her shoulder.

At the edge of my skirts a robed and haloed figure pointed its scepter toward a red sun and a black moon. I looked to Matteo.

"*God divided the light from the darkness. And God called the light Day, and the darkness he called Night. And the evening and the morning were the first day.*" He shrugged when I looked impressed. "We do bonfires up here when Jürgen's company has a little extra windfall and we can afford the wood."

"My favorite story," Gracie said, setting the small cups in their saucers on the counter. She placed the plump, drenched *Dampfnudel* between them with a pair of forks. As a regular bonfire goer, I found the choice intriguing.

"Even the part about the snake and Adam's fall because of his wife's wicked ways?" I asked.

"Especially that part," she cackled and I had to laugh.

"The fifth day." I pointed a little further afield on the mosaic to a jigsaw of fin and feather. I reached deep and found a bit of my mother to channel. "*And God said, 'Let the waters bring forth abundantly the moving creatures that hath life, and fowl that may fly above the earth in the open firmament of heaven.' And God created great whales and every living creature that moveth, which the waters brought forth abundantly, after their kind, and every winged fowl after his kind; and God saw that it was good.*"

When I turned back to the counter, life-worn Gracie had turned starry-eyed.

"You're a storyteller?"

I shook my head, but Matteo laid his hand on my arm. The warmth in his eyes could have melted me where I stood. "No. You are. You definitely are. You did things to those words Gracie and I haven't been able to do after years of practice. That was amazing."

"You should hear my mother, then. That's real magic." I lifted my cocoa from the counter. "How much do I owe you?"

"You just take that and enjoy it. Maybe you'll have time to come back tomorrow and share a little of your gift with us before you go."

"I will do that. Thank you."

Matteo led the way to a table away from the other patrons. We settled in and I leaned in.

"That is a sweet woman."

"Gracie used to own a toy store. Every afternoon she would have story time. She'd bake cookies for the kids. Her chocolate chip oatmeal cookies—amazing."

"I can see her doing that. I can definitely see her doing that." I took a draw of the sipping chocolate. It was thick and rich, lingering in my mouth like a thinned pudding fresh off the stove. The chocolate hit my system in a rush, through my tongue, through my throat, settling a contentment deep inside me. Still bundled in Matteo's intoxicating jacket, I leaned back in my chair. "Mmm, lovely. So, what did you do after abandoning your high school acting career?"

Matteo took a sip of his own cocoa. I watched him lick it from those perfect lips, watched his throat convulse as he swallowed it. Got caught watching. He set his glass down with a small smile.

"I was a high school geology teacher."

"God! You are kidding. And how many cheerleaders did you have stalking you home at night?"

"Just the two."

I watched him for a beat. "You're not kidding, are you?"

"Nope. Tiffany called the cops, but nobody took it too seriously. I'd been on the job for about four months when the principal finally sat me down for 'the talk.' She promised she was thoroughly impressed with my abilities in the classroom."

"But?"

"But perhaps this just wasn't an appropriate career path for someone like me."

"Wow."

"'Perhaps when you are a little older. When there is more of an age gap between you and the students,' she said."

I watched his face for a moment; his reaction to the memory was easy enough to read. "It broke your heart, didn't it? Your dream, everything you worked for turned into something ugly."

"Yeah. Yeah it did."

And he wasn't just referring to 'the talk,' I knew. I heard the weight in his voice, did the math in my head. He'd have been working in that school when the Sleeper's Syndrome epidemic hit. It was an easy guess that over half of the kids in that school now slept in a Castle somewhere. *God.*

Time to take the conversation elsewhere. I sat forward on my chair, speared off a piece of the steamed sweet bread, gave it an extra dip in the pool of vanilla sauce, and offered it to him. I openly studied how his tongue drew the bread forward, how his lips closed over the fork and slowly tugged the delicacy into his mouth. My stomach did a slow tumble as I blindly returned the fork to the plate.

"So," I began, trying to coax thought back to my brain. "So what do you do for Jürgen? You started to tell me about developing jobs, but you dropped it just when it was getting interesting."

He laughed, obviously not buying into my curiosity.

"Well?" I prompted.

"Alright, but just remember you asked. When we first got here, we were losing people to depression by the handfuls. It was a horrible time. Jürgen decided we needed to turn this place into a settlement, a city—give people something to focus on besides everything they'd lost. I got elected to be a glorified trainer. I research the careers involved in each business or government position that Jürgen, Suzi, and Dr. Roz decide we need. Then I go out and recruit and train people, help them get set up with the suppliers, that sort of thing. Like I told you: exciting." He glanced up at the heat lamp, then pulled his chair closer in. I chuckled. After considering for a moment, I rose. He watched me uncertainly as I pulled his jacket from my shoulders. I stepped around the small table until I stood beside him. He took his time, sweeping his gaze up my body until he reached my eyes. Then I leaned down and wrapped the jacket around him. His lips parted in protest. I shushed him with a finger.

"You can loan it to me again when we leave. I'm fine."

And I was. The feeling reminded me of sitting at a bonfire: frozen on one side, baked on the other. It was stimulating. Almost as stimulating as the high school geology teacher watching me walk away. As I resumed my seat, I reached for the fork and broke off a piece of the dumpling he had made look so tantalizing. I had just raised the fork to my lips when the plate slid off the table in a screech of porcelain against metal. I clenched my teeth to keep the vibration of the horrible noise from making a second pass through my bones.

"Luciana!"

I have no idea how he drew the air to shout. Involuntary reflex had me holding my breath. When I looked, I saw the plate disappear into the shadows of a hunched figure wrapped in layer after layer of tattered garments. The impression of a filthy face was barely discernable beneath the mounds of cloth. A set of small grimy fingers clutched the second fork and the plate. The stench sent my eyes watering.

"Luciana, if you were hungry, you could have just said something."

"Venessia sent me to see the new one." The pile of rags stabbed her fork in my direction. "She is pretty enough. Yes, she is. Will she keep you from selling your soul, Matti? Will she?"

The bent little woman tossed the plate and fork back on the table—empty.

"What is your name?" she demanded.

I hesitated, loathed to part with something so personal, so fundamental. The creature just chuckled.

"Ah, smart one, this girl. Smart one she is. She understands. Maybe she will make it. Better than you." She flicked a dirt brown hand at Matteo, began to wander back into the fog. "Better than you. Always lying to yourself. Every day a little lie. Umm hmm. Until you've lost yourself. All gone! And your soul has slipped away...."

Her chattery little voice faded away. Her scent took a little longer. Finally, I turned back around in my seat.

"Okay, what was that?"

Matteo just shook his head, a cross between perturbed and amused. "A little local color. There were a handful of 'Venetians' still living in the ruins when we got here. Luciana is sort of their leader, I guess. She always pops up at the weirdest moments. Mostly benevolent. Emphasis on mostly. I'll get another *Dampfnudel*. Oh, here comes Gracie already."

The skinny proprietress set a fresh desert down before us, collected the empty plate. I offered to pay. She just shook her head. Matteo explained.

"We always put a little extra in the tip to cover it."

"She does this a lot?"

Gracie laughed over her shoulder as she headed back for the warmth of her hut. "A couple times a week. I think our little sprite gets lonely."

For a moment I looked back off in the direction the creature had gone. They didn't try to cage her. They simply adjusted the pattern of their lives to accommodate her. As I turned toward the table, I slipped the neglected bite of fluffy, creamy bread into my mouth. When I had finished savoring the smooth flavor, I rested my chin on my hand.

"I'm speaking out of turn here. I haven't seen much, but from what I have seen, you've built yourselves a beautiful life here. You could have just come here to rot, but—"

"It's Jürgen. He—"

"Did Jürgen implement the Luciana tip?"

"No, I did."

"Did Jürgen organize the bonfires?"

"No, Gracie did, but that's not the point. Jürgen got us back on our feet. Gave us the chance to find our self worth again."

"Maybe, but you took the opportunity. You did something beautiful with it. You're creating jobs for people. You're helping people feel useful and needed."

"It's my job. It needs—" he broke off, his eyes roaming my face critically. He reached out, pulled my gloved hand from the cocoa cup. His thumb rubbed at the juncture between my forefinger and middle finger as he pulled me forward, closer, caging me with the seriousness of his scrutiny. I held off the delicious shiver my body wanted to respond with.

"You were saying?" I prompted.

"I was saying...." He looked down at the table. "When I saw your name on the guest list this morning, I thought, oh that skinny girl from drama class. Didn't she become one of those half-crazy immersion artists? It might be fun to see her again...or it might be awful. She'll probably see me and run screaming, 'Carrier!'" He looked up at me and I was riveted by the soul in those eyes. "So tell me, Alyse: How did I get you so wrong? You are smart and funny. You are kind and thoughtful. And you are so beautiful, graceful. I could sit here and watch you and the way you move all night."

I stared at him, completely taken aback.

"You look shocked. Why?"

"I...." I didn't know what to say. People didn't say things like that to me. Except my Daddy. Except for my Daddy.

Matteo seemed to understand so easily. His eyes narrowed gently.

"How long has it been since somebody told you that?"

My face pinched up with a warning of tears. I closed my eyes and tried to breathe out of a prickly nose.

"Alyse?"

"Sorry, I...I thought I was steady. I..." I pressed a fingertip to my forehead, trying to pull myself back together. How to explain without sounding oedipal?

I felt his big hand slide over my cheek, cup my face. I flinched. Then I froze. It didn't come. The horrible grinding sensation, it didn't come.

I opened my eyes.

I stared at him.

"What's wrong?"

"You can touch me?" I breathed.

"What's wrong, Alyse?"

I glanced around us, at the handful of people carefully minding their own business.

"Is there someplace more private?"

He came around the table and slid the jacket back around my shoulders. I clutched it shakily as he helped me to my feet. He held me tight as we drifted out into the fog. I burrowed closer, my mind, an empty rattle I kept a cautious distance from. We reached the small shack that housed the ladder.

But this time the gate had a guardian.

I felt her before I saw her, that same surge of power I'd felt from Jürgen, but more elemental, more penetrating. Both Matteo and I stopped abruptly. His grip on me tightened.

She took form from the shadows that clung to the structure where the light couldn't penetrate the fog. The delicate lines of her face took shape first, upward sloping eyes, cheeks, and jaw. Her skin had the same pale hue as the clouds around her and her eyes were a ghostly blue, narrowed coyly. She stepped forward and Matteo went completely still beneath my hands. Her long, long silvery hair danced around her face and her glittering gown flowed in the same mysterious storm. My whole body screamed a warning at a mind that had long since gone numb.

Then she laughed, a light airy sound, completely at odds with the seductive threat I felt coming off her.

"Ah, Matteo, are you going to hide her from Hadria? Keep her for yourself?"

Matteo jerked into motion.

"Get lost, Cirena."

Again the tinkling laugh. She tossed her head back, her hands clasped in merriment. Matteo's arm turned to steel as he held me against him and pushed his way around her. She floated easily aside, her glee never faltering as she watched us.

"Oh, little Matteo, but what if I want her for myself?"

Her overloud whisper followed us into the shack like the rush of a falcon's wings, only warning of danger after it was too late. Matteo slammed the door behind us. Her tiny giggle still filled the room inside, taunting us.

"Come on."

Matteo led the way down the ladder. I was going into overload. I had to force my body to focus on the task of lowering me down the metal rungs. Matteo lifted me off and set me down next to him. He navigated the maze of corridors and closets, then came to a stop at a door.

"Sorry about Cirena back there. She's, well, she's got a pretty fucked-up sense of humor." He glanced at the door. "Are you...do you still...?" He turned back to me, brushed a thumb over my cheekbone. "Are you comfortable going to my apartment?"

I stilled my rushing breath as his smooth skin slid over mine. *He could touch me.*

The fey woman's sinister taunting melted away as the warmth of him spread through my chill body. I looked into those questioning eyes and nodded silently.

We slipped out into the stairway and he led me down the flights until we reached the entrance level, but instead of turning toward the crystal staircase, he turned the other way and pushed through a door marked "Private." Two doors down his key card admitted us to another world. Brown suede couch, coffee table made of driftwood, ceiling of dark stained timbers. The burnt-orange wall slowly grew in luminescence as the apartment recognized its owner. The room was divided by a grey marble counter. On the other side gleamed a stainless steel kitchen.

I had invaded his personal space. He was uncomfortable. I was uncomfortable.

"Can I get you anything? A glass of water?"

"No, thank you."

A cereal bowl and a sweatshirt lay on the coffee table. He reached for them. I put a hand on his arm, pushed it down. I wanted him back. I wanted him back with me. Slowly, he raised his head. That brown gaze met mine. I held him there in that pose until the hard analytical edge wavered, softened, until he was with me once more. I lowered my hand. As he straightened before me, I traced a satin-clad finger along his jawbone. He lifted his hand to do the same, but the second before his skin touched mine, he stopped, drew back his hand. He looked from his curled fingers to me.

"What happened up there, Alyse? Before, when I touched you."

With a steadying breath, I stepped back. He watched as I slipped out of his suit jacket. Stalling, I walked over to his tall grey bistro table and hung it with precision on the back of one of the chairs.

I kept my back to him. "Can you help me with these gloves?"

He walked up behind me. I could feel him over me, around me. I tensed. He glided his finger over the skin of my arm, pulled the garter free of the hook, once...twice...three times. I lost my breath. He slid his fingers beneath the satin and peeled the glove down my arm. I pressed my lips together to keep from moaning. It had been so long.

"Alyse," he whispered. The syllables of my name fanned my ear, my neck, tasting of chocolate. I looked up. I saw him watching me in the mirror above the kitchen sink. I saw us together: him with his soft eyes gone wicked and hungry, me with my whole body gone loose and wanton, open for the taking. He tugged the glove from my fingers. He ran the cool, smooth satin up my arm, across my neck, until my head fell back against his shoulder.

We watched each other from afar as he stripped the other glove from my body, tossed it with a flick onto the table. He ran his palms down the length of my arms. I couldn't hold it back any longer. I groaned, nuzzling his neck with the bare skin of my cheek. He held me up, turned me around, his eyes serious.

"You wear those gloves on purpose. Why?"

"I'm hypersensitive. It hurts when people touch me. Skin to skin."

"This hurts you?"

I laughed a little deliriously. "No." I reached up tentatively, stroked my hand down the side of his stunned face. My hand trembled as I pulled it away. "No, it feels wonderful."

As comprehension turned his eyes soft, Matteo framed my face with his big, gentle hands. "You've been alone a long, long time, haven't you, Alyse Bryant?"

"Don't make me cry again."

"I'm not going to make you cry again. I'm going to kiss you." My heart stilled as his hands shifted to cradle my head. His thumb brushed my lips open. His lips followed in the gentlest caress. Then he came back for more and I wanted it all. I tangled my hands in all that long, thick hair and yanked him even closer. His groan rumbled against my lips.

"God, how did you get under my skin so fast?"

He didn't give me a chance to answer. He nipped at my lower lip. I tipped my head back and opened my mouth, let him in. Our tongues met. I whimpered. He dived in. My back slammed against the chair. My hands scrambled for the buttons of his shirt. I had to touch all of him. Now. I clawed the buttons free, shoved crisp cotton aside, filled my senses with him: satin-smooth skin, ridges of muscle and bone, that earthy, warm scent that only sharpened my craving. I lowered my head and nibbled at one hard nipple.

He groaned and pushed me away. "Shoes."

I balanced against his head as he pulled off my Cinderella slippers. Then he reached up my skirt and yanked down my satin leggings, panties and all.

I hesitated.

He didn't.

Matteo rose before me, suddenly bigger, stronger. He grabbed me by the waist and hoisted me onto his marble counter. The silk skirt parted, leaving me bare. His gaze lowered, then climbed back up my torso.

"You're not wearing a bra, are you?" He scooped a hand into my bodice and freed one breast from its delicate silk prison. He reached in again and exposed the other breast as well. "I've wanted to do that all night. This dress was built to kill a guy. And so were these." He caressed the generous slope and curve of my breasts lovingly. Then he dipped his head. And suckled. I cried out, bucked, arched back. He caught me. But he didn't let me go.

With his free hand, he slowly, purposely followed my center line using the firm pressure of his thumb, starting at my forehead, down my nose, into my open mouth, deep on my tongue, damply down my chin, my throat. With the moisture of my mouth, he drew the divide between my breasts, the separation of my ribs, the vulnerable give of my belly with a dangerous dip at my navel, until he reach the naked skin revealed by my split skirt. There he rubbed at the bone, taunting my most sensitive organs until I was begging.

He released my breast with his mouth, but kept me tossing and mindless with his quick fingers flicking over my nipple.

His hand caressed my inner thigh as he lifted my leg and hooked my heel on the edge of the counter. Then he guided my other foot to the cold, cold marble. He had me wide open, exposed, uncaring.

Without preamble, he parted the last of my center line. My breath caught. I reached a flailing hand toward him, to stop him, to urge him on, but he was beyond my reach. I was at his mercy. He held me open. The warm, hard pressure of his finger began tracing me in looping figure eights, slowly, faster, faster, faster. I twisted. I thrashed. I screamed.

"I want inside you, Alyse. I want to drive myself deep inside you right here." He used a pair of fingers to demonstrate.

"Please," I sobbed. "Please, now. Oh, God!"

I heard his belt hit the floor with a thump, his shoes clattered after it, all the while his fingers pumped into me. He stepped up onto something. Then he stopped, just held me open with his big warm hands on my thighs. I felt the cool pressure at my entrance. I braced myself. He rammed into me. I shattered.

He had to catch my legs as I fell limp.

"Are you alright?"

"Yes, very."

He kissed my knee as he started moving inside me. Bliss began building back toward frenzy. I hooked my knees over his arms; his hands moved back to my breasts, kneading, pulling, gripping that soft flesh to slam me against him. I strained to get closer, rocked my hips to meet his thrusts. Then my mind released and my hips were moving of their own accord, my hands groping the counter wildly, for something, anything to hold onto. I was coming apart, coming undone, I couldn't hold on anymore.

He stopped, froze above me.

I whimpered. His hands caged my hips, pinning me in place.

"Stop, Alyse. I can't. Stop."

I shuddered. His grip tightened.

"Stop," he ordered, his voice nearly a growl.

I tried to gather myself together.

"There won't be any babies. My switch is flipped," I assured him, my own voice barely a whisper.

His breathing grew faster, rougher. "Not the problem."

The note of desperation in his voice raised me up on my elbows in alarm. His eyes were closed, his face beaded with sweat, his features twisted with a terrible strain.

"Matteo? Oh, God, do you need a doctor? What's—?"

His eyes flashed open, looked straight into mine: no irises, no whites, just black glittering chaos. Soulless. *Will she keep you from selling your soul, Matti?* My own core froze painfully as I stared. His lips twisted in a snarl. Then the sound: a growl, a roar, a shriek that pierced my icy shock.

"What the fuck?!"

I scrambled backward in a tangle of silk. He grabbed my skirt, flipped me over. I kicked at his ribs, managed to swing my body head first off the counter, taking coffee cups with me. We both hit the floor. He grabbed my hair, jerked my head back. That horrible animal shriek cracked the air again, froze me. He stabbed himself inside me. I screamed, clawed at the hand that held my hair. My touch-starved body didn't care what had changed. Only a few more strokes and my muscles convulsed; his body jerked with his conclusion. I felt the slight loosening of his hand in my hair. I wrenched myself free. I rammed the ridge of my foot into his ribs. He grabbed for my foot, missed, surged to his feet before I could get fully upright. I tried to shield myself with an arm, but his blow tossed me off my feet. I struck something. My ribs gave just a little too much. My head went back, hit something hard.

I saw the bestial rage on the face of the man I'd just made love to.

Then I saw nothing.

༄

Her exquisite, pale face hovered above mine. Her silver hair still danced in its own wind. She smiled gently as her cool fingers ran lines of relief over my halo of pain.

"Sleep."

I breathed in her glittering, sweet breath.

I slept.

Chapter 6

"There she is. I told you we should have contacted her primary sooner. These high-tech patients always have little quirks you don't know about."

I heard the syllables. It wasn't for several moments that they grouped together into words, then into ideas: I was in a medical facility. I didn't want to open my eyes. Something bad was out there. Something out there was going to hurt me.

"She should be coming around any second now."

"Alyse," a woman's voice whispered kindly. "You're alright now. Come on and open your eyes." She laid a papery hand on my arm. I jerked, shrieked, snatched my arm away. A moment later, my body screamed. I couldn't.

"Up the dosage," the grey-haired, grey-bearded man told the woman standing next to me. My body shuddered as the drugs flooded into me. My breath returned.

"Sal, get in here. She's awake. Better let everyone else know, too."

A new man in a lab coat came through the door. He glanced at me with a quick nod of his balding head and turned to study my charts with the other man. The woman with her rounded figure and rounded head of black hair joined them.

"She's behaving just like a phase one patient, Dr. Franco," she told the newcomer in a low voice. As if I couldn't hear her.

Dr. Franco's Mediterranean complexion paled. Finally, he nodded, resigned.

"Alright." He turned to me. "Alyse, my name is Dr. Sal Franco. This is Dr. Neil Grimshaw and his wife Maeve is a registered nurse." The door opened again. An older, stout woman entered, looking like she had been pulled straight from her bed, her poof of sculpted blond hair flat on one side and her loud floral blouse wrinkled. "This is Dr. Roz Calles. She handles mental health issues here at the camp."

"Don't let Jürgen hear you say that," she teased, her kindly eyes twinkling.

"Right. Here at the *city*," Dr. Franco amended. "We're just waiting for Jürgen and Suzi. They should be right here."

I had to close my eyes. Too many people, too much noise. The sickening fear I'd awoken with had begun to creep back in. Bits and pieces floated to the surface of my mind: a sound that rolled through the roar of a wild cat and broke off in the two-part shriek of a hawk. Sweet, soulful eyes. A cruel hand fisted in my hair. Gentle lips. A blow hard enough to break my arm, knock me from my feet.

"Alyse, stay with us for a moment, dear," the perky psychologist coaxed.

I forced my eyes open, but I was trembling now. Dr. Franco gave the nurse a nod. She touched something on my bed. The tremors slowed, the tightness in my chest eased slightly.

The door opened one more time. Jürgen and Suzi entered the room. That aura of power filled the large, vacant space, but the pair was all grim-faced business. Suzi carried her strappy heels in one hand. Jürgen had removed his jacket and tie, rolled up his sleeves. On his forearm was a wide medieval-looking brace of beaten bronze, acting as a backdrop for a glowing row of red and green gems. A strange piece of jewelry for a man.

Dr. Franco gave the mayor and his second a nod, then approached my bedside. "Alyse, you've taken a pretty nasty beating. You have a cracked radius in your left arm and three broken ribs on your right side. Your team has been notified of your status, but we can't allow them to visit at this time."

I watched the doctor's droopy face as he spoke. Dr. Sal Franco. I knew that name.

Mo?

Dr. Sal Franco. Developer of the gene therapy cure for Brighton's Disease. Has spent the last nine years unsuccessfully researching a cure for Sleeper's Syndrome.

"Could you recount how you came to be in Mr. Ranier's apartment?"

"We were up at Gracie's and decided we wanted some more privacy," I whispered.

"Did you and Mr. Ranier have an argument?"

"No, we had sex."

"You got the fractured arm from having sex?" The doctor half looked like he would believe it—you know those wild immersion artists.

"No, he...." Now I was at a loss. His eyes turned into bottomless black pits? He howled like a feral beast? Even the flood of meds couldn't keep my voice steady. "He attacked me."

"Would you be able to tell us a little bit more about what instigated the attack?"

I let my face speak for me.

The doctor shook his head. "We're not asking out of prurient interest. In addition to creating an incident record, we are trying to determine a course of treatment for Mr. Ranier. When we found you, you were both unconscious. He appears to have had some kind of breakdown."

I shifted on my cot and my body reminded me even through the medication exactly what kind of "breakdown" he'd had. My brain, however, was refusing to have a reaction—a big black emotionless space. I used that emptiness to find my voice.

"We had almost finished having sex when he froze up. It looked like he was in a great deal of pain. I offered to get a doctor, but..." I stopped, the memory requiring too much editing. "...but he scared me. I...tried to get away, but he caught me. We finished having sex. Then I tried to beat the shit out of him and he did beat the shit out of me. That's pretty much it." Any more was none of their goddamn business.

"One last question: Did he attack you before or after you tried to get away?"

I shot him a wary look. "After."

The doctor turned back to his group. "I told you they were messing around with the braces."

"I would never have believed Matteo would be that stupid," Suzi said.

Dr. Calles, in her over-bright flowers, left the clutch of medical doctors and circled my bed to stand on the other side.

"This all probably won't hit you until the morning. They have you pretty drugged up, but tomorrow I will come back and we can talk about it for a while."

She reached out to pat my arm. I dodged her touch. Her hand darted out and caught my forearm. Her warm, plump fingers wrapped around my wrist. The pain faded. I stared at her, my heart pounding. She just smiled and nodded. With a pat on my hand, she raised her head and interrupted the low argument on the opposite side of my bed.

"This girl is worn out, Dr. Sal. Let's finish up here so that she can get some sleep."

I'd had enough of the weirdness.

"I want to see my crew."

Dr. Franco bit his lip as he returned to my bedside. I had the whole room's undivided attention. I didn't like it.

"I'm afraid you can't."

"Maybe now is not a good time, Sal," Jürgen said, laying a hand on the doctor's shoulder.

Broken bones or no I pushed myself upright. I saw my beautiful dress, Tamsin's gift, in tatters in a chair in the corner. Jürgen stepped quickly around the doctor. Gently, he lowered me back to the bed. His touch left no aftershocks when he pulled his hands away. Tears wobbled in my eyes as he leaned over me. I felt unbearably young and lost as he tucked strands of hair back away from my face.

"What's happened?" I forced myself to ask.

He paused, his regal face registering grief.

"You're infected, Alyse. You're a carrier."

For hours I fought for consciousness through a thick haze of drugs. Each time I grasped it, a fleeting thought distracted me, slid me back under. Now once more I seized at a crack in the chemical barricade. This time my desperate grip held. I felt the cool breeze of reality on my face. I snapped my eyes open, trying to lock in my return. The moving air burned my eyes as I stared at the scarred ceiling. I forced myself to trace the patterns of battered beams left behind by archeologists and looters. I traced them over and over and over. Just holding on, nothing more.

Minutes passed. I dared release a little tension from my body, let my gaze wander in a little wider sweep, still wary of distraction, just focusing on the chipped pattern of the moldings. That's when I saw him. In a blackened corner of the ceiling, he gazed down on me beatifically, a bulbous baby, naked save for a pair of tiny feathered wings—both whimsical and grotesque in his burnt out patch of painted sky.

"He's mine, you know. I saw him first, I did."

As startled as I was, my body was too heavy to react. Instead I turned my eyes, saw the nurse, Maeve, sitting in a chair beside me.

"When Venice finally died, the folk who were left took everything with 'em they could: paintings, wood paneling, marble. All of it had more value to 'em over there in those souvenir markets than left here for the sea to destroy. Then the looters came. Chipped away everything else. Like grave robbers, they were. Stripped the corpse down to the bones. Sometimes they even took the bones themselves. But they missed my little *putti*. Left him to watch over us, I like to think. Lord knows we need watchin' over."

I turned my eyes back to the little orphaned infant. I'd awoken fighting, angry. Now desolation joined the weight on my unresponsive body.

Left behind.

In the most beautiful city in the world.

In the emptiness. Someone had been left. Someone had been here in the end. Had made the choice to leave. How must it have been? How must it have been to have the responsibility for the stories and for the lives of all of your forefathers...and then one day to realize that living had to take precedence over remembering? You had to leave, knowing you had abandoned all this...to die its solitary death. Or die with it.

The choice gets forgotten. Then the emptiness gets erased.

Until it is hard to imagine.

Back home, I remembered a black and white photo—a patch of foundations: Demersville. Kalispell's great rival. Demersville had been someone's bright dream. And then it was gone. Lost to a little change in the path of the coming railroad. Its people put wheels on their businesses and their houses, dragged them across the plain, a great creaking convoy. They set down new roots in Kalispell, went on with their lives. Most of them, anyway.

But Demersville was a brash young man. Venice was a grand dame.

Left behind.

The sea dragging at her heavy skirts.

Only a matter of time.

I felt myself slipping again. The exhaustion swept forward. I fought it back half-heartedly.

"Sleep if you need to. I'll be here. I won't let you wake up alone."

The anger surged.

"Your injuries are healing very well. With a little rest you should be whole by evening. I know it doesn't feel like it right now, but you are really very lucky. You exhibit all the symptoms of the patients who respond well to the Sleeper's Syndrome treatment. There is hope, dear. You hang onto that. It's more than folk here have had in so long."

Sleeper's Syndrome.

Sleeper's Syndrome.

The anger found focus.

My DNA is not patched. I cannot catch Sleeper's Syndrome you lying son's of bitches!

Mo, you tell Margie to get these drugs out of my system right now. Do it slow. I don't want them noticing, but get this shit out of me!

The woman next to me prattled on.

"I truly am so sorry about Matteo. I know it wouldn't do a speck of good to tell you he's a good man. But maybe I can tell you he had a terrible breakdown. He's on Dr. Franco's treatment plan, but someone went and tampered with his medications. Unfortunately, you had to witness why that is a dangerous, right foolish thing to do. Jürgen and Suzi are doing their best. They will find out what happened, find out who did it. If it makes you more comfortable, Matteo will be confined to his apartment until Dr. Franco has been able to stabilize him."

I laughed. Two short barks of sound. I pressed my lips together.

"Don't worry, dear. The drugs should wear off soon. Now, I should go get Dr. Franco. Just you wait right here. I'll be back right quick."

I watched her bustle around the bed and lean through the doorway to chatter at someone else. Any other time, I might have thought she was cute, sweet even—if she hadn't been the one to drug me.

Maeve must have seen the look on my face when she turned to resume her station at my side. She looked suddenly nervous. That only made the prattling worse.

"Your friends sent ya down a change of clothes when you're feeling up for it. Didn't guess you'd be wanting to spend too much time in that gown." She hesitated at the foot of my bed, her face naked in her fear and worry. "For myself, I can't understand how ya could have become infected. I've been here nine years with Neil and never developed a single symptom. Either has Roz. I've been trying so hard to think—"

"Maeve."

Her head snapped up. Dr. Franco finished walking through the door, closed it quietly behind him. The doctor's droopy face now bore dark black smudges beneath his eyes and at the brackets of his mouth. Maeve sent him a wordless apology. Then he turned to me.

"You're up earlier than I was expecting. I would have liked to see you get a little more rest." I noticed him keeping his distance from the head of the bed. I also noticed a reddened bruise on his left cheekbone. I couldn't remember putting that mark there, but I remembered enough rage, fear, and desperation to have caused it. I kept my face, my mind blank. He kept talking.

"Jürgen would like to see you when you are ready. Your infection will have huge ramifications for everyone. He would like to call a meeting with you and Lone Pine to discuss the best way to handle it."

Of course he would.

As if the outcome of that meeting hadn't been predetermined the minute I stepped onto that crystal staircase. All the penetrating stares, the threatening innuendo, the orchestrated encounters. The warnings of my intuition I'd purposely, blatantly ignored. Was Emory so wrong about me after all? Was I actually hell bent on my own destruction?

Before that thought could take root, I locked my brain's defenses down. Silence.

I watched the doctor as he lifted my chart from the holster at the foot of my bed, scrolled through it. When he replaced it, a tremor ran through his hand, but he offered me a smile when he looked up at me again.

"We'll discuss your treatment options at that time as well. Go ahead and let Maeve know when you are ready."

And then he left. So matter-of-factly. *Here's your death sentence. Let's get together and discuss how you want to carry it out. See you then!* So much bullshit.

I tested my hands, rolling my fingers, my wrists discreetly. Satisfied, I moved to sit up. Maeve rushed to my side.

"Take your time now, dear. There's no reason to hurry."

I let her do most of the heavy lifting. When she had me upright, I released the tie on the grey hospital gown and tossed it aside. That sent her scrambling for my clothes without further argument. I gave her enough trouble with the clumsy dressing process and my little trip to the bathroom that she hurriedly called for a wheelchair when I pulled off my wrist monitor and pointed my careful steps toward the door.

Maeve drove me out through a tiny reception area and into a hallway. Little details looked familiar: the wall lamp, the arrangement of the five doors, the big solid door at the end of the hall. Adrenaline gave my heart a little twist. The second door down. Was that Matteo's apartment? Or was this a different part of the palace all together? Maeve turned my chair the other direction.

Mo, tell Tamsin and everybody I'm going to want to talk to them after this little meeting.

Maeve actually left me in peace as she rolled me around the corner of the short hall. The Venetian fantasy land looked different in the daylight—a little more worn, a little more homemade—until we got into Jürgen's apartment. His front room had been set up as an executive office, one part meeting space, one part private work area. The chairs, paint, and carpeting were all pale grays, blues, and whites. The accents slashed through the haze of color with hard lines of black. But the man himself was the centerpiece of the display. As we came in, he set aside a report and got to his feet. I had to fight the instinctual urge to rise to the challenge in those hard, considering eyes. He gestured to the guest chair in front of his desk, but I stayed in my wheelchair, the perfect picture of feminine weakness.

Maeve was dismissed. Jürgen resumed his seat, sat back, and waited.

I looked around his office, spare of furnishings, but the paintings, sheer stiff panel curtains, the wrought iron lighting fixtures were almost mystical—certainly expensive. Outside the window I saw bright daylight.

Mo, turn on my recording feature. No tell light.
Illegal function. No consent.
So is kidnapping. Turn it on. Now.
Recording feature: on.

"So," I said, finally. "I've spent the morning trying to decide if this constitutes theft or kidnapping. Since there are Built to Recycle instructions in my schematics, I'm guessing legally this is a theft. I suppose I should have been suspicious when the project spec said you only needed us for five days. A project this size would take years, decades even."

I turned my wandering gaze directly on him, let him taste my disgust. "So I'm left wondering: did you just go after me or did you leave a lure out for any of the other five? What did you try to lure them in with? Drugs, money, sex? By the way, you can tell Matteo he was a great fuck."

That got a reaction, however small: violent menace leapt up in those dark eyes.

But then it was gone.

Now it was my turn to sit back and wait.

He took his time. Slowly, he tapped his interlaced fingers against his lips. The tapping grew faster as I watched. Then the fingers dropped to his lap.

"We haven't decided what to do with you yet. Your existence jeopardizes everything we've managed to build here. You are carrying a falsified DNA chip. Not only doesn't your dog tag reflect the manipulation of your genes, but our analysis revealed a series of non-matching genetic identity markers."

And he got the reaction he'd been fishing for. I pulled the shock quickly from my face. If the rest was lies, then this would be, too. A convenient explanation for an infection I shouldn't be biologically capable of contracting.

"We had to run a full work-up when we got the positive test result. That's when we discovered the discrepancies. We're hoping they lead us to a logical explanation. So far that is not the case. In an effort to avoid providing the world's terrorists with a new bunch of targets to practice on, we are willing to wait in reporting your infection until we can locate the source of your DNA patch and confirm the circumstances of your infection. If there is anything you can tell us about your medical history that might help, we would appreciate having that information to work with."

Terrorist targets. My mom, my uncle, my aunt and her family. Despite my careful blankness, my stomach slammed viciously. All Jürgen had to do was whisper. Even an official government denial wouldn't save my family's lives. Too many terrorists, too many terrified people who just wanted it to all go away. I could feel the sweat beading up on my face.

A knock sounded at the door. Jürgen admitted Dr. Franco.

"Sal, I have just been explaining to Ms. Bryant that her cooperation in determining the source of her DNA patch could save a lot of unnecessary violence in the world. Did Tamir tell you the Seers tried to attack last night? They got lost in the fog, swept out to sea at low tide."

"Amazing they didn't get burnt to crisp in the security perimeter."

"Indeed."

Dr. Franco took the chair I'd declined. Both men looked at me.

"The patch in your DNA isn't exactly the same as the one I used in my Brighton's patients," Dr. Franco informed me. "But I've run the treatment scenarios and it should work just as well for you. Jürgen is right, though, if we could find out how you were altered, that would be very valuable information. It would help us discover if there are others like you capable of becoming carriers. I haven't had much time to look into it, but could the

DNA patching possibly have been done during your sensory immersion operations?"

I replied to his questioning look with a level stare.

Mo, I need a current layout of this place.

She turned up a rough sketch.

Map me a way out of here.

"Ms. Bryant is electing to believe she is the victim of an elaborate kidnapping plot, rather than accept her condition."

"Ah, well, I truly wish that were the case. Unfortunately, I ran both tests three times and they came out the same each time. This isn't something I would lie about, not for any amount of personal benefit. I can promise you that." Dr. Franco rose. "I think you will discover that once you have progressed a certain distance into the therapy, that you will find a great deal of release from symptoms that have been affecting your lifestyle. Matteo mentioned that you are already suffering from touch sensitivity. Bouts of severe melancholy can also be common. Especially ones related to specific locations—like an intense homesickness. You just have to give the therapy some time. If you are ready, I can escort you to the treatment center. "

The doctor took my lack of response as agreement. He walked around behind me and released the locks on my chair.

"I'll be by a little later on," Jürgen assured me. I actually saw sympathy in that lordly face. That finally got me scared.

I caught myself holding my breath as Dr. Franco backed me away from the desk and wheeled me to the door. He reached over me to push the door open. I let out the hoarded air in a rush.

The door banged against the foot rest.

I sprang through the doorway.

I turned and slammed the door shut, ramming the chair into the doctor.

Then I ran.

Mo's map pointed me around the corner and back toward the door at the end of the corridor. I reached the midpoint lighting fixture when a hand closed over my arm, whipping me around. That same hand caught me around the throat and slammed me against the wall. Impossibly, I found myself face-to-face with Jürgen. His face was remote, inhuman, terrifying.

"Don't mistake my empathy for stupidity. I will not allow you back out there. I will not allow even one more child to be locked away in one of those damn castles."

"You won't get away with this you psychopathic son-of-a-bitch."

"You better believe I will. I hold all the power here, Alyse." His breath was strangely sweet on my face. A memory tried to flit to the surface, but he gave me a shake and the connection was gone. He dug his forearm into my sternum. My hands clutched reflexively at his wrist. "One call and the whole world will have you on the Carrier's List. You won't make it two centimeters onto dry land. Think about that."

"Alyse?"

I wrested my gaze away.

Matteo.

He stood in the doorway to his apartment, his face pale, his eyes red, T-shirt rumpled, feet bare. On his forearm an antique brace gleamed dully, a brace exactly like the one Jürgen wore underneath his civilized business shirt. For a split second my heart stopped beating as a volley of terror, joy, and confusion hit it all at once. Then I screamed.

"Matteo, get him off me!"

Matteo tried to run toward me. His feet jerked to a halt. *Confined to his quarters.* Fuck!

"Let her go, Jürgen! Don't do this!"

Jürgen glanced over his shoulder. "Get back inside, Matteo. I will speak with you in a moment."

I struggled to see past the lamp that was butted up against my head. The door back to reality was so close. Jürgen's attention returned to me and I shivered. My breath was coming in gasps. Only a few meters. I had to make it—if only to get away from that soul-stealing stare.

I bucked and head-butted one of the richest men in the world. Bursts of starlight flickered in my vision; pain streaked across my skull, but I distanced myself from all of it. Jürgen blinked and I attacked, releasing all of my pent up terror into a flurry of jabs and lashes. He stumbled a half-step back. That was all I needed. I drew my knees up and rammed my feet into him. He lost his grip on my neck. I fell.

"Run, Alyse! They're coming!"

I raised my spinning head and saw two security guards, one a big barrel of a man, the other short and stocky, leaping over the capsized wheelchair. I bolted for the door. Only a few meters. I reached for the handle. His full body weight—solid muscle—struck me from behind, slammed me face first into the tile floor. I lost the air from my lungs; my intake of breath sounded like a quiet scream.

"You could have gone willingly. You could have had the support of all of us who have gone before you. Now you will sit in a jail cell and suffer your symptoms alone...until you either change your mind or lose your mind. It is your decision." Then Jürgen lowered his voice until it was barely audible. "But I must thank you, Alyse, for a beautiful hunt. We'll do it again sometime."

"We'll take it from here, Mr. Phan Mai."

I felt Jürgen's smile against my cheek just before his weight lifted from my body. I dropped my head to the cold tile. A large black boot cut off my view as my arms were wrenched behind my back, my wrists cinched together with a sharp plastic tie. My captors lifted me free of the floor.

"...arrest for carrying a false ID tag, refusing treatment for a Category I Infectious Disease, assaulting a government official..."

I looked up.

The door had only been a breath away.

Chapter 7

The door to the cell only reached my ribs. The shorter guard snipped the plastic tie binding my wrists. Blood rushed into my hands. I rubbed the purple marks left behind.

"Duck." The larger guard pushed my head down and gave me a little shove forward. I stumbled into the tiny room.

"Stay away from the walls. Turn you into a bleedin' porcupine."

I spun around just in time to see the two men's legs disappear as they pushed the ancient wood door closed, sealing me in. Through the tiny square window I saw their shadows walk away. Their footsteps receded. Then there was silence.

There was silence in me, too. An empty quiet just waiting. For something.

I turned and looked around my little wooden box in the dim light. Behind a partition: a metal toilet, a metal sink. In the center of the room: a metal cot, a pile of folded blankets, a pillow. The smell of must and disinfectant clogged the air. A thick, frigid draft rolled in from the barred window.

Shuddering, I sat down on the cot, found myself staring at a scarred wall. The old, rotting planks bore deep, angry gouges, the displaced wood fanning out in long sharp splinters. Rusted nails that once held the wood in place were now half exposed. I thought of a raging lion raking its claws through the ancient wood, desperate for freedom. I leaned down and let myself drop to the cot, stared up at the ceiling.

The gouges became the claw marks inside the lid of a coffin. I sat up.

Mo, set up that meeting. Let me know when they are ready.

The response was immediate. Mo hooked me up to my avatar. I closed my eyes and animated my representation in our digital meeting space. Around the low, battered coffee table the other three members of my team already inhabited their personas. The questions hit me at once.

"Alyse, honey! Where are you? They won't let us see you!"

"I'm 'bout five minutes from breakin' that Phan Mai freak's face. You tell him we don't give a goddamn how bad you're hurt. He can't keep you locked up like this. Don't worry, baby. We're going to get you out of there."

"What happened, Alyse?"

I raised a finger to my lips. "Shh."

I looked into each of their faces: Tamsin, frantic; Ben, angry; Ryan, grave. Something huge and horrible held me mute. I turned my gaze to the table, trying to gather the strength to break through and speak.

"I...I am fine. They are holding me, because.... They are saying I'm infected."

I felt myself start to shake. I told Mo to keep that response out of my avatar. I clasped my hands in my lap and raised my eyes. And waited.

"Oh, God. I knew we never should have come here. Alyse?" Tamsin was out of her chair. She took a step toward me, then stopped. "Oh, God, 'Lyse, honey. Oh, God. Just once, just one goddamn time could you think of somebody other than yourself? Could you just once not run and throw yourself off a cliff without any regard for anyone else around you? Did you think there would never be any consequences?"

"Tamsin, I didn't—"

"Infected. With Sleeper's Syndrome. Fuck!" She put a hand to her mouth, turned to Ben and Ryan. "That...that means they were wrong. That means any of us can get infected. We've got to get out of here. We've got to get out of here right now!"

Her avatar vanished.

I sat back in my chair. I tried not to be shocked. I told myself I couldn't be surprised. Tamsin had been the perfect best friend to me for over a decade now. But only to me.

I'd seen the signs a thousand times, the signs that I was the goddamn turtle carrying the scorpion. She dumped Nico when he moved his newly divorced Mom into his house. She never showed when Johanna finally worked up the courage to take a slot at the storytelling at the Tuesday Night Bonfire. She ditched Karen over a fucking pair of shoes! The list went on and on. The girl was a goddamn flake. How long had I expected to last before she did it to me? I shouldn't be shocked, shouldn't be hurt.

She was supposed to be my best friend.

The boys didn't move. Didn't say anything. Tears started streaming down my face. I told Mo to leave those out, too.

"They say I have a false dog tag, that I'm genetically modified. Not exactly the same as the carriers, but similar. They claim I—"

"It was you." Ryan leaned forward as he whispered, elbows on his knees, tremors visible in his clasped hands.

"What?"

"It wasn't Mrs. Patterson. It was you. Haylee came with my sister to a stunt demo you did—"

My anger finally burst free. I surged to my feet. "That's not true! Don't you get it? None of this is true! I never had gene therapy. Unless the rules have changed, I am physiologically incapable of contracting Sleeper's Syndrome! You know that!"

Ryan didn't look up at me. He just kept staring at the ratty digital carpeting. "I never put it together and then I got this job.... It was you. You are the one who put Haylee to sleep. And Mrs. Peterson, an innocent woman, died because of you."

"Oh my god, how could you even—?"

That little-boy face turned up to me and in an instant I saw ten years of anguish rise to the surface, dark colors of haggard exhaustion and impotent rage blotting out the patience and thoughtfulness I'd known.

"How many other kids have you put to sleep since then, Alyse? Has Lone Pine been covering it up for you this whole time? Is that why they sent us here? To remind you to be a good little piece of equipment?"

"How can you say that? You know me. You know I could never—"

Ryan pushed to his feet now. "*That's* why you always offer to come with me when I go to visit Haylee. To ease your fucking guilty conscience! Oh, it all makes sense now!" Ryan started forward. "How dare you—"

Ben jumped up, slapped a warning hand against Ryan's chest. Ryan's lip peeled back from his teeth as he flicked a glance down at Ben's hand. Then his avatar winked out of existence.

I stared.

Another one gone.

Ben dropped his hand and gave me a long, long look. I watched his familiar face warily, the fire draining from me fast. He was the last one left. He had the power to leave me alone. I held very, very still.

"I told you I didn't like this place," he said finally. "I should never have let you go. I let those two talk me out of doing my job. I—"

"It's done, Ben. I don't think...I think they would have found a way. These people, they're smart and...." Scary, terrifying. I closed my eyes and heard Ben sigh.

"So, you think they're trying to steal your tech or somethin'?"

I looked up. He believed me. The relief nearly collapsed what was left of my control. Carefully, I ran my hands over my face, groping for an answer.

"Yes. Maybe. I don't know."

"Doesn't this Phan Mai guy have his own technology company? Can't he just build his own?"

My chest went cold. Images of Dr. Franco's saggy face loomed over me. "You think he's going to reverse engineer me?"

"Don't think so. He'd have stole Lex the Latest Model if that's what he was thinkin'. We already checked in with the other teams. Nobody else is missing. He was watchin' you last night, baby. Just you."

I sank back into the overstuffed chair. I remembered Jürgen's hard eyes, the solid black of his eyebrows rising as I backed away. *I must thank you, Alyse, for a beautiful hunt.*

"Why?" I asked finally.

"Maybe 'cause of those six little gold men you got sittin' in a glass case back at the office. Maybe he ain't tryin' to steal your tech, Alyse. Maybe he's tryin' to steal you, steal your talent. He's tryin' to put this little island back on the economic map with this sensory immersion tour of his—and you, baby, are the best there is."

Me? He was trying to steal me? I couldn't answer. The breath had gone out of me.

"Look. I gotta take care of these guys. Doesn't matter if the accusations are true or not. We can't have these two flappin' their yaps about it. I gotta go."

A significant bit of foresight for Ben. Or an easy way to step away. But he lingered for a moment as something seemed to occur to him. I waited, bracing myself. He stepped around the table and over to me. He leaned down.

And he hugged me.

At first I was startled, but then I hugged him back with all my desperate strength. For the first time, I felt the true warmth of his friendship. No repercussions here in cyberspace. Releasing me, he squatted down in front of me.

"But you gotta prepare yourself. No one understands this disease, Alyse. You gotta prepare yourself for that."

The magic shattered. I clenched my jaw to keep from snarling. How could it be that no one believed me? I didn't acknowledge his statement. I couldn't.

"You stay strong, baby." He gave my knee a squeeze, then rose. With a little salute, he disappeared.

I was alone. Completely and utterly alone.

Mo dissolved the meeting space. The dark, dampness of my splintered wooden coffin returned. The deep cold of the room had worked its way into my bones and muscles. The lack of food shot pain through my abdomen. I pushed the pillow to the head of the bed. I unfurled the three thick, handmade quilts beside me, layered them over me one by one. Then I leaned back and swung my legs and the quilts up onto the flimsy mattress. I settled my head on the icy pillow, but the tears began pooling in my ears, so I turned on my side.

Distantly, I heard the shush of the ocean, the long call of sea birds.

I closed my eyes.

I left me, too.

Chapter 8

I opened my eyes.

No time had passed.

The light was exactly as it had been before. The weight in my chest was exactly as it had been before. I felt so lonely it was an ache through my entire body. It was ridiculous. At any other time I would have savored the silence, the stillness. Solitude was a thing I craved. But not like this.

I stared blankly ahead, my eyes focusing on empty air.

Did a tree falling in a forest make noise if there was no one around to hear it? Did a woman huddling in isolation exist if there was no one around to acknowledge her?

Profound.

But I felt nonexistent.

I could conceive of absolutely no way to prove that Dr. Franco's fabricated version of me was false. That the me right here in this room, the physicality having these thoughts was the real me. That I, the real me, actually existed. He had all the medical "evidence." All I had was my memories, my word—in other words, nothing.

I should call Emory.

He could launch Lone Pine's battalion of lawyers at Jürgen Phan Mai and Dr. Sal Franco. *They* could prove I existed. There was only one flaw in that logic: Nothing that went into Emory's office ever stayed secret. If I needed a reminder of that, I only needed to remember the little family reunion back at the Quarantine Processing and Visitation Facility.

Somehow the other two movie houses had heard Bryce and I were coming. How had they known? My team had a pool going: Ryan thought it was a lurker in Emory's comm gear; Ben thought Devon, Emory's coordinator, was on the take; Tamsin had decided Emory himself had a couple of side dishes at Enchanted Mirror and Atleiter who were less than discreet. As for me, my money was on the old-fashioned grapevine. The business was a small one. Everyone knew everyone else. Nothing covert or high drama about it.

In the end it didn't matter what the mechanism was, all that mattered was that it cut me off from my surest path back to sanity and the real world. One little word, one little insinuation that I might be a carrier and my life would turn terrifying and brief. The Flaming Sword of God and the Seers would be the least of my worries. Every lunatic left from the Zealot's War, every bereaved mind cracked by the loss of a child to Sleeper's Syndrome would hunt me like they had hunted all the others. Not even Ben with all his tools and precautions would be able to protect me forever.

Never threaten the children.

My ear was losing feeling smashed up against the hard pillow. I rolled onto my back in the deafening crackle of waterproof coverings. I groaned quietly as my ribs and my arm reminded me of the damage still under final repair.

There had to be something I could do. I couldn't just lay here and ache in the sea-borne cold. I squeezed my eyes shut, scrunching the stiff tracks of dried tears on my cheeks. I couldn't just lay here and do nothing.

Someone would come. Someone would try to cajole me and then I would know their game and I could find a way to fight back.

Someone would come.

Then I could fight.

៹

How could a day turn into eternity?

The light from the window had moved a little this time. Would I be measuring my time by which part of the wall the light hit as the sun passed through the sky? I shifted to my side. I had to stifle a cry of pain. The cold had leached its way up through the cheap mattress and into my battered body to spread tendrils of ice through the tissues of each of my joints. I needed to get up and move. I didn't dare compromise the seal on my quilt-cocoon.

How did convicts survive it? They had a routine, I guessed. They had a library and exercise equipment. They had guards and each other. And food. I stuffed my face into the pillow as my stomach tore at itself. Shouldn't have thought about food. Really shouldn't have thought about food.

I pulled my face free of the rough, plasticky pillow and glanced toward the ceiling. It was riddled with thick metal studs. In my dazed and wandering mind, one of them fell down, down, driving straight through my open eye. Lovely. Why didn't I just turn the entire room into a chamber of spikes while I was at it? I could watch the ceiling lower slowly...

Jürgen should have come by now.

He should be crouching next to my cot, his face bathed in half-light and shadow, telling me he would let me go if I would just submit to his vision, his resurrection of the dream that had been Venice. Hadn't he waited long enough by now? As much as he terrified me, I would rather have faced him than this. And he knew it. He knew things. About me. Real things. Things I didn't know myself.

Those eyes.

I shuddered. It sent me to shivering.

Tamsin thought he wanted my body. Ben thought he wanted my talents. I didn't think it was that simple at all. Power. He wanted power. He wasn't going to get it. Not over me.

I curled myself up tighter under the quilts, trying to slow my shivering. I could fight him. I could fight this. I took a deep breath and pictured those beautiful, hard black eyes. I hardened my mind and body against the fear.

Then those eyes went soft with empathy.

I crumbled.

╰◉╯

I resurfaced into a swirl of worry.

Why hadn't my team called? Where were they? Had something happened to them? Had he hurt them? I pulled a hand free of the blanket and pressed it against the frozen flesh of my face. It did no good. My hand was barely lukewarm.

Giving up, I tossed the blankets aside and got to my feet, sucked air as the cold hit me. I paced over to the window. The wide, rusted slats of metal cut the illuminated fog into neat squares. Not much of a view.

My team was unique. With the exception of Ben, we'd been together for most of the nine years I'd been an immersion artist. We got together in our off hours. We drove at Ben's exhibition races; we pounded junk food for Ryan's James Bond marathons; we feigned sophistication at Tamsin's wine and chocolate tastings. I reached out to touch the rusted metal, pulled my hand back before my fingers brushed the surface. We were friends. Real friends.

I glanced at the wall, found an unslashed section and flopped back against it. The cold wood burned against my back. They wouldn't just leave me. They would try to do something to get me out of here. I could only hope that Jürgen wouldn't find a way to use that loyalty against them, against me.

Why hadn't they called by now?

I opened my mouth to ask Mo to call Ben. I closed it.

They didn't believe me.

I turned my head to see a long line of raised splinters. A gruesome sight. For some reason it filled my head with images of torn flesh, of blood and screams. If we were such good friends, then why did my face light with a cold fire, my chest and my head fill with dead pain when I thought of them? I lost my hold on a bitter laugh. Tamsin and Ryan hadn't even stopped long enough to listen. Could I blame them? Who would follow even their best friend into a nightmare like this, a nightmare that could so easily consume them as well?

They didn't believe me.

I shoved off the wall. My shirt snapped repeatedly as it popped free of the tiny, sharp claws in the rough wood. Uncontrollable shaking rattled my teeth against each other. Getting up from my ball of tepid warmth had been the mistake I'd known it would be. I limped back to the bed, dropped to the crackling mattress. I curled up and packed the quilts tightly around me, but they brought no comfort, no relief.

I was not lying. How could the people I trusted most in the world think I was lying? Fuck them anyway.

Chapter 9

There are experiences which can make you question the reality of what you've been through, people who can make you question the truth of what you know. In the fog of half sleep, in my mind, I faced Jürgen again. His accusations of my infection, his allegation of my DNA patch held rigid authority while the certainty slowly drained from my memories. His face displayed sympathy as he stroked my hair, as I pleaded with him.

"The touch sensitivity, I've had it since I was sixteen. Haven't I? I think. No, I know that. It only got this bad lately. The last few years. I would know if that was Sleeper's Syndrome. There would be the children falling unconscious. But I move around a lot.... Maybe, maybe they fell asleep and I never knew."

He said nothing—just looked into my eyes, so sad and understanding.

"The patch. I've never had gene therapy. I would know. They would have told me, if they were changing who I was. I would have known about the procedure…wouldn't I? Are there spaces missing from my life? Are there blanks spots and I just don't know?"

His face came so near mine. His hand moved from my hair to stroke my throat seductively.

"I didn't do all this to steal your technology, Alyse. I did this to steal you. Just you. Only you."

Our breaths combined, his, so sweet, filling my lungs. The raw, leftover ache between my legs spread, opened, filled. Jürgen's face shifted. His eyes relaxed into a soft brown with long lashes, his hair lengthened to gentle brown waves stroking my cheek. Matteo moved over me, his perfectly sculpted lips brushing mine. I moaned as sensation flooded my limbs, my womb. But I couldn't let go, couldn't crest to that final release. I saw his eyes turn to molten tar, heard the sound of his animal scream. But his hands stayed gentle; his lips caressed my eyelids, traced the shells of my ears.

"I'm just a man," he whispered. His hands moved to my breasts; those lips swallowed my gasp, then my cry. "Just a man making love to this beautiful body." He filled those large hands with the weight of my breasts, teased my nipples with his circling thumbs, pumped into me, steady, relentless.

"Just a man," he promised.

"Yes," I sobbed. "Yes."

I jerked awake.

I covered my mouth as the orgasm ripped through me.

The bolt screeched on the wooden door to my cell. The hinges creaked. I sat up, my body still pulsing.

"Dr. Calles would like to speak with you."

I blinked at the man.

"If I were you, I'd take her invitation. Days can get pretty long when the only human interaction is a six-second glimpse of my face when I fast ball you your sandwich."

This was the shorter, stockier guard, a Caucasian with a good boy face and a bad case of bed head. The name Milo floated through my mind. But only one thing was important to me: he was offering to get me out of here.

I put the blankets aside and rose, forced my stiff body to unfold. My bare feet screamed as I put my full weight on them. I looked around myself for a blank moment.

"It's warmer out here."

I shuffled forward, through the door he held open for me. Despite the fact that I was a full head taller than the man, the subtle way he moved lightly on his feet had me on my guard. He didn't cuff me, just took me by the arm and guided me down the brief corridor to another cell—this one with a full-sized door.

We stopped to the left of the door and he released my elbow. I had to rest my throbbing head against the wall.

"You look green. Haven't eaten, have you?"

I shook my head. Carefully. The problem with having a body full of machines is that they expect to be fed and then they help themselves to your reserves if you don't see to their needs in a timely fashion.

Milo pulled an open pouch of energy gummies out of his cargo pants pocket and dumped out a handful.

"Here."

I took the little green nuggets and popped a couple in my mouth. My stomach was instantly appeased. I had to trust that my head would follow soon.

If the hall was warmer than my cell, I couldn't really tell. I tugged at the sleeves of my white silk-cotton blend T-shirt and tucked my frozen hands up under my arms. It pulled the draping neckline low over my breasts, but Milo had that one-step-back air of someone who has seen and heard it all before. He wasn't going to care.

He gestured toward the door.

"No attacking the doctor. She isn't the powder puff she looks like she is. I trained her myself. I'll be right outside the door the whole time. And, yes, I will hear every word you say. Ready?"

I nodded.

"Not a big talker, are you?"

I just looked at him and shivered.

He chuckled and swung the door open. The blast of hot air hit the ice of my skin, prickling as it penetrated the permafrost. Now that was more what I'd had in mind.

"Dr. Roz, brought you your new victim. Hey, Vittorio, let's go."

Vittorio unfolded himself from one of the two client seats and rose...and rose. His shoulders curled forward as he reached down to shake Dr. Calles's hand. She stood to exchange the farewell. Her poof of cheery blonde hair had been remolded into its full circular halo. A bulky, flowered sweater covered what I could see of her stout frame.

"I'll see you tomorrow then, okay Vittorio?"

The giant released her hand and turned towards us. Two ambling steps brought him directly in front of me. The low ceiling had him bent from the shoulders up. He looked down, his thick white-blonde hair catching the light, his long face surprised. I looked up, equally caught off guard.

"He doesn't talk much either," Milo informed me.

The guard gestured me forward. I took a step in the indicated direction. Milo led the big man away. The door closed and locked behind them. The giant took one last peek at me through the narrow window in the door before he disappeared.

"That man can make even me feel petite," Dr. Calles said. "Come on in. Have a seat. I just have to make a couple notes." Her stylus flew across the privacy-screened pad on her desk in big loopy waves, not so different in shape from the curls of her hair.

She chuckled as she worked. "If it weren't for that grant money, I wouldn't even bother with this. These 'Venetians' as they call themselves, I think they get lonely hiding out there in the ruins. We call them houseguests. They stay a couple days, then they disappear. In fact, I can almost promise you our Vittorio there will be gone by morning."

The doctor tapped in a few commands, then set her stylus to the side.

She sat back and gave me a few seconds to take in my surroundings. Her little cell had fresh wood paneling, thick brown carpeting, and soft cozy chairs. Brightly colored kitsch—mostly in the form of animals—decorated every available space not taken up by potted plants. The air carried the light scent of flowers and moist earth. A soundtrack played the sounds of the forest in a low whisper. Despite everything that had happened to me, despite the pain in every part of my body, I found myself relaxing.

"I talked to Jürgen a little while ago. He told me what happened this morning." She saw me tense and smiled. "I thought we might leave that for a little later on. Maybe today we might talk about what brought you here."

I knew I would have to pay for the vacation from my little meat locker. The question was whether I could do so graciously enough to receive further opportunities for escape. I wasn't sure about that part.

"By here, I mean Venice. Not this room in particular. How did you end up coming to the open house?" she prompted again.

I looked down at my arm, saw the faded answer. I tugged my sleeve back down.

"I got bit by a shark."

"You came because you got bit by a shark."

"No," I paused to look up. "I was *sent* because I got bit by a shark."

Dr. Calles scooted forward in her chair. "So how would a shark bite get you sent to bid on a project?"

"Because my dad had been mauled to death by a shark a few weeks before."

"I'm still not sure I understand."

I grit my teeth. When it came to people poking their noses into my business, my graciousness wore off way too fast. *Answer the question.* "My boss did not find my grieving process appropriate. He sent me here to...take a break."

"By grieving process, you mean getting bit by a shark?"

"No, I mean doing an enactment with a juvenile shark. It wasn't my intention to get bit."

"The bite is there on your arm?" She pointed to where I had my hand wrapped around my forearm. She rose and came around to the other client chair on my side of the desk. "Do you mind if I take a look at it?"

Yes.

I held out my arm, pulled back my sleeve. She seized my arm before I realized she planned to look with more than her eyes. I inhaled with a start, exhaled with a slow, quiet sigh as my body melted. The driving pain drained from my head, my neck, my shoulders, sliding slowly, exquisitely down my body, through my legs, out my toes, leaving me in a heavenly drift. I coaxed myself to turn my head toward the doctor. She traced my scars with a thickly painted false nail. When she raised that cutesy face to me, the cold, hard eyes belonged to someone else.

"He rent your flesh. He marked you."

The comment took a moment to penetrate my cozy lull. Then I looked down. I still had marks, purple lines across my forearm. In her grip I turned my arm over and saw the matching set.

"I still have the scars. I shouldn't have any scars."

Mo, status on repair from shark bite received at Maine Aquatic Nature Reserve.

Repair complete.

Confused, I gave my arm a tug to retrieve it, but she wasn't letting go. She pushed my sleeve up higher. Alarm shot through me at the anger subtly twisting her features. I ripped her hands away and scrambled to my feet. The energy gummies I'd held bounced to the floor. The doctor didn't move from her chair, but everything about her had rearranged. I saw the softly padded face, gently lined; I saw the motherly worry in those pale eyes. It was so real. I didn't know what to believe.

"What's wrong, Alyse?"

"What are you trying to do?"

"The shark is dead, isn't he?"

I saw that slender young body drifting to the aquarium floor, saw my father's closed casket lowering into the grave. Guilt welled up. I swallowed it down.

"What are you trying to do?" I asked again.

"I'm trying to help you, Alyse. But you have to let me."

"I don't need help. If you need another victim to pad your files with, you'll have to look elsewhere."

"Matteo—"

"—is a nice man. Something went wrong. I get it. I'm not going to hold it against him. At least I got a good orgasm out of it. Drop it."

I walked back to the door. I tried the handle. It didn't move. I beat on the door.

"Milo! We're done in here!"

"Alyse, sit down."

That voice. My heart slammed in my chest. I spun around. Somehow the doctor had managed to cross the room and stood right behind me.

"Sit down, Alyse."

She reached for my face. I arched back, but I was already against a wall. Her creased hand slid over the side of my neck. I sat down. Straight down on the floor. The jittery fear slipped away from me. I watched limply as the doctor lowered herself to the floor in front of me. Her gaze stayed locked on mine.

"Alyse Kate Bryant, you were never supposed to come within this circle." My head lolled in her hand. Her touch was so gentle, so warm. For a moment, looking into those blue eyes, I had a glimpse of soft skies, of golden sunlight calmed by the sway of green leaves. I smelled earthy loam so rich I could taste it on my tongue. Home. I sobbed as a terrible longing rose in my chest. Home. The need to get back to my trees exploded beneath my breastbone. The doctor raised her other hand so that my head was cradled in her hands and she drew me forward until our temples were touching. Slowly, slowly, the pain eased away.

"You were never supposed to come here," she whispered. "But you have. Somehow she has brought you here. And now you are trapped with the rest of us. I am sorry for that. But I can help you—when you are ready." She drew away and tilted my head back so we were eye to eye. "Until then, I need you to be cautious, be very cautious who you accept assistance from. The covenant of indebtedness, it is the currency of every transaction here. People will use it to gain power over you. You are a clever girl when you stop long enough to think. Maybe, if you are careful, you can collect that power for yourself. But spend it wisely. Hoard it—like it is the blood in your veins.

"There is another kind of power people will want from you. You will not understand it now, but you will feel it when people try to take it from you. Resist. Resist as best you can.

"I cannot force you to accept my help; you have to choose freely, Alyse Kate Bryant. You will have to relinquish your trust to me completely. Only then can I help free you."

I stared at the woman who held me up, tried to muster my will from the heavy blanket of calm she smothered me with.

"I...I..." I stopped struggling, released everything to her embrace. "I don't need your help. I need to get the fucking hell out of here. Let me go."

And then I was standing.

Once again my hand gripped the door handle; my other hand pressed against the wood. A gentle breeze caressed my cheek. The flutter of my hair startled me back into the moment. I beat my hand against the door.

"Milo!"

The door opened and Milo appeared, but Dr. Calles held the door from swinging all the way open. Those eyes framed by heavily painted lashes turned to me. The mental health professional had returned.

"We all need help, Alyse. That doesn't mean we've succumbed to the victim role. It means we are trying to understand our past, so we can build a healthy self concept going forward." She let go of the door. Milo pulled it the rest of the way open. "Milo, she can come back whenever she chooses. Just let me know."

"Yes, ma'am."

"I *can* help you, Alyse. If you'll just let me."

I didn't look back as I followed Milo out into the hall. I wanted away from that woman. Her parting words jarred my mind. Something was so wrong about it. I tried to think why, but the details of the moments before became slippery in my grasp. Then I caught one, just by the fragile, trailing edge: *the covenant of indebtedness. People will use it to gain power over you.* So then I was supposed to become indebted to her? Shit. I shook my head out. I felt so drugged. What the hell had that woman done to me?

I heard the door fall closed behind us.

I wanted to run.

Milo's grip tightened on my arm.

The guard steered me by the elbow around the corner and back down the hall to my cell. Sight of that half-sized door sent my heart racing, but when Milo swung it open, I ducked and stepped through without a fight.

"Your friends sent up a package of medication. They said you needed the meds for your AI and your medic gear. Don't go using it to overdose."

He waved a flashlight through the now pitch dark of my cell and I saw the package on my cot. My friends. A spark of hope tried to flare. I smothered it. They'd sent me my meds. The end. No messages. I should know. I waited for them. All day.

Milo switched off the flashlight.

"I just got word that dinner's ready. I'll be bringing that up in a few seconds. Then you are on your own. It's going to be a long night. Maybe by morning you'll be ready to reconsider treatment."

As the darkness swallowed my body and the jagged cold ripped at my mind, I wasn't sure I could prove him wrong.

Enough wallowing.

I dropped the plate to the floor, unwilling to bend my frozen body enough to set it down gently. Inside the blankets, I wrapped my arms around my knees and lowered my head to my knees. I had work to do.

Eventually, Jürgen would make his move and I would find a way to bust out of here. I didn't want any blip on the screen indicating to the world that this had ever happened. I would not give him that power.

Mo, pull up current projects.

Glowing white lettering danced in the darkness. *Russo's Watch*, a science fiction thriller, shimmered at the top of the list. If my facial muscles had still been responsive, I would have grimaced at the irony. I was working on the final scene. Captain Russo had used the last of her ship's power to ram the enemy ship filled with toxic explosives and to make the hyperspace jump with the two ships interlocked.

Now the pair of disabled ships drift toward the lashing embrace of a red sun. Behind the door to the bridge her own crew beats at the metal, screaming, crying for her to do something as the frigid cold of open space begins to warm to terrifying levels.

A call blips on her flickering monitor, her lover's face battered and bleeding—the handsome and traitorous captain of the enemy ship. Russo raises a limp arm to the console to answer.

"Guess you had the guts after all."

"I gave you the chance to walk away," she whispers. "Never should have given you the chance."

"You believed, Alyson. That's what the good guys are supposed to do. Doesn't matter, anyway. The next wave will make it through."

Russo smiles. "No, no they won't. Not on my watch." She presses a button and a staticky transmission comes over the com. Her lover's face goes slack with shock as he hears the crackle of voices detail the setup of the trap that waits on the other side of the system for the larger fleet of his terrorist allies.

"Fuck!"

He scrambles to warn them, but Russo only laughs. With the drag of a fingertip, she fires the thrusters one last time. Just a little nudge from the last whiff of fuel. Communications warp and die in the radiation. The voices behind the door go silent.

"Not on my watch," she whispers one last time.

She is unconscious as the first solar flare reaches out to lick the conjoined ships.

In my icy prison of a body, I asked Mo to call up my avatar. I normally lay out sensory tracks with my own flesh and blood, but it requires fine motor control I no longer had tonight. I had Mo compile my favorite files of cold and heat, of heartbreak and victory, of a limp and shaky physicality and a mind methodically in control.

I replayed the scene.

I would lay in the cold and the heat first. Sluggishly, my avatar flipped through the files, finally settling on the sharp, dry, frost-like cold from the desert winter. It cut at the throat and lungs, pierced the flesh with its serrated barbs. It penetrated differently from this sea-borne cold that weighed so heavily on the body like it had density of its own. Such a heavy, heavy weight.

I lifted my avatar's hand to the file list. I needed...something. A file. I lowered my arm. A file. Heat. I needed heat. I tried to raise my arm again.

I never felt myself fall, just felt the concussion in my skull of the impact when I hit.

Mo, tell Margie...tell Margie to...

My club limbs did not unbend to reclaim the quilts. I opened my eyes but the darkness looked the same inside as out. Here was the world my beautiful and brilliant Grandma Sam had lived within as I'd cared for her all through high school. Staring, empty eyes. Useless, empty body.

First Grandma Sam. And then Grandpa Don. And then Daddy.

All on my watch. All on me.

Not me! Please, not me!

I screamed, but the strangled sound choked me with tiny shards of ice.

The image of Jürgen's sorrow looming over me.

White hot hatred.

Not me.

⁂

"What are you doing up here?"

The question cracked through my black emptiness, left behind silence.

A long drifting silence.

"Hadria has...*concerns* about your prisoner." A rich, low bell of a voice, beautiful, echoing.

"Hadria?" Milo. Sturdy, stalwart, no-nonsense Milo.

A heavy, thick rumble vibrated my bones. A lukewarm brush of air against my cheek. My black emptiness turned gray.

"Oh, shit. What the hell did you do, Suzi? It's like a fucking cryofreeze in here!" I felt hot pressure against my arm, against my cheek. I turned my eyes in the grey light and caught a glimpse of the angular outline of Milo's face. "You'd better hope she's got a damn good medic or we're both dead. Alyse, where's that package of meds?"

I did not answer, could not answer.

The icy blanket of air around me fluttered as Milo searched. The thud of his boots returned. A press against my arm.

Pain!

My cry came out a shrill cough. That fierce, tearing pain radiated ever so slowly from the injection site. It would consume me. How long? How long! A tear cut across the bridge of my nose, sliced across my other cheek, dripped to the floor.

No, not in front of them! Oh, god!

"Do you not understand who she is? If she dies, if anything at all happens to her, Hadria will be the least of your worries. They'll cut us off. They'll cut Venice off completely. Hadria can't feed us, Suzi."

A lash of power snapped through the room, enough even to freeze the progress of my pain, if just for a second.

"You...overstep yourself, Milo. If you ever intend to step beyond the palace walls again, I suggest you correct the order of your priorities."

"I would suggest you make the same adjustment while you are inside them. Hadria isn't the only badass around here."

Leave, please, leave!

Suzi chuckled.

"Don't worry, little one, we will go. For all his bravado, Milo doesn't truly want to get between Hadria and those other 'badasses,' does he?"

I don't care. I don't care! Leave!

Blankets weighted down on me, refreezing the portions Margie had thawed.

Milo hit me with a second popper in the calf.

This time I screamed.

Chapter 10

Margie's little nanobots could repair cold-damaged flesh, but they could not reanimate it. I depended entirely on the tepid midday sun for that. As I lay there alone on the floor where I'd fallen, gently trying to coax cramped muscles into movement, I tried to keep the frantic desperation at bay.

Hadria.

The pain and cold had erased the specific words from my early morning rescue, but one thing was vivid: Hadria wanted me dead.

Calm down.

"I've got to call Emory."

I can't. I can't. I'll get my entire family killed. Don't be stupid. Think!

But I could no longer do that inside the walls of my disbelieving mind. I need someone to talk to, someone to calm me down. I needed someone to help turn my scattered thoughts into some kind of order, some kind of plan.

Then I realized there was one person I could talk to, one person who could never endanger my family with an accidental word in the wrong ear, or a hint to the wrong recording device. Nor would she criticize or judge.

I pulled myself up to sitting in my tiny patch of sunlight. Then I had Mo pull up my avatar.

And I went to visit Haylee.

Haylee Anderson's castle room took over the prison cell—the dusty flower curtains in her much larger window, the gleaming grey tile floor, the machines that stood beside her little bed monitoring her endlessly unchanging state. For a second I hesitated, expecting the program to kick me out. But the politely annoying notice never sounded. Somehow in his fury Ryan must have forgotten to have his sister revoke my visitor's pass. I pressed a fingertip to my forehead waiting carefully for the pain of his accusations to pass.

Finally, I lowered my hand.

Because the setting always seemed to require it, I entered Haylee's room quietly and settled into the comfortable stuffed chair positioned next to her. I leaned forward and brushed a silky lock of chocolate brown hair back from her pale skin.

"Hey, girl."

The doctors claimed they saw brain activity in response to interactions with the children's' avatars. I didn't know if that meant she understood the words I said. This time I would choose to believe that she didn't. After all, what kind of monster would talk *this* out with a six-year-old?

"Not sure how much longer I'll be able to come visit you. Your uncle is pretty mad at me. He thinks I somehow did this to you. He believes...they say..." I had to wait until the convulsive shudder stopped shaking my shoulders. "...they say I'm a carrier."

I popped up out of the chair.

"I shouldn't be here."

But I stopped with one hand on the back of the chair. I turned back. Her tiny little form barely took up a third of the bed, so small, so alone in her empty darkness. Like all the others. Why did I always visit her? Because I couldn't stand to think of her alone here. Alone like my grandmother, my grandfather, my dad. Alone like the solitary loved ones who stood vigil at their sides. Couldn't let that happen to her; couldn't let that happen to Ryan.

I gripped the back of the chair.

"You don't have to be afraid. I'm not a carrier. I can't be. And you and I both know the epidemics guys traced your infection to your teacher. That show I met you at was too long ago to be connected. Your uncle is just scared, scared and angry. So am I."

I lowered my head.

"These people here aren't right in the head. They really scare me. The one who seemed nice went crazy and hurt me really bad. I think...I think last night another one tried...tried to kill me."

"I don't know how to get out of here, Haylee. I've got to figure out...I just can't think!"

"Ms. Bryant?"

Mo sent a blip through the scene meant to indicate something outside the artificial environment needed my attention. I rushed over to give Haylee a quick kiss on the forehead.

"I'll be back soon."

I opened my eyes to find Milo crouched in front of me. Everything inside of me went painfully still. I took the fear that tried to flash into my eyes and crushed it into the bottom of my heart. I looked back at him with emptiness.

"Dr. Roz is asking if you are ready to come back and talk to her."

Get out of here? I nodded once.

Milo rose. I unlocked my fingers from around my knees. I pushed to rise. My knees and ankles would not unlock as easily as my fingers. Milo offered me a hand. I stared at it.

Milo squatted down again, turned his hand palm up. I started to reach for it. That's when I saw the sliver of copper peek out the cuff of his uniform shirt. A copper brace just like Jürgen's...just like Matteo's. My carefully crushed fear tumbled into my stomach. I hesitated.

"I'm not going to hurt you, Ms. Bryant. You're not going to be afraid of a guy who's half your size, are you?"

I raised an eyebrow at him. We both knew he could snap me like a twig.

But I took his hand.

It didn't hurt. His large grip surrounded my smaller one, solid, warm, and comforting. Like my dad's when I was a little girl. But I absolutely wouldn't stop to think about it. I forced myself to standing, pretended the excruciating movements belonged to some avatar I inhabited. Milo wasn't fooled. Once we cleared the door, he wrapped his thick arm around my waist, took the pressure off my battered legs. I found myself wanting to burrow into him, like he really was my dad, there to comfort me. I had to hold myself very carefully to remind myself of the reality of the situation.

"Hello, Vittorio. Would have expected you to have vanished by now."

I looked up to see pale fingers wrapped around the black bars of a tiny prison door window, pale eyes boring into me.

"Ah, you are interested in this one? Not a good idea, my friend. From what I've seen she's a bit of a hell cat."

A short laugh escaped me.

"Alright maybe not today. But maybe tomorrow after I've brought her extra quilts."

I shot a small dry smile at the floor, out of the corner of my eye watching Vittorio watching me. Then we were past him and approaching the good doctor's office. And suddenly, this doctor's visit became about more than just getting warm. And Milo was too damn observant.

"She can help you...if you let her."

I clenched my teeth and straightened, drawing myself up and out of his embrace. He just sighed and shook his head. His knuckles rapped on the rough, thick wood.

"Dr. Roz! You got company!"

The door swung open and the ebullience that was Dr. Roz beamed up at me.

"Alyse, dear! Come in, come in. I'm just in the middle of repotting some of my plants. You can give me a hand."

I watched her suspiciously as I followed her into the room, flinched when I heard the door thud closed behind me. But she didn't try to touch me. Instead she hurried back to her desk now covered by a large black tray. I approached more slowly. The dark, moist soil in the tray had a rich mineral, almost chocolate scent to it that sent my mouth to watering. I reached out tentatively and tunneled my fingers into the soft, crumbly earth. I raised a handful to my nose and drew in its heady fragrance.

"My little Myrtle here has been complaining for a new pot for months now, but I've been holding back on her. If she grows much bigger, I may have to let her go. Not enough room in here for a full grown tree, you know!"

I had a flash of Tamsin's face, the conversation we'd never had about the future of her career. I hesitated. But no, Mo would have told me if there'd been any calls, any messages. Which meant.... Best not to think of it.

Shaking the dirt from my hands, I surveyed the little work area. Three clean, ornate pots. A bucket of rocks. As the doctor worked the sapling free of its tiny pot, I layered the rocks in the bottom of each of the pots, laid down a shallow bed of soil. While Dr. Roz held the slender plant in place with her large-knuckled hand, I packed in the fill dirt. We worked in silence, transplanting each over-cramped plant into its new home, rich with fertile new soil. I imagined I could hear their leaves sighing with relief and gratitude. Such relaxing work. Too relaxing.

My body, soaking in the fragrance of the soil, the quiet forest sounds emanating from somewhere in the room, began to sway. I thought of home, my Lone Pine forest, the sharper, more citrus scent of the pine woods. My heart hurt with no sachet to heal it.

Dr. Roz took me by the elbow and led me to one of the client chairs.

I slumped against the back of the chair, closing my eyes.

"What does he want? Just tell me what you people want."

"He just wants to help you, Alyse, my child." She took my hand and I felt the familiar melting begin. I welcomed it. I could no longer think through all the pain crowding my mind and body. Somehow, her touch just bled it all away until I floated on the swaying branches crowding her tiny wooden office. The rush of leaves filled my ears. The breeze caressed my skin.

"Speak to me, dear child. Tell me. You are not alone in the darkness."

Yet out of the darkness it attacked: memory. Hour after hour of ice stilettos driving through my body, trapping me immobile, my mind desperately sluggish. The darkness. That violent chill shuddered through my languid body, wrenching me from the doctor's imposed peace.

I shoved to my feet. My body responded easily.

"Just tell me what you want! Who the hell is this Hadria? She wouldn't be the first to want me dead, but it would sure as hell be nice to know why!"

Dr. Roz's cheery, kind face went instantly grim.

"Then you can never leave the palace."

What, so you people can keep trying to kill me?

She pushed her old bones from the chair and stood to face me. I took a step back.

"Alyse, while you are here, I can keep your symptoms at peace until you are ready. I can help you find your way through treatment once you have come to accept it. Out there, you *will* die."

"I will not play your game."

It seemed the light grew dappled as the doctor's face grew brilliant, powerful, unbending.

"You have no choice."

She took another step forward. I took another step back. I had my eye on a stone wolf figurine just barely out of reach. And then she was on me, hands wrapped around my arms, draining not just the pain, but *everything* from me, as I cried out. And Milo was there, easing me to the floor.

"You don't understand, yet. But you will. We have eternity to wait."

Chapter 11

Night had fallen. With it, time slowed, turned crystalline, measured out in beats: *we have eternity to wait.* Eternity to wait.

I had the spoon gripped in my fist, all the new clothes layered tightly over me, the new quilts piled around me, shoes laced tight. But I wasn't huddled on the bed. I had my face pressed against the rotting wood of the cell door. I needed a taste of reality, just a little sip of sanity to quiet my head. But the man I would have called at a time like this was gone, dead.

Guilt.

How long had it been since I called him before he died? So long. So long I couldn't remember. My hold on the spoon tightened. No, no touching that thought right now. Let it go.

I *had* to talk to somebody. Now.

I couldn't call Mom. I just couldn't do this to her. I remembered her face after the shark enactment too clearly. This bullshit, this would just be too much for her. No, I definitely couldn't call Mom.

So who did that leave?

Sure as hell not my team. Two days now without a single word from those bastards.

So who?

I groped around my past, not willing to believe that the past ten years of constant travel would leave my social landscape so barren. When I thought back, though, most of the people I'd sought comfort from were gone now: Grandpa Don, Grandma Sam, Grandpa Eduardo. Grandma Anala and I never had that kind of relationship. She had her flower gardening and her basket weaving. I could never sit still that long.

Keats. I could call Uncle Keats! Grandpa Don always blamed my wild streak on Uncle Keats. My dad's younger brother had been the first to take me base jumping, sky diving, glacier trekking, and a whole lot of other things my mother would never hear about. At the funeral we'd joked about the look on Dad's face when I'd told him that for my sixteenth birthday Uncle Keats had let me take the helm on one of his wreckers and I'd nearly totaled the machine—myself included.

It had been years since we'd been partners in crime, but seeing him at the funeral had been good. I seized on the memory and told Mo to place the call.

"You've reached Keats & Byron Demolition, your number one source for interior and total building demolition. We specialize in disaster cleanup and historic building recovery. Please leave a message and a representative will get back to you about your project needs."

I took a deep breath to smother my disappointment. "Um, hey Uncle Keats, it's me, Alyse Kate. I..." I what? I called to beg you to bail me out of this mess? I called to cry on your shoulder? Called to make sure the terrorists drew a straight line to your doorstep when this all comes out on the flash-update news? Shit. "I...I just called to talk. Anyway, knock down a big one for me."

We specialize in disaster cleanup. I laughed grimly and wrapped the other hand around my little metal spoon.

୨

Eternity to wait.

I traced the lines of my face with the edge of my little metal spoon. Over the ridge of my eyebrows, around the socket of my eye, across the sharp bone of my cheek, down the slim line of my nose, the divot above my lip, down to my chin, up along my jawbone. I couldn't feel it. I wondered idly if it were cold enough that the spoon might stick to my face if I accidentally wet it on my lips.

My eyes ached from staring into the black abyss. My body ached from holding me upright against the cell door, from holding me awake against the night. How many hours? How many more hours?

Interrupt this, please, Mo. Tell me a story. Get me out of here for a while.

Once upon a time...

I settled back and found the edge of the doorframe to rest up against.

...there was a young man named Giacomo Casanova. He was a scoundrel and a con artist, a lover and a libertine of the quality for which wanton Venice was famed. But as in all things, Venice balanced her *joie de vivre* with a taste for dark stricture. Warned, but unbelieving, Casanova succumbed to betrayal and found himself arrested and imprisoned without trial, without the slightest whisper regarding his wrongdoing. Day after day, month after month he languished in this very cell, waiting for the mistake to be corrected, but that day was not to come. His indefatigable intellect strained at the confines of these walls ineffectually until one fateful day when he was allowed out for a bit of exercise in the attic and discovered a discarded door bolt. This bolt became his focus, his dream of salvation. In the light of a small, homemade lamp, he honed the bolt to a chisel and chipped away at the floor of his cell, using his mattress for cover.

By painstaking increments, freedom became nearly tangible as the ceiling of the room below, the Hall of the Inquisitors, began flaking away. But then fate whisked his chance out of reach. Our Casanova was granted the favor of a roomier, better lit cell. As was inevitable, during the move his labor toward liberty was discovered. Only threats of implicating the gaoler in his attempt at escape saved young Giacomo from terrible retribution. And he had every right to fear—these attic Piombi where he served his sentence were palatial chambers compared with the Wells, the basement prisons where the flood of lagoon water kept prisoners trapped on ledges, where the condemned fought with sewer rats over their stale crusts of bread.

Despite a strict surveillance by the guard, the young man would not be dissuaded from his goal. And in the exchange of books with a pair of fellow prisoners, a new opportunity presented itself. Father Marin Balbi and Count Andre Asquin of Udine of the neighboring cell succumbed to Casanova's seductive offer of escape. Casanova entrusted Father Balbi with his precious chisel and the cleric chipped through his own ceiling to the rafters and then created an entrance to the ceiling of Giacomo's cell which could be broken open with a quick series of blows at the appointed hour.

Again, however, fate tested the young man's quick wit and unerring resolve. At the moment when the father was near breaking through to free him, Casanova received a new cellmate—a proud traitor, a fallen spy for the Council of Ten. The traitor Soradaci, however, was a superstitious man, the sort Casanova had made his entertainment and sometimes livelihood duping. To secure the turncoat's loyalty, Casanova proceeded to convince the fool that the Virgin Mary would send an angel in the form of a man to free them from imprisonment. When Father Balbi burst through the cell ceiling, Casanova's vision seemed fulfilled and if the traitor were only fooled long enough for the escape to be performed, it made little difference.

Of the three fellow conspirators, only Father Balbi had the courage to follow Casanova out through the leaden roof of the Doge's Palace and across the perilous architecture to a dormer window where they once again broke into the palace. The rest of the night they wandered the empty chambers of the palace seeking a way out. As dawn broke over Venice, Casanova righted his appearance and boldly leaned out a window. He was seen by the door-keeper, but this time fate took pity on our adventurer. The door-keeper thought the pair accidentally locked within the

Palace the night before and immediately came to free them. Without a word, Casanova led Father Balbi out of the palace and straight to a gondola. From there he traveled to terra firma, to Mestre, and finally beyond the clutches of the boisterous, craven embrace of the Most Serene Republic.

With the end of the story, Mo's voice trailed away in my head, leaving the darkness somehow deeper than before, but richer, too. I freed one hand from my coverings and traced the wood by my cheek. It was soft, bloated by age and lack of tending. My fingernail caught on the seam between the boards. I unburied my spoon and aligned the metal with the edge of the wood. I pressed. I felt it give. Blindly, I followed the handle of my spoon up toward the wood. At the space where the handle met the bowl, my sturdy spoon was now bent ninety degrees.

I guessed I would have to wait for falling monks.

With my crooked spoon I found chinks in my ancient door. And I found a flange. I tapped it with my spoon, a little rhythm:

> My home's in Montana.
> I wear a bandana.
> My spurs are of silver;
> My pony is grey.
> While riding the ranges,
> My luck never changes.
> With foot in the stirrup,
> I gallop away.

I pressed my ear to the gap in my door. My little ditty echoed in the hall beyond.

With foot in the stirrup
I gallop away.

With foot...

No, that wasn't my song. That was somebody else's song. I could hear it start to take shape from the tinny echo. This was more of a lilting ballad. Mo caught the tune, played it out for me:

Mamma e papà cinquant'anni fa,
sposi a Venezia arrivarono
e per ricordo comprarono
una gondola col carillon.

Fifty years ago, momma and papa
Came to Venice and married
And for a memory they bought
A gondola with a carillon.

"Vittorio," I whispered. My voice creaked from lack of use. My lips refused to close properly over the letters. But the metallic serenade stopped, the resonance faded. Then came one clear "ding." My reply. My blood suddenly began flowing again. My mind remembered itself. I pressed my lips to the chink.

"How long have you been here, Vittorio?"

Ding. Ding. Ding. Ding. Ding. Ding. Ding.

"Seven days?"

Ding.

Disbelief returned me to silence. I stared at the nothingness. Finally, I pulled the truth free of my soul.

"I can't make it that long, Vittorio. They'll have me. They want something from me."

Ding.

The ringing of his final answer ricocheted in my head. Gradually, it slowed my mind once more. Exhaustion slowed my blood. From the hall the tune resumed. Mo sang the words:

Ma quel ricordo di un'altra età
che accompagnò la mia gioventù,
oggi purtroppo non suona più
la sua magica e cara canzon...

But that memory of another time
That accompanied my youth
Sadly today sounds like nothing more
Than the magic of a beloved song...

They want something from me. I closed my eyes and saw Matteo again, his beautiful eyes gone lightless as the pupils deepened and spread their inky blackness even over the whites of his eyes. I closed my eyes and heard Luciana's sing-song voice wondering if I would fare better than poor, poor Matti who had let his soul slip away. All gone!

They wanted something from me.

I used my cold, cold spoon to cool my eyes where they burned. I burrowed deeper in my blankets.

My home's in Montana...

☙

My spoon wasn't just bent; it was twisted. I stared at the warped metal, unable to remember how the further mutilation had occurred.

I could see it. I could see my spoon.

I looked up toward my cell window. The faintest grey light crept past its edges.

You have a call.

Go ahead.

Please be Uncle Keats! I closed my eyes and the nausea of sleep deprivation welled up my throat. I leaned my head against the door and pulled the blankets tight again. Bryce's avatar appeared in my head. I stared.

"Bryce?"

He rushed forward, stopped just short of me.

"Alyse, I just talked to Tamsin. Shit."

He paused, pushed a hand through his hair, looked up at me. "I should never have left you alone in there. So stupid. God, I should have been more careful. Damn it!"

I blinked at him in surprise.

Bryce dropped his hand and started worrying that bone pendant of his.

"Okay, I'm going to try...I don't know what I'm going to try." He took me by the arms and I nearly jumped out of my digital skin. "Look. You have to listen to me. I don't care what they tell you. They're lying. It's going to sound so real. They're going to try to twist your brain around. God."

Been there, done that already. And they were painfully close to winning.

"Bryce, do you know something about what's going on?"

He raised a hand to cup my cheek. Like on the train, those beautiful, intense cobalt eyes were all mine. So easily, I was all theirs, too tired to separate yesterday from today.

"Alyse, just this once I need you to forget about the fact we're exes. You've got to listen to me. I'll do everything I can to get you out of here, but don't wait for me. I don't care what you have to do. You have to get out of here. Trust me, Alyse. You have to get out."

"Bryce, what—?"

Bryce jerked back suddenly, quickly palmed his pendant and slipped it back into his shirt.

The call ended.

I laughed my disbelief.

The bolt of my door screeched against my skull. Sluggishly, I pulled my weight off of the tattered wood. The hinges squealed as the door swung away from me. I saw a pair of boots. Then a long, long figure folded itself into my doorway. His thick, white-blonde hair glowed in the pale morning light. His arm unfurled into my cell.

Vittorio offered me his hand.

Chapter 12

"Ah, God!"

Tiny razors ripped through my fingers and toes, sawing viciously up through my feet and hands, into my arms and legs. Vittorio wrapped his body tighter around me, his long fingers silencing my whispered scream. His body heat poured icy fire through my veins. Tears poured down my cheeks.

Never once in my nine years as an immersion artist had I considered doing hypothermia—let alone twice. I like my fingers and toes right where they are, thank you. Even I wasn't that crazy. Of course, it occurred to me then that my recording gear was still on and uploading. Ah, our twisted friend, Irony.

Vittorio had carried my curled, frozen body to this hidey-hole behind the wood paneling at the end of the hall. I'd seen a rope dangling inside before he'd sealed us in. I had to find a way to get myself up that rope. Bryce's desperation combined with my own. I *would* get myself up that rope.

My breath shook as another series of shudders rattled through me. I tried to slow it down, but it seemed like the harder I tried, the harder I shivered. I knew outside dawn was spreading and while the crack of dawn was one of the empty hours, perfect for escape, it didn't last long.

With claw-like hands I pulled his fingers from my mouth. He took my hands between his and began to rub life into them. The contact was only cold pain for now. I could handle pain, but it was so, so strange suffering in his embrace, strange being ministered to by an invisible stranger.

Vittorio was gentle and gentlemanly and so very quiet—not just his wordlessness, but even the movement of his body and his clothes. Even wordless I never misunderstood his direction. The fluid interplay between us felt surreal to my overtired mind. He guided one of my hands up. He wrapped it around the rope. I tested the grip of my hand. I tested the pull of my arm. The arm was fine; the fingers, very, very iffy. Together, we uncoiled the rest of me in the narrow space. I cut off my own gasp as my hips and knees and ankles had their revenge. My body is tuned for, accustomed to the rough and tumble. Unfortunately, this means it has been roughed up and tumbled a lot in the past. Cold conjures up the worst of these physical memories. I forced my body to stretch through it.

I had no idea how the fuck I was going to get up that rope.

Vittorio's huge hands closed around my hips. I could actually feel his fingertips meet below my navel. Unbelievable. Willing a miracle, I stretched and flexed my bloated fingers, then I slid my hands up the fibrous cable, softened my knees, and Vittorio launched me up into the darkness.

I tightened my hands until it felt like my fingers would burst. I began to slide. I hefted my weight a handhold higher. The sudden move cracked my skull against something in the darkness. The pain went straight to my stomach. My hands loosened.

My descent stopped—abruptly.

Somehow, Vittorio had found my foot. He placed it on his shoulder. His fingertips took the ankle of my dangling foot and drew it forward. The sole of my shoe contacted a solid surface, a beam. I stared ahead of myself, forcing my eyes to use the hint of light up here to form images. Lines began to connect.

Rafters.

We were under the roof. I reached out and pulled myself into one of the geometric grids. Clinging to the splintery wood, I breathed in the earthy scent of it and took a moment to calm my mind and body.

The thing I couldn't calm was the fear—the fear that if I couldn't get myself collected and moving that Vittorio would decide to make his escape solitary after all.

The tall man began to rise hand over hand before me. He transferred easily to the vague outline of the rafters across from mine. He turned and began moving away from me through the gymnastic course. Quickly, I reached out for the spot he had just deserted. My hands held solidly as I swung myself over. One thing about that rap on the head: It had gotten my blood pumping.

Vittorio never looked back as he navigated the angles and empty spaces as they gradually tapered. I knew then I was right. I was in his proving ground.

Well, screw that. More and more readily my body answered my commands, stretching, sweeping, leaping, and pulling. And he wasn't the only one who could move quietly. I landed on his beam. He was patting down the ceiling when he turned abruptly, suddenly realizing I was crouched beside him. The grey dark hid his expression, but after a moment I saw him nod his head once.

He turned back to his work and all at once a rectangle of light opened above us. With it, a gust of frigid wind slammed over my recently thawed body. *Oh, damn!* We both coughed as the wind forced its way into our lungs.

He led the way up. I followed.

Dawn made the remains of the fog luminous as we bellied our way across the roof. I wondered how many times the Venetians had "disappeared" from Jürgen's jail during mornings where his all-seeing eyes up in orbit were blinded by a haze like this one.

Supports for the structure above us interrupted our progress at intervals. I assumed that structure was the park Matteo had introduced me to. Those supports were the only thing saving us from a steady slide over the edge. For every few meters we scooted forward through the moss and the muck, we slid down the grade an equal number of centimeters. If this had been an enactment with the proper safety equipment, I would have been exhilarated. As it was, I kept all my focus on Vittorio and counted the breaths until we reached the security of the next support.

Vittorio reached a grey post at the edge of the park above us and looped an arm and a leg around it. He sat up. Then he stood.

I froze in my position, knowing there was nothing I could do for him if he slipped. He was two meters from the edge of the palace roof. It was a three-story drop.

The frigid wind swirled in the cavern created by the intersection of the park and the palace roof, flicking my hair in my face. The sharp stings brought licks of muck with them. I watched through narrowed eyes as Vittorio looped a new rope around the post and bound it with an autorelease clip. This just kept getting better and better. People called the damn things suicide clips for a reason.

I closed my eyes. Was I really this desperate to get away? Plastered to the roof like this, I could feel Jürgen's weight pressing down on me, feel his cheek pressed against mine.

Yes. God, yes, I was this desperate.

Just breathe. He knows what he's doing.

I opened my eyes.

Vittorio didn't walk himself backward over the edge, but instead leaned over the edge of the roof, wrapped his hand around the rope and swung himself over.

He was going to lose his wrist. No, he was going to lose his life.

The rope stayed taut as I worked my way over to the post to which it was affixed. I had to know.

I gripped the rope and, staying on my belly, worked my way down to the stone ledge. Cautiously, I peered over. I saw that large white head dropping steadily away.

Okay.

The rope was knotted, I saw, much to my relief. Below my guide, a huge pile of rubble butted up against the aquarium glass and connected the palace to the battered ruin on the other side of what had probably been a canal.

The rope went slack in my grip. Vittorio had landed. Alive.

Which meant it was my turn.

Great.

I'd learned long ago not to hesitate. If you hesitated, your brain might actually kick in. I pulled up a length of the rope. I wrapped it around one leg, then clamped the soles of my shoes together over the top of one of the thick knots. No jungle girl swings for this fugitive. My fingers were still too thick and stiff for my liking. I eased my lower body over the edge. Then came the full commitment: I released the masonry and transferred my hands to the rope.

Holy Jesus.

I didn't wait for the dizzying swing to stop. Immediately, I inchwormed my extremities together and reached with my feet for the next knot. Again. And again. My ass connected with a piece of protruding rockwork.

"Shit!"

The fragile morning silence felt shattered. I cringed as my voice ricocheted through the rooftops, waiting for a head to pop out of one the windows below and shriek: *There she is!*

Time to pick up the pace. Together and down. Together and down. I kept my eyes, my body, and my brain focused on the rope. I was sure the view of Venice must have been spectacular, but I would wait to appreciate it until some other time. I comforted myself with a single thought: If that fucking suicide clip broke, I'd be too dead to care. There was no way that violent pile of broken rock below me would let me cheat death.

One knot. Two knots. Three knots.

Out of nowhere a huge gust of wind tossed me against the wall. I sucked in my breath as I was reminded with tiny slices across the entire front of my torso and thighs, that I now wore a layer of soggy muck on top of my two layers of clothes. The shivers started again.

Not good.

I raised my eyes to collect myself and found myself facing a window. I nearly lost my grip. Mere centimeters away, Matteo stood watching me. He wore navy drawstring pants and nothing more—so sad, so beautiful...so real. I hesitated, trapped in that soft gaze. He raised a hand to the glass.

I caught myself lifting my right hand from the rope. I snatched it back, my heart jackhammering in my chest. Eyes. I couldn't tell the color of his eyes!

The bones around my heart and lungs cinched tight, too tight. Shivers lengthened into tremors. I fought to breathe, to keep my grip on the rope.

I saw Matteo say my name as he pressed his palm against the transparent barrier. The pain in his eyes; tears rose in my own. It started out so beautiful. What the hell happened? Why couldn't it just once...just one damn time!

The rope snapped against my foot.

Get moving, Alyse!

I dropped my head, cut out my view of him, cut the connection. It felt like ripping a hole in my own damn chest. I didn't have time to be one of the crazy doctor's goddamn victims right now!

I looked down. I was right above the thick wall of aquarium glass. I let myself drop to it.

Vittorio was less than a full body length below me on the shattered blocks of brickwork piled in the canal. Cautious of the jagged edge, I levered myself over the side of the glass. The giant man caught me at the waist when I pushed off. He lowered me to the crumbling pile beside him.

With a flick of a switch, he released the suicide clip. The unit came toppling toward us, cracked against the glass above our heads. Vittorio reeled the rope in expertly until it was a tight little bundle. He tucked it into a cubby hole in a broken sheet of marble. Without a word or a look, he set off across the pile of debris.

I wasn't going to look back.

I wasn't.

But I did.

Through the reflection on the window, I could see Matteo still standing there, still watching me, still with one hand pressed to the glass.

Chapter 13

The man was a mountain goat. A really, really tall, two-legged mountain goat. I wasn't used to being the one trying to keep up. It scraped at my pride, but it forced me to keep my mind absolutely clear of everything and everyone. It forced me to focus only on unpicking the navigational knot ahead of me. Right now that consisted of keeping my balance on a shatteredbrick wall, while dodging dangling boards that had once supported the floor above this one.

A chunk of plaster from the surviving ceiling spun down directly in front of my face and tagged me in the foot. I clamped my lips together and rolled my eyes.

I took just a second to shake out my foot. Just one second. When I looked up, I saw Vittorio in his shadowy grey sweater and slacks duck through a window frame. And disappear. Again.

Don't you dare abandon me here.

I wanted to rush it. I wanted to surge forward until I was caught up with him once and for all. Except that rushing was dangerous here, so I slowed my brain and lowered my body. A less than graceful duck walk brought me clear of the beams. I straightened, but my attention stayed trained at my feet. The salty brick exploded at each placement of my shoe, chasing me relentlessly forward. It reminded me of walking on a shale slope. Which meant I was going to land on my ass. Of course, there was nowhere here to land.

Better not fall, then.

No sooner had the thought entered my head than my arms began spinning. My body tilted. I threw my weight forward and ran until I slammed myself against the building's outer wall. I took a deep gulp of air as I dug my fingers into a patch of exposed brick dusted with crumbled plaster.

"Okay, that was one way to get to the other end," I muttered.

I reached across and heaved myself up onto Vittorio's windowsill. As I straightened, I laughed in disbelief. A bridge. A freaking rope and plank bridge right out of some bad jungle flick. Where were the howling natives when you needed them? Of course, I didn't really need the threat of poison-tipped spears to get my butt across. Oh, no. I had Jürgen and friends who were going to figure out any minute now that I was missing. And the minute they did, they would be after me. Maybe without their handy satellites to guide them, but they would be after me just the same.

And I had no idea where I was.

Or where I was going.

Shit. Vittorio had to be a whole building ahead of me by now. I leaned out and grabbed the rough rope railings with both hands. The bridge dipped with my weight. I put a firm test foot on the center of the first plank. It was surprisingly stable. I looked down to the flooded street below. The tide was low and the apex of a doorway was visible through the black sludge. The water itself looked just like it smelled. Nasty.

Here we go.

I loosened my grip and began to move. The bridge sank with each step. Down, down, closer to the thick water. That shit had to be toxic. I charged it. The ropes squealed with the strain. The planks bucked and clanked as I pumped my way up the slope created by my own weight.

I dismounted with a leap onto another windowsill.

Stepping down from the windowsill, I entered into half a palace. An artist should have painted it. Glassless windows poured soft light over a floor of crushed marble. The floor promised to expand out into a sweep of ballroom—only to be severed brutally, leaving a ragged edge of wood and stone over empty air.

I was the only dancer at the ball.

Vittorio was nowhere to be seen. There were no footprints on the dusty floor.

I tried to stay reasonable. I tried to stay linear: Go forward. You'll see him. You don't see him, you keep going forward. I wasn't an idiot. I knew he had no investment in me, that I should be grateful he'd taken the risk of popping the lock on my cell. He'd gone far out of his way for a stranger. I should be grateful. I should be grateful.

I jogged across the huge floor to where it dropped away into a pile of marble and brick a full story below.

Nothing.

I turned to scan the room a second time.

Nothing.

A greasy, chill sweat crept over my skin. I ran to the bank of windows. There. Another climbing rope two windows back. I dashed back and scuttled down the rope, slipping as I went. I dropped the last half meter and quickly pressed my raw hands to the backs of my thighs, the only clean place left on my grey cargo pants. I'd landed on the backside of a pile of building debris. A glance to my right showed that the carriers were building out a raised alley, maybe a pier. To my left was only the slosh of green sea water.

I went right.

He had to be here somewhere.

The newly built alley was short. At the end, I poked my head around the corner and saw that the next alleyway opened up into a square paved with stones in a neat herringbone pattern. I darted across the intersection and clung to the shadows of the buildings. It was still brutally cold here, out of the vague sun. I hugged myself as I crept to the corner. Carefully, I peered into the square. I ducked back into the shadows. People. Just two or three. Shopkeepers for crying out loud.

Unless my coating of grime had me fooled, I smelled bread...and coffee. My stomach rumbled violently. Oh, and there was a salty, lingering base note of ham. Mmm, lovely.

He was here somewhere. He had to be. Hunger was a pretty universal motivator. I pressed a hand to my stomach. It was all too easy to put myself in his oversized shoes. I needed to eat. Now.

I looked down at my attire. There was no way I could play the lost tourist and stroll into that coffee shop. I had to look like the Swamp Thing's younger sister. I pulled at my hair. My hands came away black and speckled with moss. I lifted my black roll-hem sweater. My white T-shirt was no longer white.

There had to be a way to do this. I heard an alarm clock on the other side of my wall. The regular world was waking. It was now or never. Come on! Think like Vittorio. How would a fugitive giant go about securing breakfast?

Mo, I've got to get my bearings. Can you find an aerial image of this square?

Mo pulled up a satellite picture of the city. The backdrop of exposed brick disrupted the details of the image, but I didn't dare close my eyes long enough for a close study. I was roughly in the middle of the east half of the city, in a tiny square reclaimed from the ruins, stark against wreckage of the rest of the island.

Pull me in closer.

How would he get into one of those shops? I didn't see a back door the way the buildings butted up against each other. Just a couple of side windows. I looked up. Side windows.

I switched off the image. The yellow building on the opposite side of the square from me had side windows. Centimeter by centimeter, I scanned the slice of the square I could see. He had to be somewhere right there.

A soggy lock of hair fell forward and pinned one eye shut. Just as I raised my arms to twist the whole mess back into a bun, I saw a flash of white. It bobbed briefly in a darkened doorway in the building kitty-corner to mine. Gotcha! I finished securing my muddy hair as I checked to see that the shopkeepers were done setting out their tables and securing their canopies.

One last woman remained, a short, cute blonde. I tapped my thumbs on my thighs. With careful consideration she set rich green potted plants out on each of her four tables. I willed my ghost guide to stay put while the little woman puttered. She turned to pull a chair over to the hand crank for her awning. I ran for it.

I shot through the side door into the empty building. The hallway was scattered with construction materials—wood, brick, metal, even sheets of glass. Tools lay piled neatly along the wall. The doorway where I'd glimpsed my ghost guide was halfway down the building. I sprinted my way through the obstacle course. I nearly flew right past the corridor leading to the second doorway. It was the glint of sunlight off that pure white hair that stopped me.

Vittorio crouched, readying himself for a sprint of his own. I slowed to a stop beside him, making enough noise to announce myself. He glanced at me. Our gazes connected, but there was nothing there, no acknowledgement, no surprise, or annoyance. It frightened me.

I had no chance to process it. The moment he turned away, he took off toward the side of the blonde woman's yellow two-story building. One foot on the window box, one set of fingers dug into the ledge between floors. A shift of weight: both hands on the window sill above. He levered himself up onto his elbows, raised the window, slithered inside.

Well, naturally. My arms and legs felt like limp noodles and the man had two, maybe three heads of height on me. I wiped the sweat from around my mouth with the back of my sleeve. Shit. At least I could say I died for a good cause. I've always considered coffee a good cause.

I made it up onto the flower box, caught myself by pressing my palms up against the roof of the window sill. I shifted one set of fingers to the top of the sill, adjusted my weight, dug a second set of fingers into the top of the sill. It was a stretch, but I managed to work the fingers of my left hand up and over the dividing ledge. When that hand became the one bearing the weight, it began trembling uncontrollably. I barely got my right hand up there in time to catch myself from slipping. I still had to make the shift to the second-story window ledge. I reached. I scrabbled with my feet against the sill below. I wasn't going to make it.

I looked down. When I fell, my feet were going to get caught in that flower box and I was going to pitch straight over backwards. I was going to dash my brains out on the pavement. After all of this, what a stupid way to go.

Vittorio's huge hand wrapped around my forearm. He yanked.

༄

I sailed into the room, rapping both of my knees soundly on the stone sill, then the wooden window frame. I was out of patience and out of pain tolerance. I got to my feet ready to rip his throat out.

He handed me a sandwich.

I kept my mouth shut.

The sandwich wasn't the croissant and black forest ham decadence I'd smelled outside. It was the kind you find in the convenience store fridge, prewrapped with wilted lettuce and soggy bread. Thieves can't be choosers.

I sank to the floor to unwrap my little meal. And to guard the window exit. Vittorio wandered the labyrinth of crates, peering into boxes as he munched on his sandwich. The man was truly the incarnation of silence. Not even a squeak of the floorboards marked his passing. I never took my eyes off of him as I ate. He was not disappearing on me again.

He raised his head, tossed me a box. I reached up and caught it. A box of insta-hot coffee. I had to smash the back of my wrist against my mouth to keep from bursting into hysterical laughter. For this, I had nearly killed myself. I saw Vittorio watching me cautiously. I tipped my head back and let the tears of laughter drain away. I popped the heat tab on the waxy box and chugged the drink before it could get too hot. Not exactly the fresh-roasted elixir wafting through the square below. In fact, I noticed a remarkable similarity in flavor between the beverage and the grit in my hair. Definitely worth dying for.

Vittorio wound his way back to me, crouched down in front of me. His expression was curious, not the "I wonder if this works" kind of curiosity, but the "I wonder if this is broken and I can take it apart" kind of curiosity. But his hand was gentle when he turned my leg and brought my attention to a long scrape on my ankle and the rip in my pant leg below my banged up knee.

Being handled so carefully brought all my ricocheting emotions crashing down.

"Thank you. Thank you for getting me out of there."

Abruptly, he let go and rose. He reached into his pants pocket, pulled out a handful of energy bars, dumped them in my lap, and walked away.

When I remembered his initial fascination with me, the initial ease with which we had worked together, I couldn't help but take this treatment as a rejection. Which was ridiculous. For all I knew, the carriers had him in jail, not for being a pest like Luciana, but because he was picking them off with arsenic. He certainly dressed too high brow to fit in my imagined casting of Luciana's rag tag band. That soft grey sweater of his had to be cashmere. Very, very filthy cashmere.

Currency of indebtedness. I picked at the battered corner of the coffee box. The idea seemed cold, but then so did his behavior. But what could he possibly want from me? Maybe it was Luciana that wanted something. I set the box aside. Luciana had said she was sent to meet the new one. The new what? Girlfriend? Why would she care who Matteo shared hot chocolate with? The new target? Had the carriers pulled this power play on other people before me? Could the Venetians actually be trying to rescue me from Jürgen's evil clutches on purpose instead of by accident? I wished I could surrender my fear of abandonment to the idea. It would be so much easier.

I watched Vittorio polish off a second coffee as he kept a safe distance. I was going to absorb every second of rest he allowed. Wherever he was guiding me to, I knew the path would be just as brutal as before. I looked down, fisted my right hand, and felt the muscles move under and around the scars of my shark bite.

That beautiful blue ribbon of a fish, so vivid, so fluid. I saw that maw coming at me again. I flinched. *Geezus.* Mom thought that was my dad coming back to give me a message, a warning. I flashed back to Dr. Roz's reaction to my story and the scars I shouldn't have. Whatever else was going on in the doctor's warped head, even I could see that the shark attack was more than a botched enactment. It had changed everything. Things hadn't been quite real since the moment those teeth had sunk into my arm.

And I hadn't been quite real since the moment my dad had died.

In my memory, his glittering eyes laughed, that same vivid blue as the young shark. *Oh, Daddy.* The crushing pain in my chest emptied the breath from my lungs. I jerked myself upright, forced myself to breathe through the ache. I couldn't keep this up forever. Dodging all these memories, all this pain. There would come a time when I would have to let them out. But that time just couldn't be right now.

Pulling on my game face, I shoved the energy bars into the pockets of my cargo pants and got to my feet. I looked at the crates around me. This had to be the carriers' grocery store. I felt disturbingly clingy as I walked over to where Vittorio dug into another crate. That feeling irritated me enough to snap me out of my grief.

As I stepped up beside him, I was overwhelmed once more with how huge he was. His elbow was level with my shoulder. Without looking back he handed me a pair of water bottles. I shoved them into the pockets at my thighs. It made things snug. I did a test crouch. It would work. I felt the weight of all we had taken. I thought of the short little blonde I'd seen outside getting this shop ready to open for the day. I could hear her moving around her little shop downstairs.

Mo, sometime today, find a way to pay for this stuff—anonymously.

Yes, ma'am.

Thanks.

I covered my eyes with my hands as a horrible exhaustion crashed down over me. Screw Dr. Roz. It was probably just like Matteo said: the Venetians were mostly benevolent. Vittorio probably wasn't coldly collecting markers; he was probably just irritated with me for slowing him down, that was all. I would be if I were him. I lowered my hands and turned to him. He was gone. I spun around.

Just in time to see him pop out the window.

I wanted to scream.

I forced myself to walk over to the window and lean out of it. A little surge of surprise zipped through me. Vittorio was standing on the tiled pavement below, looking back up at me. I pulled my head back in and collected myself. I could do this. Feeling a hundred years old, I climbed back up on the sill and swung my legs over. Vittorio caught me at the knees as I lowered myself down. My sweater and my T-shirt were hiked up to my breasts by the time I slid down him to the ground.

He even paused while I adjusted myself. We took off down the alleyway at a trot. This little town square of civilization was brief. The brackish water and blackened walls of low tide returned. We picked our way across a fallen wall in the growing morning light. The fog was going to burn off. It was going to be a beautiful day. Suddenly all I could think of was sleep. Even after the coffee, the vise of sleep deprivation cinched tight over my eyes. My thoughts were growing blurry.

Ahead of us, across a stretch of water, an old, filthy stone staircase rose. It looked like a great place to curl up. Vittorio strode right into the water. It came up to his knee. It hit me on the upper thigh. I reached the stairs with a few strides. My pants sucked in tight around my leg as I stepped up. Then I went down hard. For a minute, all I could do was lay there, trying to breathe. I knew I was lucky; my hands had already been stretched out in front of me. I closed my eyes. The stone was so cool and I was so queasy. I actually began drifting.

Distantly, I felt Vittorio's hand close over my upper arm. I fought returning to full consciousness, then caught myself doing it and opened my eyes. I helped him right me. He released me and continued on his way up the stairs. My legs were shaking.

Mo, you have to talk to me. Keep me going. If I keep thinking about it, I'm going to puke and then it's all over.

Britta Niles is requesting first review on Russo's Watch *by October 10th. You currently have ten incomplete scenes left to go on the project. Alexia Brandon has returned* Whale Song *for extensive revisions on the lost calf scene and the lonely call—*

Stop, Mo. That's not helping.

I got to the top of the stairs. Of course, Vittorio was gone.

"Oh, come on. Where the fuck is he? How am I supposed to find him when I don't even know where the fuck *I* am?!"

The Palazzo Bragadin Carabba.

I sighed, staring at a pool of sunlight on the cracked and crumbled tile floor in front of me. I'd never seen a more inviting place in all my life. Was that a rat over there? I'd heard they made good cuddle toys. God, I wasn't going to make it.

The Palazzo Bragadin Carabba, I repeated. *This should have significance to me why?*

This was the home of the jurist Matteo Bragadin, the home of the man your arrogant young Casanova convinced to become his keeper. This was where Casanova lived in luxury and decadence before he was sent off to prison.

I looked up from my pool of light.

"Really? Now that is interesting."

Move the feet. Find him. Get yourself unlost.

I fought to keep my brain engaged by keeping my eyes darting all around me. It was impossible to guess by looking at this half-gutted mansion what it would have looked like in Casanova's day. But dressing it in my mind's eye got me past the rats and into the next room. I gave it white molded ceilings, gilded claw foot chairs and couches, a big crackling fireplace, and a large, lovely mahogany desk. I didn't know a damn thing about the décor of the period. I didn't know a damn thing about the dress of the period either, but I put my anti-hero in hose and heeled shoes with one of those long brocade coats with lacey shirt sleeves covering his hands. And why not a goofy powdered wig while I was at it?

Still no Vittorio.

A flush of fear bloomed along my hairline.

I pushed on to the next room.

"Keep going, Mo," I warned.

The Bragadini family itself has a Venetian hero: Marcantonio Bragadin. Marcantonio had been commander when the colony of Cyprus fell to the Turks. However, the turkish Pasha turned an honorable surrender into a macabre entertainment. The Pasha captured Marcantonio before he could return to Venice with his remaining men. In a long and pitiless torture, the Pasha ordered his men to cut off the commander's nose and ears. Finally, the villainous Turk publicly flayed the proud man alive and re-stuffed his skin with straw—

"Okay, you can stop that one right now."

Mo didn't have a sense of humor, but I got the undeniable sense she was laughing at me as I rubbed my hands over the clammy skin of my face. The image of Marcantonio the Scarecrow was not mixing well with the adrenaline. I heard a board clatter. Had my silent guide actually made a sound? Was that too much to ask for? What kind of jackass couldn't even wait ten seconds for a girl to catch up?

I passed through a smaller room and out into a hall. The ceiling had caved in here. I had to pick my way over beams and exposed nails. I couldn't help but think this didn't match the flavor of Vittorio's previous paths. Everything up until now had been treacherous, but clear. I stopped in the middle of the dusty pile. I'd bet half my library I was following my cuddly little rat friend.

The floor beneath my feet softened.

I lunged forward. My mistake. If I'd crept, I would have made it. Instead, the thrust of my leg rammed the rotted floor out from beneath me. My lead foot caught my weight and I pushed off of a dangling beam to give my momentum a forward direction. I dove for the safety of a windowsill as fallen beams crashed through the flooring I had punctured. I heard a startled chattering. Then I saw them: my cuddle toy's friends and cousins.

"Ah, shit!"

I cocked my head around to peer out the window. *Please let there be an obvious way out of here.*

By pure chance, I spotted the blonde bastard mounting a small bridge between this palazzo and the next building. That bridge was at least two rooms away—two large rooms. I looked down. Five or six of Cuddly's closest friends scurried around the dusty floor beneath my window sill. I waited. One headed back toward the darkness of his home. One raised his whiskered snout to examine me. I slipped off my shoe and smacked him on his twitching nose. He backed off for a second. He would either head home or come back for more—in which case it would be survival of the meanest. And frankly, I was feeling pretty mean.

He began to edge toward me. His four friends seemed to realize something was going down and joined his advance.

"Yeah, Tamsin. I'm great with animals."

I slipped on my shoe. They edged closer. I read once that you can get chewed on by a rat and not even know it. Probably a myth. I caught myself checking to make sure all my fingers were still intact. I shuddered.

Worse than vanishing digits, of course, were all the horrible diseases available from those sharp little teeth. And me out here with no access to a doctor. The alpha rat put a paw to the powdered plaster of the wall. I tucked my feet beneath me. The second one raised up on his hindquarters. The third one vied against the other two for the same section of wall space. *Not good. Not coming up here. Stay down little nasties.*

I risked a glance up. My audience was attracting attention. Some of their little rat buddies had returned. I had to get out of here before I got myself bit. Did I dare try to jump over them? Would this part of the floor hold? I leaned forward. I felt a weight on the back of my shirt.

I shot straight up. And landed right in the middle of the rats.

"Oh, shit! Get off me! Get off me!"

I swung around, trying to dislodge my attacker, stepping on tails, and feet, and even a full body. I saw the alpha charging me. I was now officially a territory invader.

Shit.

I ran. As I hit the first doorway, I swung sideways and bashed whatever was clutching my shirt against the doorsill. It knocked free. The shrieks and squeals grew louder. The clinging material of my soaked pants added to the muscle fatigue slowing me down. The water bottles dug into my thighs. I glanced back. The rats had doubled in number. They spilled out of the doorway. I promised my legs that all they had to do was make it across that bridge. Just keep going. If they could make it that far, I promised we would find someplace rat-free to lie down and rest—elusive white-haired giants be damned.

I found another one.

"One about a woman who was eaten alive by rats?" I wheezed.

One about a party and a scandal.

"Oh, I definitely see the connection." In my mind Cuddly exchanged places with my well-groomed Casanova. Would he waltz with a little lady rat with wedding cake hair? God, just let me lie down!

I flew past a large section of missing flooring, caught a glimpse of my bridge out the broken window. Almost there.

The last room brought me to a standstill. Nearly the entire floor was missing. The ripped out balcony where the bridge connected lay on the other side of a vast chasm.

"Giant boy cleared it. How did giant boy do it?"

As I spun around, I saw the rat swarm surging across the room behind me.

"Rope. Giant boy likes ropes."

I looked up. There, strung from doorsill to doorsill. I jumped. I caught the taut rope with my battered hands and knew I had only seconds to switch my grip before I fell. No hand over hand for me right now. I arched back and swung. And shrieked as a rat went flying off my shoe and into the chasm. I swung back again. My foot smacked something and sent the pack chattering. On the upswing, I caught the rope with one ankle—rat free. I got the other ankle hooked. Against my will, my fingers were opening. I twisted and shoved one forearm up and over the rope. I hugged it to me as I wrapped the crook of my other arm around the rope. Flesh peeled as I worked my calves over the rope as well. Below me, the rats milled frantically.

More rat trivia: rats boarded boats by doing tightrope walks on the docking lines. Move!

I scooted across that rope with amazing speed, expecting any second to have a fat ball of greasy fur and sharp teeth drop onto my head. I dropped to the floor on the opposite side and spun around.

I straightened.

"You lazy sons of bitches."

Bobbing sets of whiskers explored the edge of the chasm. Others examined the wall. None of them broke out their rat magic and ascended the doorsill to the rope. I was almost disappointed.

I kept a baleful eye on them as I dropped my hands to my knees to slow my breathing and calm my brain. Vittorio was somewhere up ahead. I was no longer sure I cared if I found him. Was there any point to this endless chase, anyway? He could just point me toward the goal. Mo could guide me the rest of the way. Mo was reliable. Mo didn't stay just far enough ahead to keep me in a constant state of panic. Of course, Mo's data on this particular landscape was centuries out of date and would certainly not include all these aboriginal ropes and bridges. Giving up, I turned back to the bridge. I plodded forward. Once I'd crossed the wide canal, the bridge structure continued inside the building, the floors having fallen away decades ago.

Go ahead, Mo, tell me about the party. Just please keep talking.

The Bragadini once hosted a party so popular, so well attended that they had to reinforce the floor of their ballroom against the sheer weight of the attending masses. But it was one guest in particular who gave that party its legend. She was Maria da Reia, a nun from the Convent of San Lorenzo, the convent for leftover noblewomen. This bride of Christ had found the holy marriage bed a bit chilly and invited the French ambassador to share in those neglected marital privileges. But this was not thrill enough for the ambassador. That fateful night he slipped the fair sister out of the convent and brought her with him to the party in the most indecent disguise imaginable—he dressed her as a man!

I chuckled at the horrified shock in Mo's tone. I passed by one, then another, and then another support wall and then the structure opened up into a balcony. I stepped down into the cushioned tiers. The carpeting let out a puff of something I was sure I shouldn't be breathing. A broken chair here and there had been left behind by otherwise very thorough looters. Over the edge of the balcony lapped a great oval lake. The roof was merely a fringe of splintered beams around the edges of the room, leaving the morning sun to shine so brilliantly that I almost thought I could see the submerged stage. Somehow that struck me as horribly, horribly sad.

A lot of piety mongers consider sensory immersion artists to be adrenaline junkies or carnally obsessed. I've always thought of myself as an extension of the storytelling tradition...and here was part of that tradition that told stories no more.

"An opera house?"

Teatro Malibran built over the remains of Ca' Milion, the palace of Marco Polo.

I smiled and nodded. Storytellers and adventurers. That was...perfect.

And if I didn't get moving I was going to sit down and never get up again.

I picked my way across the balcony. I stopped at the entrance to another bridge and shook out my limbs. Follow the bridge. I could do that. I glanced back at the abandoned stage.

You know, Mo, I almost wish this Venice project had been real. I could have brought Mom along. It seems like every bit of mortar and stone here has a story. It would have been incredible. We would have been perfect for this job.

Yes, we would have.

The bridge led upward. I climbed it on autopilot. Mo seemed to be out of stories and I couldn't think of a prompt for her. I emerged onto a red roof—and nose to chest with Vittorio.

His long face remained inscrutable as usual as I craned my head back to see his eyes. He glanced at the now clear sky, then dipped his hand into his pocket and pulled out a pocket watch. The satellites. How could he possibly know when they were turned toward us and when they weren't? Trial and error? Even Mo didn't have access to that kind of data. Vittorio tapped a thumbnail on the face of the antique timepiece. He looked out over the red roofed landscape, then back at me. Sliding the watch back into his pocket, he made his decision. He turned and clambered up to the apex of the roof, kicking chunks of tile at me as he went.

I sighed. So he'd waited. After leaving me lost for the length of two buildings. Definitely a jackass. I waited until he began rapidly walking the spine of the building before I followed. I could feel a second wind coming. Second winds are dangerous. That last burst of energy comes with a certain reckless inattention, a superman mentality that leads to injury. Reckless inattention wasn't something I could afford up here. Unfortunately, in this environment I couldn't have Mo chatter at me to keep me awake either. I kept my focus by picking out a goal and staring it down until I reached it, then picking out the next one. At least the steady breeze kept the nausea down to a bearable level.

As I clambered after him, I kept mostly to all fours. We were following the roofs of five buildings cobbled together to circumscribe what had once been a square. Each building insisted on its individuality with a roof at odd angles with itself and the one next to it. At one point I simply sat down and let gravity do the work of getting me to the next level. It wasn't really the height that had me worried. After the run-in with the rats, my concerns were more immediate—namely the structural integrity of what lay immediately beneath my feet.

Our circular route gradually took us down to the roof of one of the lower buildings. Vittorio stopped at the edge with his back to me. It took me a minute, but I slid feet-first down the last bit of roofing and managed to land beside him. I pushed myself upright next to him. Together, we stood overlooking a church whose roof had more or less completely caved in. The work had been done by the rust-red bell tower which had toppled crosswise across the structure. To my surprise, Vittorio took my arm and began descending into the building. Our path was built of artfully arranged remnants of the church. Shit, more rubble to climb. And this stuff wasn't even firmly attached to the wall.

But we descended below the fan of rotten floor boards and our goal came into view: a rickety floating patio of sorts. The square, four-walled raft held its position via tethers tied to the church wall. Floats fastened to its facing benches kept it stable. I glanced up over my shoulder. Absolutely no way Mo and I would have found this little hideout, even with detailed directions.

In a hail of rock and brick chips, Vittorio and I reached the lap of the water's edge. Even as I was getting my legs back under me, he laid his hands on my shoulders and turned me to him. I looked up in surprise. He studied me for a moment, then offered what I could only call a grudging smile. He released me. I just stared after him as he bent that huge, fluid body to pull on one of the tethers and bring the raft closer to us. He offered me a hand up. I took it. Midway between land and water I noticed there was no waterway out of the church. That struck me as odd. But then one foot was on the bench and Vittorio was helping me hoist my weight forward. I clambered down onto the floor of the raft.

I turned around.

He was gone.

Chapter 14

You're shitting me.

Above me, through the slats of wood, a seagull cried as it rode a current over my cavernous, echoing church. The air had a tang to it from the gently rolling seawater beneath my feet.

I remembered to breathe.

I watched the bird disappear over a tall wall where red brick had begun to bleed through the bleached plaster. I looked down at the raft. After all this time of wishing for it, I had to think to sit down. I perched on the edge of the bench, at a loss for what should come next.

My ghost guide had abandoned me.

I stroked the rough wood beneath my fingers.

I dropped my head into my hands and swore.

I thought about scrambling out of the boat and going after him.

I didn't move. This was where he was taking me. This was the end.

Of what?

I raised my head and looked at the shimmering green water all around me that hid who knows what. What the hell was I doing? What the hell had I done? Why had I taken his hand? I'd made it through the night. I should have stayed and.... What? I couldn't fight back against them. They shut me down every time.

So now instead I was stranded on a rickety old raft.

Out there, you will die.

I grabbed my knees and squeezed hard. The din quieted. Just a little.

I released my knees. My legs itched. No, my body itched. It was the stagnant seawater weighting my clothes. I slipped my shoes from my feet. My double layer of socks sucked tighter around my feet. I worked the soaked cloth clear of my feet and stretched my toes.

I still itched.

Methodically, I moved on. Pants. I could feel each line of stitching distinctly as it chafed my tender skin. First, the unloading. Slowly, deliberately, I emptied each pocket of my cargo pants: an extra pair of panties, an extra bra, two bottles of water, four energy bars, two travel maintenance packs for Mo and Margie. Problem. I stared at the two sealed foil packets lying on the floor. Once we used up those supplements, the girls would slowly start leaching minerals from my body. Eventually, they would kill me.

Not going to think about that right now.

A small swell lifted one end of the raft, slid my little collection to the opposite wall, then slid it halfway back to me. I looked around myself for somewhere to stash it. I saw the hinges on the bench across from me. My legs trembled in protest, but I rose and shuffled across the raft, popped the lid open.

I thought it was garbage at first, little foil and plastic packets, dirty little coffee boxes, but I ran my fingers through them and realized they were full. I sifted through the collection only half reading the smudged labels. Deodorant wipes, plaque fizzies, lotion samples, trial size shampoos. I felt a large packet on the bottom. I tugged at it. It popped free from the sticky wood. A bath-in-a-towel. I managed a smile.

The promise of being clean eased a little bit of the weight from my mind and body. Balancing against the side of the raft, I peeled away my cargo pants, then, much more painfully, my snug black slacks. It was my lace panties, however, that felt like they were actually removing flesh. They rolled up into a tight scroll before I could even get them clear of my ass. After an awkward struggle, I finally kicked free of them. The sweater and T-shirt I took off as a piece, trying to spare my face. I flicked open the catch on my bra and tossed the lacey bit of lingerie in the pile with the rest.

I paused and looked down at myself. The damage was worse than I had thought. My feet were red and angry looking; my knees were black and blue. There was a ding on my hip. A long red welt from the stairs rode low across the tops of my breasts. My forearms were similarly bisected. My hands showed patches of raw meat and the nails were torn and bleeding. Even my face was stiffening from a scrape.

I hadn't been this beat up since...well, a very long time. I felt Margie start to kick in. I hesitated. Should I waste resources on bang-ups like these? In the end I let her keep working. These bang-ups had been dipped in some sickeningly filthy water. I wanted them closed up.

Carefully, I lowered myself down to the floor of the raft. I winced. Even my butt hurt. Twelve hours on a stone doorsill would do that. I leaned my head back against the edge of the raft and unwound my hair. I was about to abuse my resources. I opened one of the bottles of water and poured the tiniest bit over my scalp. Using the tips of my fingers I worked shampoo through my roots. I rinsed it as best I could with the small amount of water I'd budgeted for the task. The length of my hair I combed out with my fingers, trying to knock most of the dirt overboard. I sectioned my hair and wiped it down with the bath towel. My hair still crackled with bubbles when I wound it back into a knot. It would have to do. I lowered my arms to my sides.

I didn't want to move.

But it was worth it. That first caress of the towel across my face pulled a sigh from me. The slight swirl of a breeze retraced the line of moisture. I took my time, using the towel to guide the breeze down the line of my neck, sloughing off the crumpled and ancient, leaving me long and graceful. The soft cloth made a sweep across each breast, reminding my heart to beat as first my left, then my right nipple came slowly back to life. A sweep under the weight of each breast relieved the pressure where the dig of my bra was remembered.

Gently, I drew the chill tingle across my belly, around and over the length of my back, drawing me up straight and light. Then the breeze followed down, down the lean muscles of each arm to the throb of my fingertips, cooling, gentling, softening. I shifted the towel to hold it loosely in both hands and began drawing it through my toes, over my arches, up my ankles. The moving air brought cold kisses to the hot-cold muscles of my calves, my thighs. I let my legs fall limp. The last patch of white on the towel cleaned the space between my legs.

I set the towel to the side and tilted my face up. The sun was just beginning to peek over the walls of my sanctuary. I sat open to the sun and the wind, drinking in the warmth and the chill of both. Feeling alive for the first time in days.

Someone had touched me.

Not teased or tormented. He had actually touched me. It had been so long I'd truly forgotten what that felt like. If I closed my eyes, I could feel his skin against mine, feel his breath moving against my ear. A tight sense of loss wound around me. I pulled my head and my limbs back into myself. That look of awful sadness when he'd said goodbye at the window. Why did I have to lose what had promised to be so lovely? What the hell had happened?

Futility turned sorrow to anger. I shoved those thoughts away. The sting and burn from my scrapes drew me back to the present. I looked at my pile of soggy clothes in the corner. My skin crawled at the thought of putting them back on.

I looked around myself. The bench where I'd boarded had hinges, too. I leaned over and peered inside. A fur blanket, a giant jug of water, and a half crushed first aid kit.

I pulled out the blanket and sniffed it, stroked it. It was clean. I nearly rolled myself into it and gave up, but the two watts still left glowing in my brain forced me to break into the first aid kit and steal the last remaining vial of anti-bacterial solution. Treating my scrapes took the whole thing.

    I got up and wiped down the floor, then spread half the blanket over it, leaving the other half to pull over me. I stretched out on the blanket and drew it tight around me. I shivered now, exhaustion and exposure drawing my body temperature lower and lower. The soft fur of the blanket soothed my trembling, cradled my aching flesh. I fell asleep in its embrace and dreamed of laughter and dancing. And forgot about the monsters.

Chapter 15

Something rocked my raft. My eyes opened reflexively. My brain did not follow suit. I heard footsteps. Then came the smell.

Ah, God!

I held the fur blanket to my breast as I struggled to sit up. I'd slept so hard that slipped joints snapped as I righted myself. I wiped an indelicate smear of drool from my cheek with the blade of my right hand.

Luciana perched in a faceless ball of tatters on the left bench near my feet.

"Vittorio, Vittorio, he has no manners. Hospitality for our guest. Our guest will know Venetian hospitality."

A pretty white dish painted with tiny purple flowers emerged from the shadows of her costume. In it were two squares of grilled polenta, overlaid with sliced salami. A bit of clear sauce swayed in the bottom of the bowl. She placed a fork in the bowl with a little "tink."

I hesitated. Her aroma overpowered all my senses. I couldn't imagine ingesting anything that had been too near that filthy body.

She shoved it at me.

"Eat."

I adjusted the blanket, so I could hold it up with my knees. Then I took the bowl. *They sprang you from prison. Eat.* I took a bite. I let her see my pleased surprise—the creamy, smoky flavor of the polenta, the salty, spicy richness of the sausage, all tied together with the tangy sauce.

"Thank you, Luciana." I stopped midway through another bite. I looked up at her again, finding the place where I thought I'd glimpsed a face in the shadows of all those layers of rags. "Thank you for everything."

She shifted her little sneakered feet. "You couldn't save our Matti, could you? Too bad. Too bad. He was a good boy—kind." She hopped down from the bench and scuttled over to the other side of the raft, lifted the bench seat to peer in and paw through the collection of samples. "He fought it. But he didn't really believe in it. Now he's changing. He's becoming one of them. Too bad. Too bad."

"What's 'them,' Luciana?"

"A *fata*."

Help me out here, Mo. What's a *fata*?

In Venetian folklore, a fata *is a combination of witch and fairy.*

I hid my indulgent smile in another bite of my lunch. "Matteo is becoming a *fata*?"

"It was too late for him. I had hoped. But you couldn't do it. Now he's going to lose his soul. The *fate* will steal it. Steal it away from him and give it to the Devil. Steal away what poor, poor Matti never believed in."

She turned on me abruptly. I saw her eyes, a sharp emerald green, piercing—and without a trace of the lilting, crazed chant of her little voice.

"Do you believe in your soul, Alyse Kate?"

My smile fell away as another set of eyes stared back at me from my memory, eyes black as emptiness, deep as eternal night. I couldn't answer.

"You better decide, Alyse Kate. You better decide soon."

She snatched the plate away from me, shoved a bag of warm cookies into my hand. Before I could react, she tottered away again, started picking through my discarded clothes.

"Look at this. Vittorio didn't like you. Didn't like you at all. Took you the hard way. Too strong. Didn't let him show off, did you? Look at this." She gathered all my ruined clothes into a ball. "Don't want these now, do you? I'll take them. I'll take them for you."

"What?!" I started to lurch forward. Every abused joint, every overused muscle in my body chose right then to seize up. I pressed my lips closed over a cry of agony. I dropped back down. "Luciana, give those back."

The little demon just laughed at me. "Matteo sends a gift. A little trinket." Two large white plastic bottles came sailing at me. I caught one, the other tagged me in the chest. I turned over the bottles. One was a tech-specialized multi-vitamin, the other a high-potency mineral supplement—both violently expensive. I let out a little breath of disbelief. The man had just saved my life.

I looked up.

She was gone.

So were my clothes.

"Oh, fuck!"

I wasted the energy looking around the church for any sign of her. There was none. Gracie's little sprite had disappeared completely.

That little turn of my head reminded me of my exhaustion. The images of my surroundings stuttered into each other until I had to close my eyes to settle my senses. I felt sick. And now I felt vulnerable, too. I've seen women wear their natural form with such a powerful confidence that not even the crassest guy in the room leered or snickered. Maybe it was the exhaustion, but I wasn't feeling like one of those women right now. I felt trapped and pinned down—naked.

I picked up the bottles of supplements from my lap where they'd fallen. Beneath them in the fur something gold glittered. I set the vitamins aside. With careful fingers I pulled a shimmering filament free: a delicate, nearly translucent gold chain with a simple golden topaz pendant—in the shape of a tear.

"Matteo," I whispered.

I held the pendant to the sunlight, watched it pick up the warm glow. I don't wear jewelry. It's dangerous in my line of work. I've always said Bryce was a fool for risking his life over that little bone pendant of his. I unhooked the catch, slid the feather-light chain around my neck. The pendant hung low, resting gently between my bare breasts. I felt the tears begin to well and blinked them back.

"I'm too tired for this bullshit!"

I tossed the blanket to the side and got to my knees, whimpering pitifully. I should have done it before I slept. I would take care of it now and hope it made some kind of difference in the level of lactic acid build up that was kicking my ass right now.

I opened the bench. Four large bottles of sports drink had been added to the pile of packets. A twisted sense of angry gratitude seized me. I took a second to breathe it out. I'm old enough to recognize irrationality when I feel it. Most of the time. I popped two of Dr. Keith's maintenance pills, tipped back the purple bottle of sports drink, and chugged. When I set it down again, it was more than half gone. I added two of Luciana's little cookies. The delicate almond flavor clashed with the syrupy sweetness of the drink, but it would all serve to keep the medication from burning the shit out of my stomach. I rested my head on my knees.

"How long was I asleep, Mo?"

One hour and twenty-three minutes.

"No wonder I feel like shit."

Again I got to all fours and stowed my new supplies. I balanced myself with one arm against the side as I straightened my blanket. It was from this awkward position that I saw it: a big black eye staring up at me from the water. I shrieked and jumped back from the edge of the raft.

"What the hell was that?!"

Loligo vulgaris. A squid.

I couldn't help it. Despite being marooned buck naked on a raft in the middle of a deathtrap that could collapse on me at any second, despite having been locked up by lunatics and having everything that constituted my life threatened with destruction, I broke down into hysterical laughter. I wrapped up in the fur blanket and curled up into a quivering, giggling ball. Even the twinges in my freakish shark bite couldn't shut me up.

"Some fucking tough shit immersion artist you are, Bryant."

Then something bumped my raft. Hard. I sat up, abruptly sober. The raft was nowhere near the wall...or any of the other obvious debris in the water. I made a quick survey of all four sides of my floating patio. Nothing. A random thought floated through my head: *Sharks eat squid. Squid are shark caviar.*

Ike coming back to haunt me. My heart started beating triple-time.

"No, no, no. I will not develop a shark phobia. I will not. I will not."

I curled back into my furred cocoon. I settled my head on my throbbing shark-bit arm, using the pressure of my head to contain the pain. I closed my eyes. My raft jerked again. That hit had come from the left. I scrambled to my feet, stared hard at the green water. Were those ripples in the surface forming a line? Was that sleek shape in the murkiness a body or a shadow? I waited. The ripples faded. I waited. The shadow seemed to slide away. Maybe it was never there to begin with. My arms began to tire from holding me up over the side. Still I waited.

Nothing happened. My visitor was gone. Slowly, I sank back down to my blanket. I blew out a breath and rubbed my hands over my face. My scars ached sharply, though I could feel the pain beginning to fade. I cradled my arm against me. I had to sleep. Just holding my eyes open was agony. I lowered myself back down to the floor, reached behind me, and drew the blanket over me one more time.

Just the local wildlife saying hi. But my eyes wouldn't stay closed. Sighing, I pressed my fingers over them. Maybe I should relocate to somewhere up off the water. Even as I thought it, I knew it wasn't going to happen.

"God. Where are we, Mo?"

She flashed a map into my brain. *Approximately one block from the Grand Canal in San Giovanni Grisostomo, the Church of St. John, the Golden Mouthed.*

"The Grand Canal. We don't have a boat, Mo. What good is that going to do us? Golden Mouthed. That's good. Maybe old St. John will come talk our way out of this. Shit."

My eyes slid shut from pure muscle fatigue. But shadow sharks cruised the backs of my lids. I couldn't relax.

At one time this church housed the finger bone of Saint Onophrius. It is said that the saint was once a girl who beseeched God to change her into a man to preserve her virginity from a persistent suitor.

The chuckle that escaped me released a few of the sharks from their endless circling.

"Mo, although we do seem to be suffering on account of a persistent suitor, I don't think any deity is going to intervene on behalf of my long lost virginity."

In another version of the story, the saint is a beautiful, but lecherous young girl who repents her wicked ways and beseeches God to save her. She wakes up the next day as an ugly old man.

I laughed and the sharks were gone.

"Shut up and go to sleep, Mo."

※

I was climbing a staircase, racing forward as each step crumbled away behind me. Faster, faster. I could see the landing ahead of me. If I could just run faster, I would make it. I would be safe. A piercing shriek speared my brain. The staircase exploded beneath my feet. I fell.

My body jerked. My eyes snapped open.

"Ah, shit! Turn that off, Mo! Turn it off now!"

I clamped my hands over my head as my AI ran a mad series of security scans. The shriek cut off. The connection popped open. Fucking Phan Mai and his high-tech booby traps. How the hell did he get my address?

The caller wasn't Jürgen, though. It was Dr. Roz Calles. But judging by the way her eyes moved and her careful posture, she wasn't alone in the room. Big surprise. Just to be on the safe side, I closed my eyes to shut off any view of my surroundings and told Mo to keep tabs on my tracker to make sure it stayed off.

"Alyse, are you alright? Are you injured? You didn't answer—"

"What do you want?" My voice was a gravely croak. I hazarded a quick glance at the sky through the slats of my roof. The sun was straight overhead. Great. One more hour of sleep for the home team. The sleep deprivation alone was going to kill me.

"Alyse." Dr. Roz leaned forward. "Please come on back. You're going to get yourself hurt out there, honey. I know you don't believe us, but give us a chance to help you. We'll set you up with an apartment; we'll tell the press you're working on the folklore tour. You can try the treatment plan and see for yourself if it doesn't clear up some of your symptoms. We just want to help you."

All that motherly concern made it hard to remember why I was out here, when I could be back there, being taken care of, being loved. I fought it.

"No." Why? Where were the memories? "You...you locked me in that room. I almost froze to death. You tricked me. You hurt me. You...lied."

Dr. Roz's attention went off camera. "We've got to get her back here right now, Jürgen. Something's wrong. What does she mean 'almost froze to death'?"

Jürgen came into view. He stood behind the doctor, his face, the methodical approach to crisis where Dr. Roz was pure worry.

"I'm going to trust you with something, Alyse. I'm going to send your AI my personal address. Now I need you to trust me.

Have your AI send me your location. The doctor and I will come out and pick you up ourselves. Whatever's happened, we'll see that you get the help you need."

"Jus' need some fuckin' sleep." I cut the connection. Consciousness drifted away, then back.

You have a video message. It is one hour old. Would you like it?

No. Sure. Who is it?

Tamsin.

Tamsin sent me a video message? Why wouldn't she just use her comm gear? Play it.

Tamsin's familiar face appeared in my mind with a backdrop of the peacock wallpaper from our hotel room. She was using the hotel comm system. That's how Phan Mai had gotten my address. Thanks so much, Tamsin.

"'Lyse, I'm getting the hell out of here. There's a boat leaving right now." Tears started rolling down her face. "I'm...I'm just so mad at you right now. I told you not to go with him. Why didn't you listen!? You never listen. Now you've gone and thrown it all away—our lives, too. I'm...." She turned away from the camera. "I'm leaving. Don't call me back. I won't answer. Goodbye."

The message ended. I opened my eyes, stared into pale fur. My eyes burned, but not worse than the huge hole in my chest. I stared forever with empty eyes. Sometime—without my knowing it—sleep slipped in and cooled the terrible fire, released me from despair.

This time when I woke, it was an easy stirring. The water rocked me gently. The wind had grown heavy, wet, and cool. I opened my eyes. The sky between my slatted roof had turned grey. There was rain coming. I looked to the left. Ben was admiring my exposed breasts. After a little start of surprise, I pulled the blanket up.

"Ben, you have absolutely no class."

He grinned. "Hey, just enjoyin' the view."

"I'm sure Steffi would buy that."

"Not for a damn second."

"Didn't think so."

I smiled back at him. We sat in the lapping quiet for a while just feeling the sway of the water. Finally, I sat up. My body still hurt, but I could move and I could think and that was an amazing improvement.

"How on earth did you find me?"

"You didn't get my message?"

I shook my head "no" just as Mo so helpfully informed me that I had a message waiting in the queue. Thanks, Mo.

Ben shuddered. "Ah, man, this foul smellin', goddamn nasty homeless crazy chick snuck into my room. Told me to pack some stuff for you. Led me here. Got a little boat thing out front."

"Luciana."

"That what that thing calls itself?"

"She and her friends are the ones that got me out."

"They also the ones that left you here bare-ass naked?"

"Yeah."

"Good thing I brought this then."

He tossed his dark green daypack at my feet. His was waterproof. Mine wasn't.

"Change a clothes in there, the rest a your meds, your workout shoes. Stole all the snacks from Tamsin's bag and stuffed 'em in there. Couple bottles of water."

"Thanks."

"Yeah."

"Found one of these, too. No reloads, though." He pulled it from his pocket and held it out to me. A stinger. An expensive one. It was done up to look like a wedding ring, but activated would produce a stinger filled with knock-out toxin. A rich woman's self-defense weapon. I took it, slipped it on my finger. I didn't ask where he'd "found" it.

I ran my hands over the straps of the pack in front of me. I wasn't shaking anymore, but I was scared. Scared to hear what he would say next.

"I gotta get back. They notice I'm missin', they're gonna...Alyse, they're holding you hostage. They took us into this office; they explained the 'consequences' real carefully. We don't show on that boat back to Padua in an hour, they're gonna tell the feds you got infected; they're gonna throw all those people at the party to the loonies."

"If I got infected, anybody who came could be?"

"They made damn sure that picture was clear. They knew the people who got killed when the carriers first got outed. The stories they told was vivid down to the last nasty detail. That

Phan Mai freak of yours even got tears in his black eyes. He's got a wife and two kids back in Germany. Wife lost an arm in a bombing. This was even after he got quarantined."

In the space left after Ben's words, I fixated on just one word: hostage. How could Jürgen even consider a threat like that after what he admitted his own family had been through? How psychotic was this man?

Ben drew breath to speak; I exhaled to brace myself.

"Alyse, Phan Mai mighta done the weepy thing when he talked about his wife and all the rest of them, but he got stone cold when he talked about his two boys."

I looked up. "Boys."

"Yeah, three and five years old."

"Oh, god, I can't handle stories like these."

"Alyse, what if they're not lying? They said you got a different DNA patch from theirs. The doctor is looking into your surgeries. He thinks—."

"It can't be that. All the other immersion artists are here. I bet they've been tested under one pretext or another. None of them came up infected, did they?"

"None of them screwed a carrier."

"It doesn't take physical contact. If you've got the DNA patch, all you have to do is be in the same room with a carrier and you're done."

"Hey, I'm no sideline med student."

"Well, me neither, but something's wrong here. You haven't been close to these people. You didn't see Matteo whack out; you didn't see Jürgen's face when he jumped me in the hall.

These people are not okay." I pressed my hands over my eyes. "He hunted me. That's what he said, 'Thanks for the beautiful hunt.'" I pulled my hands away and looked up at Ben's worried face. "How can I possibly trust what these people say—"

"When it's impossible? Alyse, Sleeper's Syndrome is impossible."

I blew out a breath. It shook. What did it mean that I was even entertaining this line of thought? Out of the corner of my eye, I saw Ben shake his head.

"I'm sorry. The freak gave a damn convincin' speech. Guess I went off and fell for it."

I stared out over the murky water, only able to nod. Breathing was getting harder and harder.

"I...I have to go. I have to be on that boat. They're...um, actually clearin' everybody out, called the whole party off. People are really pissed."

"Yeah?" I cleared my throat. "What are they telling them?"

"Some people tell you it's the palace. The guests is too heavy and the damn foundation is crackin'. Some people tell you it's the carriers. Too hard for them to be around so many regular people all at once. They're 'overwhelmed.'"

"Hmm."

Our wandering gazes came back together. He cupped a hand around the back of my head and pulled me forward until our foreheads were touching. It was awful; it hurt even worse than before. I endured it. I had to. I didn't want him to let me go.

"I don' wanna leave you, baby. I'm not supposed to leave you. It says so in my goddamn contract."

I laughed, but my voice was wobbly. "You have to Ben. I don't think Jürgen Phan Mai bluffs when he makes those kinds of threats."

"What you gonna do? You know they're gonna lock this island up just as soon as that last boat slides through. How you gonna get out of here?"

"I don't know, Ben. I'll have to figure that out."

I couldn't stand the grinding pain of contact anymore. I pulled away. Ben got to his feet.

"I...."

I waved him off. "Go."

"Yeah."

He jumped from the raft to the rubble stairs and started climbing. Halfway up, he leapt from the pile to the fallen bell tower. When he landed, he turned back to me. I could just see him through my toppled roof.

"I love you, Alyse."

"I love you, too, Ben."

He turned away again and jogged his way up the battered structure. At the top, he vaulted the wall. And then he was gone.

I rose from the cover of my blanket. I dropped the backpack on the bench and pulled it open. Ben had made good choices. The scoop neck, long-sleeved T-shirt looked lightweight, but it was winter-weave. Black cargo pants went with the army green T-shirt. Even the underwear was practical. The clean fabric felt so good sliding against my skin as I dressed. And it felt so good to be dressed, wrapped up, protected, mobile.

I pulled my hair into a high ponytail with the band he had provided. I laced up the training shoes. When I was done, I stowed the backpack and the blanket in the bench and stood in the middle of the raft, hands in my pockets, staring up the ramp of the steeple. I let out the tight breath I'd been fighting for so many long minutes now.

"Ben, you fucked it up again. You were supposed to say you didn't care what they threaten. You were supposed say you'd stay with me no matter what. You were supposed to stay!"

"Stay" echoed shrilly around the walls of the church, becoming more and more hollow as it faded. A chunk of bloated brick toppled from the wall across from me and fell into the water.

Something occurred to me then as the ripples rushed toward me: Luciana had brought Ben to me. And then she had taken him away. The security perimeter would be deactivated and she wasn't trying to slip me out with the rest of them. She'd sprung me from prison, but she wasn't planning to set me free.

Shit. What was I? Some kind of fucking damsel in distress? Time to get a clue. No one was going to ride in and save me. It was time to take Bryce's advice and save myself.

Mo, I need a map.

Chapter 16

Us city girls forget what true night looks like. How the stars can be so silver bright, so individual, yet so impossibly many. How the moon can be so liquid, so vivid. How the dark can be so consuming.

My movements were sharp and quick as I worked the zipper closed on Ben's pack. I pressed the water seal shut over it and checked the entire pack over for any leaks. My first escape had been spur of the moment, unplanned for, sloppy, and reckless. I wasn't getting pinned down naked and dependent again. I'd packed all the food and fluid that I could fit into the backpack. Now I deliberated how best to carry the fur blanket. I wasn't leaving without it.

With Mo's aerial images, I'd located the shipping and receiving dock for the little town square Vittorio had shown me. It was my best chance to get out of here. I'd have to do some reconnaissance, find out how the supply boat guarded against stowaways, hope it wasn't by irradiating each load before they returned to port.

Pointlessly, I poked around the storage benches, wishing for something I could seal my blanket up in. I spotted the cracked first aid kit. A bio hazard disposal bag! Ha! I wrestled the kit open again. There was one bag left. I unfolded the ultra-thin plastic. I looked over at the heap of blanket. This was going to be a trick.

Without warning a stabbing shrill alarm pierced my head.

"God! Stop! Just let him in. Geezus!"

He is requesting an avatar meeting.

Without warning a stabbing shrill alarm pierced my head.

"God! Stop! Just let him in. Geezus!"

He is requesting an avatar meeting.

"Fine! Shit!"

I dropped to the floor of the raft, clutching my ears, squeezing my eyes closed. Abruptly, the alarm ceased. I sat up, shook the tension from my body. I had a moment to let out a breath, then Mo transferred my avatar to Jürgen's meeting space.

The digital meeting space was a dimmed replica of Jürgen's office back in the palace, a soft gray haze of furnishings and window treatments that left the man himself a visual slash of dark power against its backdrop. Jürgen stood leaning against his desk, his arms folded over his chest. His white work shirt was loosened and he'd rolled up the sleeves again, revealing the antique metal brace that covered his right forearm. Maybe vanbrace was a better word for it. It reminded me of armor. It was set with seven rough cut gems that bled a spectrum from a darkened ruby's blood red to the luminescence of an emerald's vivid green. All but the last, purest emerald glowed softly against the beaten bronze.

He shifted, rose to his feet; my attention rose to his face. Another thing I'd forgotten—the pure physical push of his presence, the simmering threat. I stayed where I'd entered, just a few steps inside the door. He took his time, his eyes on mine, his steps toward me slow and deliberate, stalking. God, had I forgotten.

"Night has fallen, Alyse."

Another step.

"Your friends are gone. They've left you, run away. They feared this place."

Another step.

"You should fear this place, Alyse."

Another step.

"Out there, in the dark, there are shadows, dangerous shadows, violent shades and you are beyond the circle of my protection, outside of my contract for free will. Out there, Alyse, Hadria can do anything she wants to you. Anything at all. I can't stop her."

He halted his advance. He was so close I had to tip my head back to watch his eyes. I had to watch his eyes.

"Come back to us, Alyse. Come back to us and be safe. Let us help you. Let us take care of you. Come back inside."

I swayed. He wrapped warm hands around my shoulders. He brushed at my collarbone with his thumbs.

"Where are you?"

I took a trembling breath. "I...."

Outside, in the night, something bumped my boat, rocked me.

"What was—?" My arms flailed as my body tried to catch its balance, confused between two contradictory realities. Jürgen's grip on me tightened.

"Tell me, Alyse. They are coming for you."

I took a step back, hit the door, the bench? Maybe both.

"No. No, stop this. Mo, turn it off."

Nothing happened. I shivered. Jürgen leaned closer, his eyes gone cold.

"You are too strong willed for your own survival." He dropped his hands. He took a step back. He turned away. I could breathe. I watched him stride toward the opposite door. Pausing with his hand on the door handle, he looked back at me. "Your AI knows where to find me...should you decide you need saving." He opened the door, stepped partway through, the smile on his lips just visible. "Just don't wait so long that there is nothing left to save. Hadria is not a gentle mistress."

He closed the door. The program released me.

൙

The rocking of my raft was the first thing to register as my senses reacclimated to reality. My unease transferred its focus from Jürgen's dark eyes to the dark waters surrounding my refuge. I peered over the edges cautiously, half expecting a toothy maw to shoot up from the glassy shadows. This time, like the last, I saw nothing. The deepening darkness assured it.

Out there, in the dark, there are shadows, dangerous shadows, violent shades and you are beyond the circle of my protection....

I drummed my thumbs against my thighs. If he'd wanted to make me fear the dark, he'd done a damn good job.

"Fuck this. I've rested; I've eaten; I'm going."

I grabbed the bag with the blanket and put my full weight on it to get the fur far enough away from the closure to seal it. Then I balanced the package inside the straps of Ben's pack up against the back support and pulled the whole thing on. I cinched all the ties. I rotated my arms. The blanket stuck out a little ways to either side, but it should work.

Using the tether, I pulled the raft closer to the rubble stairs. I jumped. I landed badly, just barely missing the water, scraping my hands on loose brick. Not a promising start, but my proximity to the water's edge sent me scuttling upward. The path was grey on grey. I felt my way along on all fours, crushing ancient plaster and toppling carefully balanced beams as I went.

I reached the top of the wall. My heart was pounding. In the distance, stars were being swallowed by a filmy blackness. The clouds I'd felt earlier were coming in.

I looked out over the rooftops I would have to traverse.

You never listen. Now you've gone and thrown it all away— our lives, too. I'm.... I'm leaving. Don't call me back. I won't answer.

It wasn't Mrs. Patterson. It was you. You put Haylee to sleep. An innocent woman died because of you!

I don' wanna leave you, baby. I'm not supposed to leave you. It says so in my goddamn contract.

Your friends are gone. They've left you, run away. They feared this place.

The empty breeze skimmed my body, fluttered through my ponytail. I pushed a cold fingertip to the center of my forehead. Damn the bunch of them anyway. Damn me for being lonely for them. I sank down on the top of the wall and pressed my face into my hands. Slowly, I forced myself to stop fighting the ghosts of my friends. I forced my head clear.

I sat up. This was stupid.

"No. No, despite what the whole world thinks, I am not suicidal. I am not going to throw a self-destructive temper tantrum. I am going to wait for daylight." I stood up and started picking my way back down. "I am going to get some rest on my rat-free raft between love taps from the lagoon monster and I will wait until I can tell the difference between the hand in front of my face and a chunk of rock three paces away."

I reached the water's edge and pulled the raft back over to me. My leap back aboard was a little more graceful than my departure. I stepped down onto the floor from the bench and began undoing the straps to Ben's pack.

The raft bucked.

I stumbled and caught myself on the sidewall.

Hadria is not a gentle mistress. Was that Hadria? Was Hadria my lagoon monster?

I righted myself and looked wildly around me. The shark bite on my arm shrieked with pain bone-deep. I clutched it and breathed through my teeth.

It struck. I heard wood crack as both the raft and I were tossed into the air. I landed on the backpack, cracked my head on the raft wall. I rolled to my side, snapped to my feet. The water around me churned.

"Shit!"

I grabbed the tether and heaved the raft to the wall. In the shadows I was blind, but I managed to tie the rope off. I wouldn't chance a water landing this time. The rear edge of the raft jostled. I leapt. I heard the raft crash behind me. I didn't look back. I fought my way up the slope. Debris rolled away in a loud series of crashes. Only at the top did I glance over my shoulder. The water below was still again. But I heard a distant clatter, then the sound of rocks falling into the water. Not right below me, but near. Very near.

I shoved myself up onto the roof. I padded across the spine of the building, but had to stop at the first juncture. The clouds were coming in too fast.

Mo, I can't see what I'm doing. I need some kind of overlay or something. Help me out here. I was glad I didn't have to speak the command. My voice would have shaken.

I heard the tooth-drilling sound of shoes scraping against tile. I turned. Put my back against the wall. A figure hung on the wall of the church, a shadow in the shape of a human. The shadow pulled itself up and over the wall, then disappeared over the other side—into the place where I had been hiding.

Then I heard it: that same paralyzing cry that had burned into my mind and body. It began low in the throat like a big cat's warning growl, growing, building from a snarl to a scream, breaking off in the two-toned shriek of a hawk. It echoed off the buildings. Struck me in the ear. Anger, vicious anger, murderous rage.

A cry like Matteo's when the soul had gone out of his eyes, when he'd attacked me like a rabid animal. That shadow entering my former shelter was a carrier, a carrier gone feral.

The trembling started low in my belly, rose to my lungs, then shot out through the rest of my body like lightning's fire.

Mo, hurry the fuck up!

The overlay came up. I found the handhold I needed and hefted myself up to the next roof. I trotted forward. This was dangerous. The feeds were always talking about anti-terrorist force guys getting killed doing this sort of thing. The overlay didn't always line up perfectly when you turned your head or, since the file was created by what you recorded the last time you came through, a critical detail might have changed since your AI made that file. And you might end up falling three stories through a hole in the roof that hadn't been there earlier that morning.

I dropped to all fours and climbed a tiled slope using sheer momentum. At the top I looked back. Another feral carrier had reached my hiding place. It stood at the top of the fallen bell tower. I flattened myself against the roof and spidered my way forward. They knew. They were looking for me and they knew. The lagoon monster's attack on my raft had given me warning, enough for a head start, but just barely.

I was almost to the theater. I heard noises up ahead. I froze. My position at the crown of the roof was too vulnerable, too visible. I let myself slide down the side of the roof where it met with the theater building in deep shadow. Carefully, I got to my feet. I marked where the entrance to the theater lay roughly three feet ahead of me. Then I had Mo turn off the overlay and followed the building with my hands. I needed to be able to see what was coming.

The shape of a man emerged out of the dark onto the moonlit slope of the roof. I stopped breathing. My body remembered the strength of Matteo's blow. The raw power. There were three of these guys out here. Jürgen's warning echoed in my head: *Just don't wait so long that there is nothing left to save.*

Too late. I made myself and my pack small in the shadow of the building. *Don't see me. Don't see me. Please don't see me.*

He turned from his ascent.

No, no, no, no.

He stepped down toward me.

In a deafening crackle of cloth, I lowered myself, patted around my feet for a piece of tile, a rock, anything. With a cock of his head, the man took another step in my direction. My fingers closed around a jagged piece of terra cotta roofing. His rear foot slipped. I braced myself for the impact of his fall. He caught himself—in a beautifully graceful, utterly impossible backward shift of his weight, lift of his arms.

Something crashed in my church across the square. The monster man with his clean cut business man's façade turned toward the sound. If he'd lost his balance again, he would have hit me in the face when he raised his arm to catch himself. His body dropped into a comfortable all fours no human could manufacture. He climbed the roof to its peak. Then he loped off toward the others at the church.

I covered my mouth as my gasp for breath nearly turned to a sob. The shriek, the call went up again. Not from this pack of three, but from somewhere else in the city. Another answered the first, then another, then another. They were everywhere. *They're coming for you.*

Oh, geezus. Oh, fuck!

I edged my way toward the window entrance to the theater. *There was going to be one on the bridge.* I grasped the windowsill. *There was going to be one on the bridge.* I forced one foot up and over; then the other. *There was going to be one on the bridge.* I rushed it. I didn't run; I hadn't lost that much of my mind to blind fear, but I plowed ahead so fast, so steady that anyone in my way would be laid out flat. I finally saw the grey outline of the exit. The line to it through the void was clear. Please let the absence hold. Please.

Then I heard it: the dull thunk of a ring against metal. Someone was on the balcony. I ran. I would not be caught out here with no room to maneuver and nothing but freefall below. I made it to the doorsill.

The frustrated snarl took all my bravado away. I saw her back as she looked out over the lake of the orchestra level—a big woman, intimidating without animalistic rage, strength, and agility. I closed my hand over the stinger ring on my finger. One shot. If I missed and that woman got her hands on me, she would crumple me like I was a chunk of two-thousand-year-old plaster. It had to be my last resort. I stepped back out of the moonlit threshold.

She turned toward me.

Her lip curled.

Her eyes glittered black.

I only had a second to react. A metal bolt held the bridge's rope railing to the wall. I grabbed it and ducked through the side of the bridge. By some miracle my pack didn't tangle in the fiber architecture. I handed myself down to dangle off of the boards of the footpath.

I hadn't crossed out of the deeper shadow of the wall. What were the chances she saw me duck for cover? Middling to good.

I closed my eyes.

The bridge still swayed from my abrupt departure when I felt the woman step out onto the first plank. And right onto my fingers. I lost my breath in a silent rush. Tears started streaming down my face as she mashed the edge of her tennis shoe over my fingertips. She took another step forward and released my fingers. And another step. I opened my eyes. She wasn't stopping! She wasn't hurrying either, though. My elation slowly turned to agonized frustration as she took her goddamn sweet time walking the rest of the length of the bridge.

At first I didn't move when I felt the jerk that said she'd dismounted the footpath. When I finally dared raise my fingers, the pain was more fantastic than I could have possibly imagined. Slowly, I shifted my grip to one side of the bridge. Getting up was more complicated than getting down. I chinned up to the lower bolt, got one foot braced on the rope, then lunged for the upper bolt. I caught it. A good thing, too, because if I'd missed, I'd have gone straight over backwards. Not my most well-thought-out strategy.

Mo, please have Margie take a look at these fingers.

I sat on the planks, hunched over my smashed fingers. I tried to breathe my way through Margie's repairs and promised myself the pain was probably worse than the damage. But I had to get off the beaten path. I wouldn't last long flinging myself off bridges and sacrificing my fingertips to the boot heel press of every feral carrier in the quarantine camp. I stretched my fingers. They screamed, but they were functional.

I peeked again out into the balcony level. It was empty. I darted out. I hesitated. I was not getting on another one-way bridge. At the top of the balcony's aisle stairs stood the remains of three sets of French doors. I climbed the empty tiers. Glass covered the floor up here. I placed each foot with precision as I approached the exit. With my good hand, I carefully pulled open the door. The sea breeze took a swirling swipe at my face. The reek of mold made me blink. I looked out over the floor. The moonlight lit most of the reception area. The center had collapsed into a huge ring of blackness. That left a fringe of flooring along the wall.

I heard the squeak of rope. The squeak became rhythmic. I stepped through the French door and pulled it closed behind me. I only had moments until whoever was on the bridge made it to the balcony.

My crushed fingers felt like they were being severed as I popped the ties on my pack and slung it around to the front of me. Plastering my back to the wall, I began to scoot my way around the perimeter. I had to be out of this room when they got here. Stupid to take the most obvious exit! What the hell had I been thinking?

The squeak of the rope became louder. I'd reached the door to the men's room. I pushed through. Softly, I closed the door behind me. The floor was intact here—at least according to my gradually sharpening night vision. Exposed plumbing and wiring showed where the fixtures had once been. I kept to the edges of the room. The windows were intact. I shoved at one with everything I had. It raised just far enough for me to stick my head through the guillotine opening.

I was directly across from another, smaller building. It was so close! Only about as far away as I was tall. Could I jump it? No. Yes. No.

I pulled my head inside and turned in a circle. A beam from the ceiling. Part of the frame for the bathroom stalls. No tools. The hooked end of the curtain rod. No rope. Not even an extension cord.

Come on, come on!

The curtain rod. It had serviced all three windows: it was long enough to reach. There was no way that thing would hold me. I picked it up. This was no tin foil tube. God, it had some serious heft to it! And a slick of dust. I bobbled it. I snatched it out of the air before it could clang to the floor. Maybe it could hold me. Maybe I was fucked in the head.

I dropped my pack in front of me. I dug into it, pulled out the two bottles of supplements and transferred them to the thigh pockets of my cargo pants. I secured my blanket to the pack. Then I got my full body underneath that window and shoved. I got a handful more centimeters for my efforts. It would have to do. With all the racket I was making, I had to get out of here now, before I didn't get out of here at all.

Sliding the curtain rod along my hand to keep it quiet, I aimed toward a window sill slightly lower than mine. The closer I got to my target, the more wildly my pole swung. I hung my whole body on the remaining length, trying to counterbalance it. It was going to be close.

The metal scraped the plaster of the opposing wall. I braced myself against the windowsill and swung with everything I had. The other end cleared the window sill. I shoved. It locked into place against the window frame. I rolled my end to the corner of the window sill and whimpered. I had about eight centimeters of play.

I heard the crunch of glass. No. I could not possibly be hearing the crunch of glass all the way in here. I wiped the sweat from my face with the back of my sleeve and dried my palms on my pants. Calm it down. Calm it down.

I snatched up my pack and burrowed it and the front half of my body out the window. I reared back and shot-put it through the window on the opposite side of the canal. It cleared. I drooped with a moment of relief; then it was time to get the rest of me out on the window ledge.

I turned around and wiggled myself out backward. Hanging on to the window frame, I swung my legs over the side. I gave the rod a test yank. The hold was firm, but I knew it was the bowing when I reached the center that I had to be worried about. I wiped my hands down one last time. Then I transferred my weight. My body dangled over at least two stories of nothingness. Water rippled in the canal below. The wind wrapped a lock of my ponytail around my forehead.

"Oh, this was a bad idea."

I remembered the giant woman from the balcony. I remembered the animal-like business man from the roof. I took a deep breath.

Move. Now.

I slid one hand out in front of me. Together. Apart. Together. Apart. I kept my hand placement as wide as I dared. It was so close. No slipping. No slipping. I reached the middle. Together. I heard the metal grind behind me, felt the abrupt sag.

Apart! Apart!

Only a meter left to go! The pole popped behind me. I reached the window sill. I hooked my fingers around the window frame, praying there was no glass left in it. I wasn't that lucky. Something pressed easily into the palm of my hand. I pulled my weight up to the ledge, hooked my right foot on the corner, then worked the rest of my body up and over. I pulled my hand free from the glass, let myself drop to the floor.

The thing about cuts like these is you don't feel them for a few minutes. I had to take advantage of every second of that time. I grabbed my pack, opened the straps, and secured it around me. It took a couple blows to release the curtain rod from the window sill. Using the wooden window frame to muffle the noise, I reeled it in. The smears of black blood grew larger and larger as I worked. I tucked the rod out of view.

I took a steadying breath. My time was almost up on the signal delay from the slice. I pressed my thumb to the cut and took off at a cautious clip across the room.

Mo, get Margie to work on this. I'll pop some of the supplements as soon as I find a stopping place.

This former apartment I found myself in was in better shape than the theater. I passed a bathroom with the tub still in it, a kitchen with the cabinet doors intact. I had to unlock the door to get out into the hallway.

My face scrunched involuntarily as Margie's little bots got to work on my hand. I needed antiseptic for this thing. The best I could hope for was that the bleeding was cleaning it out. I wasn't going to pour sports drink over it.

Without windows for moonlight, the hallway was deeply dark, but my eyes were catching up to the night enough for basic maneuvering. The pills in my pockets jangled while I walked. My nerves jangled with them. Why didn't I just blast a horn to let the whole damn city know where I was? But I was too scared to stop. Just a little further and I would be far enough away. Then I'd take a batch and put them back in my pack. Just a little further.

My head snapped back. Warm pain spread from my left eyebrow and my cheekbone, tears streamed from my eye. I reached out with my good hand. I'd walked right into an open door. If I swung my head side to side, I could just barely make out the outline.

"Shit."

I dabbed at the tears with the sleeve of my T-shirt. The next steps I took were cautious and probing. My breathing grew jerky.

"No, no, none of that," I whispered to myself. No tears. No meltdown.

Wall.

I sniffed back the threatening waterworks and tried to force my eyes to see what was in front of me. A small oval of gray shone at thigh level. I crouched down. A moonlit floor was all I could make out. I measured the hole with my outstretched arms. I should fit.

I pulled my pack off and pushed it through ahead of me. The wall was at least twice as thick as my forearm was long, probably the walls of two adjacent buildings. I reassembled myself on the other side. There was more light on this side of the wall, but that would change when those clouds hit the moon.

More light meant more caution was necessary as the light was coming through a dilapidated roof. On my third step into the room, I hit a soft spot. I used rocking test steps to find my way around it. Finally, I made it to the hall. This must have been an office. Doors and/or doorways lined the corridor. I hurried down the length of it. I saw another knocked out tunnel at the other end.

On the other side I would stop, I promised myself. I would find a secluded corner to hole up for the night. I would take my supplements, so Margie could stop the achy leeching from my body and start healing things properly. Without missing a step, I burrowed my way through to the next building.

A hotel, maybe? My eyes were drawn down the row to the doorway with most light. There. I could rest there, put myself back together. I pulled off the pack as I strode into the room. A huge window pulled light from an already partially eclipsed moon. The room had a table, the remains of a chair.

And a carrier.

Ah, shit.

Chapter 17

The woman was curled over her knees, rocking steadily back and forth. I froze. She raised her head. I knew her. My vacant brain grasped after the memory—the cute little blonde from Vittorio's grocery store.

She looked just as shocked as I felt.

"No," she whispered. "Not here. Not...." She began panting through gritted teeth. She squeezed her eyes shut, but not before I saw her normal eyes, perfectly normal, haunted eyes.

I took a step back, reaching for my bag.

"No. Don't. Don't. Run."

I stopped mid-reach, but kept my crouch. She was fighting it. Matteo had fought it. I got the shit beat out of me.

She hissed. "You. Hadria wants you. Ah! She wants you bad."

"Hadria?"

The woman shivered. "Should have stayed with Jürgen! Now everyone she's gotten her claws into...she's ripped their minds away. They *hunt* you. You poor idiot!" Her head snapped forward, rammed into her knees. "God, I can't!"

"Can I hel—?"

"Shh!"

Her breathing became shrill. She was losing. Shit. Don't run. That was a rule for facing predators. Don't run.

The high-pitched intake of air stopped. The air around me relaxed, darkened. The girl unfolded fluidly to perch on her fingertips and toes. She turned her face to me. Through a mass of fair hair, I watched her pupils expand, obliterating those pale irises, wiping out the whites of her eyes. Her eyes became the night sky: fathomless, glittering.

Anger twisted her features into a snarl. It should have been ineffectual on that gentle face, packed in that small, soft body. Instead it stopped my heart.

The rain clouds finally consumed the moon. I kept my eyes on the shadow that was left of her. Slowly, I straightened. The girl began circling. Moving as little as possible, I kept myself facing her, hoping she would circle her way to the door and bolt.

Her loose, cross-step prowl slid her up to the door...then past it. *Damn.* She was getting closer. I wasn't going to just stand here and get jumped. I took a test step toward the door. She stopped, bristled. Not good. I glanced toward the exit. My fifth or sixth calculated risk of the night: Could I make it to the door and slam it in her face before she got me?

I took another step. She matched me. I took another step. She hissed and followed.

I ran.

She slammed into me, knocked me to the floor. The moment we hit, she sprang off of me, grabbed my arm, and I went flying. I hit the wall with my shoulder and punched through the old drywall. As I pulled myself out of the dent, I saw her toss her head back. The growl started so deep it rattled my bones. She was going to tell the whole fucking city where I was.

I tackled her.

We went down. Her claws sank into my ribs. Her tiny teeth pierced my shoulder. She tossed me up and over, landed on top of me. I fought to break her grip—knees and elbows had no effect on her. I finally got my nails dug into her ear. I yanked. That got her attention. She reared up and punched me in the jaw. My body went slack. My senses flickered. I felt the ring on my finger smack the floor, the ring Ben "found," the stinger. I saw her raise her fist again. I dug my thumbnail into the back of the ring to activate it. I rolled my head to dodge her blow, snaked my arm through, and jammed the stinger into her rib cage, right above her heart.

The girl released me, clawed at her T-shirt, blinked once.

Then she collapsed on top of me.

୭

I deactivated the ring with my thumbnail.

Now I was the one breathing shrilly. I'd had the wind knocked out of me and the girl was a dead weight on my chest. My hands were loose as I tried to get hold of her to roll her off me. Finally, with a twist of my torso, she tumbled away. Her cloud of feather-soft hair swept over my face as she fell.

It smelled of lavender and roses.

My hands started shaking. I curled into a ball next to her. Lavender and roses. I jammed the heel of my palm into my mouth, muffled my own sobs.

※

Eventually, pain drove me to my feet. I stumbled over to my pack and dragged it to a heavy, dusty chair.

Mo, how long does the toxin usually last?

Twelve to twenty-four hours, except in rare cases where it is fatal.

My hands were still shaking as I opened the bio hazard bag and pulled out my precious blanket. I laid it on the floor. I pulled the girl onto it and covered her snugly. Her eyes didn't pop open. She didn't rake her claws down my face. She just lay there, sweetly serene, childlike.

I felt a scrape of guilt.

I turned away.

On the table next to me, I unloaded my supplies: a bottle of sports drink, the supplements, and an energy bar. I popped the supplements, then stowed them in the bag. I dumped half the bottle of sports drink down my throat, then settled back in my chair to look out the window and chew on my energy bar. It was peanut butter, Tamsin's favorite. I hate peanut butter.

Margie's microscopic bots were drilling through my system like little lines of fire, streaming to my shoulder, my hand, my ribs, my jaw. Margie herself prickled warmly beneath my rib cage.

Hadria. Everyone kept warning me about her. I was no longer inclined to think she was my lagoon monster. Sharks didn't rip people's minds away. Drugs could do that. Hadn't that nurse said Matteo's breakdown was due to medication? Someone had messed with his treatment meds? Maybe that's who Hadria was, someone who had figured out how to manipulate the carriers' meds until she could control them. But so many? Including Grocery Girl, I'd seen maybe five feral carriers so far. But I'd heard far more. And why could she possibly be hell bent on killing *me*?

I must thank you, Alyse, for a beautiful hunt.

A hunt. I slammed a hand over my mouth as my stomach heaved. Could it be as simple, as sick as that? Thrill of the chase, of the kill? I couldn't help remembering the surge of wicked power I'd experienced stalking Bryce through the fog. I forced myself to breathe through the nausea. God, it couldn't be.

And how much longer could I keep this up, being hunted? Would the hunt continue through the daylight hours, too? Geezus. Should I give up and go crawling to Jürgen? Grocery Girl seemed to think I should. But that would mean staying trapped here on the island. That would mean surviving that predatory presence day after day. No, hunted or not, I had to get out of here.

But I had to rest first. Distantly, I heard another of the feral carriers belt out that horrible scream. The girl had come here to hide from the hunt. Maybe this place would be safe enough for me, too. I leaned my head back into the dirt-filled upholstery and closed my eyes, ignoring the slight tremor that still rattled through me. I only needed forty minutes or so for Margie to finish her repairs. Then I could replenish whatever she had depleted and be on my way.

With a deep breath, I began again to gnaw on that peanut butter bar and concentrated on relaxing the tension from my muscles. I felt the moment when the supplements reached my system. The sharp ache fell away, leaving me with a more natural muscle soreness.

As my mind began to clear, my conclusions began to look hysterical. A hunt? That was absurd. Why pick me? What on earth could be the motivation? But as I looked down at the girl wrapped and sleeping in my blanket, my brain offered up one option: Sleeper's Syndrome. If the lies about my infection were true, then that set me apart from everyone, made me a threat to everything the carriers had established, destroyed their chance to build a bridge to the outside world—just like Jürgen said. Because it meant that Sleeper's Syndrome might not just be the curse of those treated for Brighton's Disease, it might actually be contagious.

God.

And for the first time it hit me: What if the lies really *were* true? What if I had just lost everything, my entire life? What if my career and everything I'd dreamed of creating had just been ripped away from me? What if I had just lost my twilight walks under the swaying branches of the pines? What if I'd just lost my evenings at the bonfires, my bizarre trips with my team, shopping with my flake of a best friend? I released a shaking breath. What if I'd just lost forever the chance to finally patch things up with Bryce? What if I couldn't be there for my mother as she rebuilt her life without my dad? And something I'd never even considered before this moment: What if I never had the chance to have children of my own? What if the choice had just been completely taken away from me?

A glance down at the girl in front of me brought my mental chatter to a halt. This girl had lost all of that years ago.

Enough. I sat up. What if, what if, what if. I was turning into Tamsin. What if I got off my ass and got the fuck off this little slice of Hell?

I jumped to my feet and walked to the window, brushed the dust from my hair and clothes. Below was another flooded street, maybe a canal. The water was growing choppy.

I opened a pane of the window and leaned out into the thick darkness. The wind had picked up. The rain would start any minute now. Below I could just make out a tiny dock on the side of the building. Is that how the girl had gotten here? By boat?

I didn't see a boat below, but that didn't mean there wasn't one. I couldn't believe that the natives would play Jungle Jane through the ruins just to get to work every day. Time to get moving. Time to find the staircase. I skirted around the woman and slipped out the door. The hall ended only a few meters away. I got lucky. The staircase was stone and intact. I followed it down to the next floor. The moving air guided me to the open window which had been built up to become the building's new entrance. And there, tucked in the shadows was a tiny little canoe and a paddle.

A quiet laugh of surprise escaped me.

I hurried back upstairs. I repacked my bag as I finished chewing that nasty little peanut butter bar. I shook out the bio hazard bag. I looked down. I sank down into the chair.

Twelve to twenty-four hours.

"Oh, fuck me anyway."

I couldn't leave her here. The ceiling would collapse on her in the storm. She would have a reaction to the toxin. She would die of exposure.

The other carriers would find her and rip her to pieces.

She'd tried. She'd really tried not to whack out on me. I couldn't glance at her without thinking of a hundred different movies where the good guys won by blowing away an innocent randomly inhabited by the big bad evil. Could never stomach it.

I groaned. Why couldn't I conjure a bit of Tamsin at times like this? I stopped myself. That wasn't fair. Sort of. No, Tamsin usually either sweet talked or oblivious-ed her way out of situations like this. And idiots like me fell victims to our own more literal consciences.

I knelt down next to my angelic little attacker and pulled her free from her cocoon. I stowed the blanket, then strapped on Ben's pack. Every fiber of self-preservation in my body screamed in protest as I knelt down and shifted her into my arms.

"Good God, you are heavy, Grocery Girl."

I was headed to the square where she worked anyway. I would dump her in the coffee shop. Surely, feral carriers weren't sane enough to think about things like business. Matteo had only succumbed to the madness for a short time, so I chose to assume the shop owner would be rational again whenever he came down to open for the day. He would take Grocery Girl to the doctor; they would give her the antidote: all better.

I hurried us down the hall and down the stairs. I didn't want to tire my arms out before I got down to the rowing. Gently, I lowered my charge to the floor. Propped against the doorframe was the small, yellow canoe. I untied it and pulled it down to see what I was dealing with. It was a one-person rig. This was going to be snug. I transferred the lightweight vessel to the dock and dropped my pack and the oar into one end. Then I went back for my passenger. I held her upright around the ribs as I toed the boat into the water. Then, sitting down on the dock, I transferred us both inside. The canoe rocked wildly as I got us situated with her head propped up against me. Finally, I decided it was the best I could do. I reached around her, grabbed the oar, and started pulling at the water.

Mo, give me that map to the warehouse again really quick.

I traced the flashing path indicator. Via the waterway, the square I'd taken hours to get to through the ruins was just up and around the bend.

I looked up and saw the rope bridge between the palace and the theater pass above us as we glided forward. Just as I lowered my head, we crashed to a halt. I took one stroke back, waited. I blew out a breath of relief when after several seconds I felt no water collecting around my feet. I turned the canoe sideways and used my oar to feel out the shape of debris. I wasn't finding a chink in the dam. How had she gotten through here? Did we have to get out and carry the boat across it?

A low growl sounded above my head. I didn't even look up. I tightened my grip on that paddle and I pressed it against the water with every muscle in my body. In seconds, I had the boat turned around and gliding in the opposite direction.

Not fast enough. The shriek was growing familiar enough that I could tell this one was different. This one said: I found her!

Sweat sprang up on my face, turning the storm wind arctic.

Mo, you said we were close to the Grand Canal. Point me that way.

First right turn.

I took the turn as fast as my amateur oarsmanship would allow. We ground past another pile of hidden rubble, but I was not stopping. I dug the oar into the side of the building and shoved. The boat tilted, scraped...and broke through. The city walls reverberated with a sickening chorus of howls. The pack was descending on us.

We shot out of the drowned side street and into the Grand Canal. I immediately regretted it. The water was more primal here, closer to the wild sea and the tide was coming in. I gave the oar a couple of hard pulls. The little canoe glided forward with amazing speed despite the conditions. Grocery Girl must have put some money into this thing.

Huge, ornate palaces slid past us in the dark, loomed over us with the shadows of toppled gothic architecture. We had the advantage here and I tried to keep it, focusing on the pacing of my strokes. Chasing us via the ruins would hamper the ferals—a little.

As I paddled, I tried to think. Staying out here on the water was like pointing a spotlight on myself. The ferals would find me. Then all they would have to do was wait me out. I had to get back to the city. The Doge's Palace stood at the mouth of the Grand Canal. I could dump the girl on the doorstep, tell Jürgen she was there, and go lose myself in the ruins. Vittorio's path would at least give me a good start. I could branch off from there.

I heard rock fall in the stormy quiet. A head and torso appeared at the top of one of the palaces. The howls started anew. I rounded a long bend. Immediately, I had to swing wide to avoid a mountain of rubble in the middle of the canal. I slowed our pace; each stroke became a careful exploration of the water.

The moon slipped free of its shadows. I saw a feral defying gravity as he skittered down a wall that had adjoined the fallen palace. He dropped to a rubble sandbar about three meters from us. I tried to keep one eye on him and one eye on the jutting stones around me. I glanced away to maneuver around a chunk of marble column. I looked up. He crouched on the other side of the marble. I jabbed my oar into the stone. The chop of the water sent us vertical instead of horizontal.

Oh, damn.

The man reached for us. His fingernails scraped the side of the canoe. The canoe scraped stone. *Oh, please don't let us run aground. Please. Please.* The sea swelled. I plunged the oar into the water and gave a short, hard stroke. We slid free and started moving. The water was so shallow, though. I gave another quick pull, then pulled my oar up and turned, ready to fight.

But the feral just stood there, water only up to his calves. He looked from the water, to me, back to the water again. Slowly, he backed away, watching the water like it was a weaving serpent.

He reached the crunch of dry brick, tilted his head back and sent up the cry. I snapped around and paddled like a woman possessed.

We tapped a couple more rocks, but then the water cleared. The little boat sliced forward under my rapid urgings. I saw another feral silhouetted at the peak of a palace ahead. I leaned frantically into my rowing, then stopped myself. No. No. No. I'd heard of packs of predators that would run their prey into the ground. The poor animal would lose its life because of simple exhaustion. That was not happening to me.

It was hard, nearly impossible to tune out that fierce howling shriek, but I sent it as far from me as I could. I breathed my muscles loose, relaxed my grip on the paddle, tuned into the rise and the plunge of the water. I dipped my paddle in and returned to a fluid, easy motion.

Not one bit of my careful distancing calmed the slamming beat of my heart.

The curve of the canal continued. Light appeared up ahead: the arcades of the Doge's Palace. The soft glow was such a relief. I hadn't realized how much the disorientation of the dark had me on edge until it was interrupted.

But that relief was tainted. The ferals had to know by now where I was headed.

Just haul her up the stairs and run like hell.

I played the scenario repeatedly in my head as we neared the crystal staircase. Climb out, grab the girl and the pack, hustle up the stairs, dump her at the door, run down the arcade, vault over the edge to the top of the aquarium wall, drop down to the bridge of rubble, disappear into the ruins. I didn't want to think about anything once we reached the dock. I wanted to be pure motion.

Rain freckled my face—at first gently, sporadically. But the droplets quickly grew in size. This was going to be a serious storm. *Shit.*

We reached the staircase. Pure motion.

I wriggled free of the girl and rolled out onto the dock, keeping one hand clamped on the boat. Using brute force, I jerked the tiny craft up onto the slippery landing. I pulled on my pack, then pulled the girl from the boat. I got my arms under her and heaved. And went down on my ass.

"Don't goddamn have time for you to be a fucking klutz right now, Bryant!"

With that one botched move, I swore I could feel the shadows coming alive. Scrambling, I dragged the girl to the stairs. I propped her up. This time when I lifted her, my balance held. My thighs and calves burned as I pushed us up the flight of stairs toward the beckoning light. There were only three steps left to go. My legs begged to give out. I ground my teeth. I was not letting those things beat me to death. I was going to make it up these goddamn stairs!

I reached the top and stumbled across the landing to the great wooden doors with their ornate black hinges and door handles.

"Ah, my little fleet-footed deer, were Hadria's hunters not fast enough to catch you?"

My gut clenched. That bright, tinkling voice. I gave my head a half turn. She pulled free from the shadows to stand in the pale light of the arcades, her long, silvery hair flowing on the wind, her glittering dress snapping in the dancing air.

Cirena stepped toward me.

"I knew Matteo wasn't strong enough to hold you. And after so long a chase, Hadria will be so very angry." She giggled. My stomach lurched.

I felt a hard pull in my chest as she glided toward me with her head tilted to the side. She was trying to catch my gaze with hers. Somehow I knew I couldn't let that happen. I turned my face to the door. The cold, hard air around me softened and stirred. My ponytail tugged as she coiled a lock of it around her finger. With that one finger, she drew my head back until I was off balance.

"But anger is a kind of delight for Hadria and we wouldn't want her to be without her joy, now would we?"

Cirena's lips brushed the edge of my ear.

My arms trembled under the weight of the girl in my arms.

And I heard the scrape and clatter of motion in the featureless night beyond.

"Let go of my hair."

"You came to me, Alyse. You came to me and I think I will keep you."

She gave my hair a hard tug and I stumbled back toward her. I jerked my head forward and spun around.

"I don't have time for..."

It was the look on her face that stopped me: shock, relief. She stared at the girl in my arms as if seeing a long lost love.

"Anna," she whispered. "You found my Anna."

My hair was released and she reached a slender, pale hand to stroke Anna's face tenderly. She drew the rain-dampened hair back from the girl's forehead. Cirena raised her eyes to me, but the threat was gone, the giddiness replaced with concern.

"She sleeps?"

"She's unconscious. She'll wake up in a couple hours."

Cirena raised her hand to my face. I fell a pace back to dodge it—a pointless maneuver. Her fingers brushed my cheek like the breeze. She looked thoughtful.

"You did this to my Anna."

"She attacked me."

The sound of the sea grew muffled. The air grew heavy on my shoulders, in my lungs. Anna slipped in my weakening grasp. Cirena held out a crooked arm to receive her from me, as if taking an infant to cradle rather than a full-grown woman. Anna settled easily against her, a daughter finding safety in the arms of her mother.

I felt a slice of guilt again at the sight of that gentle face. What the hell was I supposed to have done? Let her beat me to death?

The pressure on my body released. The rush of the sea against the aquarium wall, the shush of the rain returned.

"You could have left her to die, but you brought her to me. You saved my Anna." I hadn't noticed Cirena's hair fall slack, but now it lifted again into the wind of the storm. Though the sparkle returned to her eye, her bearing grew tall and regal. "For bringing my Anna back to me, I will grant you a boon, one wish, anything you ask that is within my power to grant, you shall have."

The currency of indebtedness. If I'd just been given power, why did I feel as though she had just trapped me somehow? She stepped toward me and the wind roared into the arcade. She grinned as the driving gusts sent the tendrils of her hair snapping around her face. Her dress billowed and she loomed over me with her too-large child cradled in her arms.

"Anything at all. If...you survive the night. They come now, Alyse."

She leaned toward me until the breath I breathed was hers.

"Run."

Chapter 18

I ran.

My body didn't want to at first. I'd been still too long. My movements were stiff and sluggish. But my heart rammed hard enough against my sternum to force blood and motion into my icy extremities.

They come now, Alyse.

I made it to the end of the arcade and swung myself over the railing. The top of the aquarium wall was lower than I thought and I took the shock in my shins and my knees. I didn't like the way my legs shook as I skirted the corner of the palace, close enough to the surging waters below to taste the salty spray.

The next thing I discovered I liked even less: My night vision was gone.

The further I crept from the light, the thicker the night became. Why had I not thought of this before?! I'd walked right into that lighted arcade without even considering what it would cost me. I didn't have thirty minutes for my eyes to recover. I put my pack to the wall, leaned my head back and swore. This time my curse was drowned by the wrath of Mother Nature.

If...you survive the night.

I squeezed my eyes closed and counted methodically to twenty. I opened my eyes. A few edges began to take shape in the dark. A few windows on the palace glowed dimly. I knew I was quite a ways from the rubble bridge. I followed the wall with both hands and scooted forward, hoping my sight would improve enough that I wouldn't scoot right past my goal.

One of the lit windows drew near. The lower sill was head height. I ducked down, but not before I saw Suzi curled in a chair by the window with a book and a cup of tea. She looked vaguely amused by what she was reading. She looked warm. She'd tried to kill me.

I rubbed at my stiff nose, then returned my stiff hand to the wall and hurried under the window. She didn't burst through it and grab me by the hair.

Only one other window was lit. I found myself hoping it was Matteo's. I couldn't understand that. He was the one who had gotten me into this insane mess, but still, I wanted someone to be up worrying for me. Wanted someone to care that I was out here alone in the dark and the rain, running from murderous madmen and from wild women whose whispered threats were even more terrifying. My hand rose to my throat. My fingers brushed the fine filament of gold chain, pressed against the cool edges of the tear-shaped topaz pendant. If I could just see his face again, maybe some of this, any of this would make sense. Against all the dictates of rational thought, I stretched up and peeked in that second window.

It was his room.

It was empty.

I felt like someone had stamped on my chest with their boot. I crouched down and lowered myself over the side of the slick aquarium wall, but my hands wouldn't really hold. I fell. I landed on my hands and knees in the water. Was it really so much to ask that someone cared that I was out here, struggling so hard to save my life? Or was it really true what they said: We all die alone?

Stop that.

I shoved myself to my feet. I'd found the bridge. I would cross the bridge. Then I would climb the ruins. Then I would do whatever came next until I could find a cubby hole to curl up and hide in.

The rain pelted my skull, my shoulders, and thighs. The incoming tide swept at my legs with every step I took. After six steps, I was no longer confident I was pointed in the right direction and was damn sure I wasn't on the part of the bridge meant for walking.

Mo, I need an overlay. I can't do this.

After a tense moment, Mo filled in the details of the fallen building in front of me. I was three steps to the left of my goal. I hurried forward.

I cleared the ruins of the first building before I heard the first carrier. It was on the floor above me, creeping forward with hard-soled shoes. I looked frantically around me. I couldn't remember this portion of the path.

Mo, which way did we go?

Down the hall straight ahead. Along the top of the exposed wall to the left.

I ran in my silent trainers, pushing to get ahead of the tapping on the floor above me. The exposed wall appeared so abruptly I almost went over the edge. I caught myself on a dangling doorsill. The tapping grew closer. I stepped out onto the wall. Even with Mo's overlay and my slowly strengthening night vision, I didn't trust it. My legs trembled too hard, numb with the wet and the cold.

I was going to turn into that stupid mountain goat the wolves ran down after all.

Except for the stupid part. If my body was done, then it was time to hide.

Now.

I teetered forward. Each time I passed the shadow image of a perpendicular wall, I reached out with my foot to test the air for a floor. At the fourth wall I found a solid beam. I transferred my weight onto it. It creaked. The tapping stopped. I froze. As I clung to a decayed stone wall with my fingertips, balanced on a beam on the balls of my aching feet, the rain turned from drops to sheets. I could barely breathe through the force of it. Blindly, I slid forward. The beam creaked again, but I didn't think the feral would hear it over the thunder of the rain.

I reached the first slats of a floor and carefully felt my way out onto it. After a few shifts to the left, the floor above me fended off the violent onslaught of water. My body sagged with relief. Once I felt confident enough to release the wall, I stepped away and wrung out my hair, slicked my hands down my face. At this rate I would leave a clear trail to any cubby hole I managed to find.

Mo's overlays couldn't help me in this unexplored territory. I stared fixedly ahead, willing the hallway to take shape as I moved forward. I cracked my shin on something hard and sharp. I bent over with a silent scream, the wet and the cold making the pain twice as amazing. Gasping, I reached out to identify the obstacle. A stone staircase.

I smoothed my hands over it. The side wall was ripped away at the bottom. I felt, almost thought I could see, a wooden frame—the remains of a small closet or cupboard. I pulled off the backpack. Reaching with my leg, I felt around the space. I hit something soft. It shrieked. I jumped. Tiny claws clattered along the floor. One of Cuddly's cousins.

Swallowing my heart back down from my throat, I folded myself up and squeezed into the cupboard. I patted around in the darkness until I found my pack. I pulled it in after me. It hit the cupboard frame. The frame fell, hit the floor. The crack of contact hit my eardrums like a shotgun retort.

The night paused, listened.

Oh, damn, damn, damn!

I jerked the bag up against me, hid my face in my knees.

The first call went up tentatively.

The second cry went up a few moments later.

The third belted out, piercing the roar of the rain, pinning me where I sat huddled.

In the distance, the tapping shoes began running. I turned my head. Two figures dropped to the exposed wall at the head of my hallway. They trotted past. Something heavy hit the floor above my stairs. A cacophony of feral cries answered the call, ricocheting off my stone hideaway, bouncing off the walls, stealing my breath.

    I was dead.

Chapter 19

I didn't want to be dead.

The tap shoes started their way down my stairs.

I didn't want to be dead. A vision of Jürgen flickered into my head. I didn't have to be dead. I could be a prisoner of that threatening perfection, of this savage horror for the rest of my life. I could be a captive of this terror that rippled through my limbs right now, the blinding fear, the nauseating expectation of violence.

I didn't want to be dead.

You have a call, Mo told me.

Jürgen. I closed my eyes, buried my head in my arms. I heard footfalls on my hallway floor.

I'll take it.

An avatar image appeared in my mind's eye.

It was Ryan.

I lifted my head. A foolish wave of euphoria flooded my body.

Alyse?

Yeah?

About the other night...I'm sorry. I... That was stupid and mean and I'm sorry.

Even as I smiled, the tears started. *Thanks, Ryan. Thank you more than you know. I'm sorry I can't talk right now.* I saw a pair of legs outlined against the square of grey moonlight from the end of the hall. I stopped breathing. *They are hunting me. And I think they just found me.*

Don't hang up! Ben and I are here. I've got us a way through the security perimeter. We're at the security station in the ruins of Le Zitelle. I'm sending Mo the coordinates. We've got a testing kit. You get here, we'll run clean tests, and we'll get you out of here. Get here, Alyse. I know you can do it.

I just stared, mesmerized by those legs.

Ryan, I've gotta go.

The knees of those legs bent.

Mo cut the connection.

All I could think was: At least I didn't die alone.

Chapter 20

The man picked up the frame from the front of the cupboard. He snapped it against the floor as if in confirmation.

Then he reached into my cupboard.

He touched my pack first. He pulled it out. The blanket fell from the straps in a crinkle of plastic. I squeezed against the back of the cupboard. It went deep. He couldn't see me. Maybe...maybe...maybe. His fingertip brushed the sleeve of my shirt. I held my breath in the blinding darkness.

Fingers dug into my arm and yanked.

My body uncoiled out of the small space and sailed across the floor—right over an exposed nail in the cupboard frame. I went sliding back down the hall, jerked from the man's grasp by the force of his own pull. I spun to my feet and ran.

I swallowed my scream as the nail line down my back and my left leg turned to flame.

I made it to the edge of the broken floor when his deep growl stopped me. I turned. He stood right behind me. My vision had returned. He was a short, balding Asian, his white business shirt plastered to him by the rain. Two other voices picked up the snarl behind me. I glanced over my shoulder across the expanse of missing floor to the path wall, saw a tall, skinny woman and a big, burly man. Even as I looked, a fourth torso lowered upside down from the floor above. Shoes beat a rhythm on the stairs. Multiple sets of shoes.

A sound—half laugh/half sob—escaped me. I squeezed my eyes shut to clear out the tears. When I reached up to wipe them away, he made a grab for me. I swung my body back and to the left. He ended up with a handful of shirt over my right breast. Two men and a woman walked up behind him.

Oh, God!

I grabbed at his hand, clawing. I heard a seam rip. He buried another hand in the fabric, picked me up, and slammed me to the floor. I saw him pull back a fist. I screamed. I rolled. Right off the edge of floor.

He kept his grip on my shirt, grinding my collarbone into a jagged beam. The rain was coming down fast enough to choke me. The torn side seam ripped another few centimeters. The beam bit off those same centimeters worth of skin. I grabbed for the flooring, but everything here was wet, slick, and crumbling. The feral gathered together fistfuls of my shirt. I felt pressure against my throat. He was trying to strangle me with my own shirt!

The other ferals crept forward.

My legs dangled over nothing.

I wrapped both hands around the beam and shoved. The seam ripped all the way down to the hem. I dropped another six centimeters as his grip on the fabric slipped. I saw him glance at my ponytail.

No!

I bucked wildly.

He had two choices: come with me or let go.

He let go.

෴

I didn't really feel the water when I hit it. In the pitch black it was more as though the air had thickened and wrapped around my body, sliding so quickly up my ankles, calves, thighs, squeezing over my belly and chest, closing over my neck, my face, my head. My feet hit something. I pushed upward.

I broke the surface. I couldn't breathe. Something was glued to my face. I clawed at the slime, but my hands were covered with more of the same. I got hold of something large and slick and ripped it away. I gasped desperately.

Above me, six heads peered down at me. Growls turned to snarls, then the rumble swelled to a roar and as one they lifted their heads and let out that last piercing shriek.

Which way is the canal, Mo?

To your left.

I turned. I could just touch bottom with my toes. I pushed my upper body forward with my arms. The seawater stabbed tiny needles into all my cuts and scrapes. I saw no exits ahead, but there had to be one. The water swayed from more than just my movements.

I heard running over head.

I pushed faster.

I found my first wall. I found my first doorway.

Still I saw no exit ahead.

I swept my arms forward. I reached for the floor. I went under. I protected my face this time when I kicked to the surface.

I had to stop a minute and catch my breath. I looked up. The ferals above me seemed to run in every direction. As I bobbed on the water, watching their imagined rabid frenzy, I bounced into a wall. I turned myself to face it and hooked my fingers into it. Hand over hand, I ran myself down the length of stonework.

Another doorway.

Now I saw an exit. A huge exit. Most of the exterior wall of the building had fallen into the canal. Debris littered the water before me. I climbed up onto a section and into the wash of the slowing deluge of rain.

My Asian was the first feral to reach the exterior of the building. His head turned this way and that as he calculated how to get down to me. I turned and started scrambling my way over the chunks of stone, brick, and marble. The rattle and pound of movement behind me increased. I heard a scream.

Someone slammed into the water.

I cleared the fallen wall.

A huge section of brick crashed into the rubble just six centimeters from my feet. I looked up. The burly white guy tore off another chunk of the building and reared back to hurl it at me.

I ran toward the water, saw the length of the canal stretch out toward the rubble bridge. My teeth chattered as I clambered down the debris. The water felt warm this time as it slipped itself around me. I pushed off and began to swim.

I didn't want to die.

Ryan.

Ryan and Ben were at *Le Zitelle*. They were waiting for me.

Mo, where is Le Zitelle?

On the island of Giudecca. Across the water, approximately 700 meters south of the Doge's Palace. She flashed me a map. I connected the dots.

I needed that canoe back.

⁂

I watched the walls as I swam. Like the guy at the sandbar, no one dived in after me. They didn't need to. About ten meters ahead, Vittorio's rubble bridge was going to take me right up into their waiting arms.

My hand brushed the slope of the bridge. I stood up. I felt every shadow around me rush forward. The rope. I dove for the cranny where Vittorio had stowed the rope from our escape. I yanked it from its hiding place and unreeled the end with the suicide clip as I backed toward the sea.

The tall skinny lady was first in line. I snapped the rope out at her. She leapt back, landed in a crouch. The bald Asian and a fashion geek in a shimmering shirt and drenched silk slacks stepped forward.

The water was at my knees, rocking me with every surge. I drew the suicide clip back. I whipped it at the geek. The Asian sprang. I hurled the heavy coil of rope at his face, turned, and dove.

I struggled to stay underwater and out of sight. I hadn't prepared my lungs for it. The oxygen-deprived burn finally forced me to burst through the surface. I cleared my eyes. I was halfway to the corner of the Doge's Palace. A spray of rock chips tagged me on the back of the head. The burly white guy. I pulled in a series of breaths, then slipped back under.

Smaller chunks of rock pelted me gently as I pushed forward. Like with the rowing, I tried to keep my pace even and fluid, tried not to feel with the half naked muscles of my back the thump of broken missiles. They were staying out of the water and I was out of their reach right now—as long as the big guy didn't get lucky. I needed to conserve my energy.

The hail of rock stopped. I gave a few more good pulls and came up for air. I had cleared the canal. I was a few meters out in front of the palace. The soft light of the arcade illuminated the crystal staircase.

It wasn't there.

The boat wasn't there.

I laid out into a series of powerful, clean strokes that brought me to the platform. I heaved myself out of the water and onto the dock.

Empty.

I looked out around the water. Nothing. I headed up the stairs. I got halfway up.

I stopped.

They were there. All of them. The business man, the big woman, the balding Asian, the fashion geek, the burly white guy, the tall skinny lady.... All of them. Standing at the top of the stairs in the light of the arcade, drenched, radiating fury, pacing and weaving, all of their black, soulless eyes trained on me.

On the easing wind, I thought I heard a high, tinkling laugh.

Slowly, I backed back down the stairs.

As if we were bound by a tether, they came down the stairs, matching each step of mine, pace for pace. I stumbled, went down on one knee. I saw something dangling from the pocket of my cargo pants, a slimy piece of ribbon.

My sachet.

The sachet of leaves and lichen that my widowed mother had made me before I left on this hellish trip. I laid my hand over that pocket.

Mom. I'm not leaving you alone in the darkness. Not ever again.

I looked up at the lead feral as he snarled down at me.

700 meters. That was nothing. I'd done crazier shit just to put together ten seconds of sensory footage for a dumbass movie. I could do this. For Mom.

I sneered back at the lead feral. I turned; I ran; I dove.

Chapter 21

No one followed me in.

The first few meters I swam with everything I had, terrified the sea would toss me back to the mercy of the hunters. I could hear them howling their rage, even above the roar of the water.

700 meters. I could make it.

But to where? Beyond the circle of light I saw nothing but blackness.

Mo, tell them I'm coming. Tell them I need a light to guide by. Something. Anything.

I glanced back to see the platform had receded to a safe distance. I evened out, lengthened my strokes, pretending that the nail gouge tightening my back and leg simply didn't exist. I set myself an easy rhythm. The sea rocked me up and over each incoming wave. I tried to pace each breath after the passing of the crest. Up, over, breathe. Up, over, breathe.

Too soon I'd swum beyond the outer limits of the light. The standoff at the palace had obliterated my night vision again, leaving the water something I felt rather than saw. The rain fell gently against my face. It felt cold and clean. The sea felt like frigid sludge.

The constant push and pull of the water up and down and up and down lulled me. I wanted to take a break, stop and float for a moment, just rest for a spell. No. Just hold on, just a little while longer. Keep moving. This is almost over.

I forced my slowing limbs back into motion

Then I saw it: the light. Just for a flicker. Then it was gone. Then it came back for a glimpse. And vanished again. What the hell?

The waves.

I corrected my course slightly and waited. I spotted it again. It was so far away. No, no thinking like that. Keep kicking. Keep paddling. Keep moving.

What the fuck was I doing out swimming at night in the rain in the Adriatic, the most toxic of all the seas in the world? At least that toxicity meant the sea life was wiped out. Except for a large white squid and my lagoon monster.

Even the feral carriers wouldn't come in the water.

Goddamn it! Don't think about that kind of shit!

But I had and I couldn't stop my heart from revving or my adrenaline from begging for a little extra speed. Soon every brush of my pant leg sent a tremor through my chest, every ripple of my torn shirt against my torso had me jerking in surprise.

No, I'm a fucking immersion artist! I don't jump at every little shadow. I jump into the damn shadow just to see what it feels like.

The edge of my shirt teased my ribs as I pulled through another stroke. Ignoring it was torture. Torture. The same kind of torture I'd put my mom, my dad through every time I'd gone out on an enactment. Every time bigger, badder, a better rush.

Torture.

I'm going to come home, Mom. I'll take you shopping, take you to the bonfire. I'll show you some of the legends I put together. You can tell me your stories. It's just you and me now, but we're going to be fine. Emory's right. I don't have to work so hard. I don't have to run so fast. I'm going to be there for you. We're going to be fine.

My shoulders burned. My thighs seized with every kick.

Focus on something, something else. I watched for the light. It bobbed up, then down, then gone. It wasn't bigger. 700 meters. Not even a full kilometer. Had to be halfway by now. God, my eyes. Where was the light? Gone.

Lift, plunge, kick. Lift, plunge, kick. Lift...

I remembered a story. An awful story. A girl fell in love with an island hermit. Would swim through the dark to be with him. Used a torch on his hut to guide by. Dumbass brothers heard about it. Had to preserve the family honor. Little brother distracted the hermit. Older brothers strapped a torch to their boat. Set out for the open sea. Girl swam and swam. Couldn't under...couldn't understand why she hadn't reached her lover yet. Boys put...put out the torch.

Left their baby sister to drown.

Couldn't lift my arm.

700 meters. 15-degree water. Incoming tide. Body past the point of exhaustion.

Fucking second wind. Always makes you think you're superman.

Mom....

The water closed over my head.

※

Panic surged through me. I flailed. My face broke through the surface. I gasped.

So close. I'd fought so hard.

Couldn't die out here.

Couldn't leave my mom alone.

I slipped back under.

※

Something hard rammed my thigh. My head and shoulders cleared the water. I slammed back down.

Oh, God. Oh, no.

I couldn't feel. Anything. My leg.

I twisted. A giant dorsal fin severed the wave. The sea pulled at me...down, down. The shark charged.

※

In the silence of the water, time slowed to a languid, liquid pace. I could see him as he curved his beautiful, sleek body to shoot toward me. I could see him. He was huge and powerful, a silvery white god, streaked with black. His eyes held me as I floated loosely in the empty ocean. He watched me, eyes flat, black, judging me without piety or disdain.

His snout reared. His mouth opened.

All those terrible, horrible teeth. I wanted to scream. The water held me mute, still.

He seized me around the waist. Was that a quick way to die? I felt no pain.

I must have screamed after all.

My lungs were filled with water.

༄

Daddy?

Strong arms cradled me close to a cold, pale chest. I snuggled closer.

I'm sorry I came so soon, Daddy. I should have stayed with Mommy. I promised I'd stay with her. She needs me right now. I'm sorry I wasn't there when you needed me. I didn't know Fiji didn't have a decent hospital. I would have gotten you a medic unit. What's all this stupid money for if it couldn't save my daddy's life? You died because I wasn't paying attention. I haven't paid attention to anything in years. I didn't even come to your retirement party. I know you missed me. Mom told me you missed me. I miss you, Daddy. I miss you so much.

The arms shifted me. I raised my head. Flat black eyes looked down at me from a chiseled white face. Long black hair floated in silken clouds around him, caressing my skin.

Not my daddy.

Who are you? I know you.

※

I embraced a hard, smooth body. His fin wedged into the pit of my arm. I pressed my cheek to his back to hide from the force of the sea as his great tail rocketed us forward.

I know you.

A flash, a memory: the curiosity of a young blue shark juxtaposed against the relentless purpose of the ancient fish that had scarred my arm. This fish.

Ike.

I killed Ike. He was yours. I'm sorry.

The sea slowed for a moment. Sorrow.

I held him tight, my hair undone from its ponytail, my legs flowing out behind me. We hurried on.

The image of a slender, young ribbon of blue, such a young, tender animal.

He was beautiful, so fragile. You're not fragile. But I'll take care of you.

I'll keep you safe.

I want to be safe.

I'm so tired....

※

Cold.

Cold clenched my skin. Water sheeted off me. He carried me up from the depths, up the sea-blackened staircase. He laid me out gently on a bleached plank of shattered marble. The edges should have pressed my flesh. I didn't feel them. My chest didn't rise and fall. I drew no breath.

He wrapped his hands around the neckline of my T-shirt. He pulled. It tore away. My other clothes came away easily, as if they were nothing more than ancient rags from the corpse of a long dead sailor. I felt the moonlight. It brushed my skin tenderly.

He ran his hands over my face, through my hair. His cool hands framed my neck, remolded my arms. Life flowed back into my flesh as he lifted my breasts, pressed down my belly, my hips. Long firm strokes lengthened my legs, my feet. Still, I did not breathe.

He leaned over me, those huge black eyes watching me as he slipped one hand beneath my back. With the other, he lifted my head. My warm, full breasts pressed into his chill nakedness. Hard lips brushed mine and still he watched me. I opened for him. His arms around me became crushing. His tongue sought mine, found it. He tasted salty, yet sweet, his breath pushing into me, pushing, pushing, pushing...

My body whipped back as the life slammed back into me. My heart clenched. My lungs spasmed. My stomach spasmed. He flipped me, held me across the hips and the shoulders as I returned what I had taken from the sea. My lungs made a sound like a scream as they tried to draw air—and failed. He rolled me back to him, cradled me in his lap. His embrace pinned my head to his chest. He inserted his finger into my open mouth. Methodically, he wiped over every surface as I kicked at nothing, clutched at the impossible muscle of his arm.

Then, still pinning me, he shifted me up and sealed his lips over my own. As I writhed and struggled, he drew me in, drew in my tongue, drew in my breath. All at once something popped, released inside of me. I fell slack against him, drew in the salty scent of him. Air.

God, I was alive!

His lips still pressed against mine, my tongue still held his. I slid my hand up his chest, around his neck, to tangle in his satin hair. I slid my tongue over his smooth, slick teeth. My nipples rubbed against his chest, sending an electric tingle down both my arms. My womb ached. I wanted him. I wanted him more than I had ever wanted anyone in my entire life. His hand smoothed down my back, then up my ribs to clutch my breast.

I whimpered and my thighs fell loose. I pressed into him, desperate for more. He rolled my nipple between us; my eyes went blind. I felt the cold night air between my legs. His hard hand glided down my breast and over my belly to settle just below my navel. He pressed the heel of his hand into the soft flesh and began to knead.

My body responded instantly. I tried to curl inward, tried to scream. He refused to relinquish my mouth. He never entered me, but it felt like he caressed my womb itself. I shook. I trembled. I opened my legs wide. I tried to raise my hips, but he kept me shoved tight against his knee.

Then he released me. I fell splayed, helpless across his lap, the top of my head resting on broken rock.

He leaned over.

He pulled the tip of one nipple into his mouth. He pressed one finger just inside my opening.

I exploded.

My whole body folded in on itself, then unfurled into the air.

With tender strokes, he gentled me, held me as I came to settle in his arms. Air, beautiful air moved in and out of my lungs in quiet, precious gasps. My breathing slowed, my mind and body softened, drifted on a glittering expanse of darkness. Life and love and the immense power pouring free from the crux between creation and destruction. It cradled me, body and soul.

Beautiful, so perfect.

Finally.

I tilted my head just enough to see his face. Those flat eyes looked down at me, watched me. He brushed his fingers over my face, drawing my eyelids closed, shushing the words from my lips.

My eyes drifted open.

His skin gleamed silver in the moonlight, the sea breeze tossed his waist-length black hair. The sea embraced him as he walked down, down, down. Then his muscles flexed and he sprang, dove, disappeared into the glittering black water.

Chapter 22

My body rocked. I was floating on black water. I was sinking. Huge leaves of seaweed covered my face, my mouth. I couldn't breathe. I was going to die!

"Alyse, baby, come on. Come on."

I burst awake.

Not drowning.

"Ben?"

His perfectly sculpted mustache and goatee had gone scruffy. His eyes were red. I sat up. My fur blanket fell from my shoulders.

"Oh, God, Ben!" I reached out to touch his face. It hurt. It hurt so bad, but it was wonderful. "Oh, God. I thought I was going to die. I thought I wasn't going to make it. They were chasing me. I was swimming. I..."

He pulled the blanket back up around me and held me, rocked me. "It's okay, baby. I gotcha." He raised his voice. "It's her! I told ya it was her, ya dumb fuck. Get your ass down here!"

Through my sobs, I heard a slide, then a crash. Over Ben's shoulder I saw Ryan land on a stack of mossy brick that had been piled in front of the sheer white façade of the church. He skidded his way down it, landed on a platform, then dropped onto the rubble "shore." I watched Ryan as he ran. He stumbled to a halt at my feet.

There was a torch in his hand.

My brothers. They didn't leave me to drown.

Ryan hesitated. I pulled my arm free from the blanket. I held my hand out to him. My skin glowed silver and gold in the fire light. He lowered his eyes. When he lifted them again, he reached out and took my hand. My nerves screamed, but I squeezed his fingers in mine. It wasn't an eloquent apology for his lack of faith—or for mine. But between the two of us, it was enough. We released each other.

Ben helped me to my feet and pulled the blanket tight around me, leaving one arm free for balance. I smoothed my arm down the silken fur. I looked down. My fur blanket. I looked back over the water. My fur blanket. How?

"What the hell did you do to these clothes?"

I turned to see Ben holding up my shirt. The side seam was ripped out, the neckline torn to meet it, so that when he picked it up, it unfurled. The front and back showed semicircles, rows and rows of slashes. I stared at it.

"I drowned."

"You swam?! Are you goddamn crazy?! Your goddamn eyeballs will start melting out of your goddamn head any second now! Jesus fuckin' Christ!"

Ben threw the shirt down on the rocks. I still stared at it. I opened my blanket. I looked down at my belly, smoothed my hand over the unmarred skin. I pulled the blanket back around me. I brushed back my loose hair, clean, dry, so very soft. Low, low in my belly I felt a faint throb.

And beneath the blanket, my left arm, my bitten arm began to ache gently.

I looked up at Ryan as Ben ranted and cursed and kicked things.

"I drowned," I repeated.

Ryan reached out, put his hand on the back of my blanket-clad shoulder, gave me a little tug. "Come on, Alyse." He raised his voice to Ben. "Let's run these tests. Think we'd better get her to a hospital."

On bare feet, I slowly followed them across the "beach" and up to an old slab of foundation where they'd made camp. My big enactment pack was there. Ben and Ryan gave me a moment of privacy to pull on a loose sweater and jeans. I found a pair of soft, thick socks and my heavy boots and pulled them on, too.

Finally, I walked over to where Ryan and Ben stood silently waiting. I wanted to hug them, hold them, but somehow I knew I didn't have the right until this was done. Together they turned. Ryan gestured for me to take a seat on a little stub of wall next to him. I felt my face go pale. Ben gave me a bolstering smile, fidgeted for a moment, then walked away toward the pile of our gear.

I sat down

Ryan produced the little black box which would verify my DNA matched what was on record. It didn't take much, just a scanner and a finger pricker.

He laid a second device next to my bench. Sleeper's Syndrome had not yet been tied to a specific virus or bacteria. The clear plastic dish contained skin cells taken from a child. The press of a button would inject an aging accelerant into the dish. A small indicator light on the side would say whether or not the cells "slept." That simple.

I held out my hand. Ryan pressed the corner of the little black box to the outside edge of my finger tip. It bit me. I bled. It drew that blood into itself. The first green light blinked on. I staunched the flow against my jeans. Ryan stepped around beside me. I leaned over, swept my hair to the side, couldn't help but think I was preparing my neck for the executioner's sword.

I watched Ben unpack an inflatable as Ryan lifted the neckline of my sweater. I felt the cold plastic run down my spine from the base of my neck to the bottom of my shoulder blades as it read my DNA dog tag. Ryan withdrew the scanner. I sat up. A fine sweat covered my forehead.

Ryan crouched next to me as we waited. I forced myself to breathe as we watched the row of little lights. The middle one snapped on. Two greens.

"That means the markers match. Now it's going to run the random checks."

The third light stayed stubbornly black. I looked up at Ryan. "Is it brok—?"

"Shit!"

I looked down.

Three flashing red lights.

Ryan turned around and bashed the box against the wall behind him. He dropped the pieces on the ground, grabbed the torch, and stabbed the internal transmitter with it until it melted.

I stood up. I opened my mouth. I couldn't speak. I looked from Ryan to Ben to the warped plastic on the ground. The inflatable fell from Ben's limp fingertips.

My DNA markers were false.

No. It absolutely could not be possible.

I grabbed the Sleeper's Syndrome kit from the ground. I snapped off the lid and fogged the gel. I slammed the lid back on. The fucking thing wouldn't close. It slid in a circle around to the left, to the right. Ryan reached for it. I shoved it at him and walked away.

My steps took me down to the rubble beach, across to the stairs connecting the church to the sea. Where my shark god had descended. My hands shook as I clutched my arms. Over the water I could see the lights of the Doge's Palace. I could feel the pulse of the place, the anger, the desperation, the dark, monstrous beauty. There? That would be where I would live out the rest of my days? How could—?

"Alyse."

Ryan. I pressed a hand to my trembling lips. I kept my back to him.

"Alyse, it's positive."

"They weren't lying," I whispered.

"No. No, they weren't."

I turned to him, saw Ben standing back at the camp, tears glistening in the light of the torch he held. My body remembered that deep, resonating growl, growing, penetrating, bellowing out into a bone-rattling roar, then tightening into an aerial cry of a thwarted bird of prey.

"They've murdered me, Ryan. They've murdered me."

Epilogue

Dawn had begun to steal the shadows from the ruins of Venice. The toppled buildings still resisted the beat of the water against their shattered foundations. The effect was melancholy, romantic.

There was nothing romantic about imprisonment.

My life had been stolen from me.

Le Zitelle, Mo had told me, meant "the maidens." This had been the convent where the city had sent girls of "dangerous beauty" who might turn to prostitution as a means of survival—or escape. I thought of the nun Maria da Reia and her wild night with the French ambassador at the Bragadin party. I wondered if she'd survived it. Or if zealots with midnight eyes had hunted her down, killed her for trying to steal her life back.

One difference between Sister Maria and me: I was going to find out who did this to me and they were going to pay. Maybe the Brighton's patients had signed on for an experimental study.

Maybe they could forgive Dr. Franco for unwittingly setting them up for a lifetime of seclusion. I had signed on for no such thing.

Someone had purposely fucked with my DNA. Maybe it had been Jürgen. Maybe Dr. Franco. Maybe this Hadria woman. Or even worse, maybe someone had rewritten me before I'd come to the island. Then that someone had knowingly endangered thousands of children *through me*. Sick. Sick. Sick. Whoever it was, they would find out there were things worse than exile.

I shivered in my frozen rage, terrified of my own anger.

Because yes, there were things worse than exile.

There was a disease that ripped your soul from you and left behind only violent fury in your depthless black eyes and in your mindless animal scream. There was waiting, wondering if that ultimate destruction of the soul was going to happen to you. There was waiting, wondering if the others already lost to it, those feral, relentless hunters were finally going to pull you down…or if you would succumb to a different, more subtle predator who wanted something unnamed, yet much more terrifying than just your life.

I was going to find out who did this to me and they were going to pay.

If the island didn't get me first.

"Alyse."

I pulled the blanket tighter around me.

"Alyse, baby. It's morning already. You gotta sleep." Ben crouched in front of me. "At least try."

I shook my head, my eyes tearing up just at the sight of his face.

"You guys gotta get the hell out of here. It's too dangerous. You...."

Ben sighed, his own face twisting. He reached up and brushed my hair back from my face. I didn't flinch when his fingers trailed down the side of my throat. Then I felt a sharp prick at my neck—a medicine popper.

"Ben!"

"I know you hate messin' with these sleeping drugs, but you gotta sleep, girl."

I didn't get the chance to finish my protest. The smothering exhaustion was immediate. My eyes slid closed as Ben lowered me to the ground.

Slowly, my mind lost its thoughts of vengeance and became a whirl of the impossible: a dark prince in his castle, luring, coaxing; a defeated young knight straining against invisible prison walls; a white-haired guide running through the woods always just disappearing from view; a crafty water sprite, stealing possessions, leaving bits of food in their stead; a fae of light and shadow with her dangerous, fickle wit; the night's relentless hunters slathering in the shadows; a sea king with power over life and death; a pair of steadfast brothers whose love and loyalty tried to save me.

And through it all, Venice, her aging stones and murky depths giving life to the dark-hearted wonder, the tempting horror of that from which she was created—from legend.

Read on for a special preview

...coming Summer 2012!

We all have lies we tell ourselves in order to survive. We breathe life into these lies, set them before our eyes, and see the world through them. We create safety that way, order.

Maybe that's why what I was doing felt so dangerous.

I was trying to see through mine.

I crouched on a half-submerged rooftop and watched as my fingers drifted back and forth through the filmy green water of the former Venetian lagoon. And I tried to feel the truth. I let the electric charge of the coming storm envelope me, rushing cold over the flesh of my exposed face and forearms, flicking sharp fingers up the legs of my cargo pants, up the sleeves, down the neckline of my winter-weave t-shirt until I shuddered in the charge of too much awareness.

But I had to know.

I *would* know. A far off island—marked only by fallen walls and rooftops protruding from the sea—became my focal point as I fought to release what I'd always believed. As I narrowed my world to those distant walls, the clouds above them began to roil, blocking out the early morning sun, casting me in pale darkness. It was in that darkness that I reached down deep, deep into my lie. And beyond it. I reached past the idea of a healthy body so carefully tended for a physically demanding profession. I strained to feel the stark reality of the disease crouched within me, a disease so vile it would send any child I met into a stasis-like coma—forever. Sleeper's Syndrome.

I couldn't feel it.

It wasn't true.

It *was* true.

I'd run the goddamn test myself. I shoved to my feet, my eyes riveted on those clouds as they slammed and billowed out their destruction. Their wind whipped at my clothing, ripped at my long black hair. Even as I closed my eyes against it, my mind spun out into the violence. *The test. That goddamm test. Three flashing red lights and my life is over.* I raked my hair back from my face, fisted my hands there, tossed my head back to face the sky.

And screamed.

A petty indulgence.

It had its price. My foot slipped. I threw my weight forward, but I knew, I knew it was already too late. I couldn't even work up the give-a-shit to flinch. *Fine,* I thought. *If this is how it is going to end, then this is how it is going to end. Just make it go the fuck away.*

My plunge toward the toxic water and jagged masonry jerked to a halt. I registered an ice-cold hand wrapped around my upper arm. Shock sent me scrambling to set my feet under me and I spun around.

"What the hell—"

The snarl dropped from my lips as I looked up into those flat, unblinking eyes on that too-white face. Wet black hair hung down his naked chest; a few strands of it clung to my cheek. My fingers wandered up to brush it away. I stared at it, black satin against my white fingertips.

"You're real," I whispered.

He loosened his grip enough that I could turn to face him fully. His hard alien features did not bend in expression, but I felt sadness seeping from him as he scooped my own hair back from my face. He backed up the roof, drawing me with him.

Short flashes of memory assailed me, half-remembered images of two nights ago, the night I'd died: Desperation as the waves knocked me under. A scream that filled my lungs with the sea. A white and black shark charging with teeth bared. A man, this man cradling me as I died. I raised my hand to his arm.

"Before. You saved my life. You..."

I left the sentence unfinished in case the rest had just been a beautiful dream, fed by an undernourished libido. But then he drew me up to my toes and what I felt matched that dream too perfectly. His cold, hard lips brushed mine, his strong fingers cupped my head, bearing the weight for me. I reached for his tongue with my own, tasted his salty essence as he opened and let me slide into him. So perfect. I leaned into him. His arms wound around me, pulling my shoulders and hips tight against him, protected, safe. For the first time in days I felt the dark coil in me loosen; the tension in my shoulders eased so fast my head floated. All I could do was cling and watch those dark eyes as they stared inside of me, as they drew me up and in until the body I'd just tried so hard to know loosened its hold on my mind.

And was gone.

I was in darkness. But it was not emptiness. I felt him, my shark god, wrapped around me, protecting me from the open wildness around me. Unleashed energy, emotion raged all about us, threatening destruction, creation, explosive life. The sheltering cocoon of him kept me centered in the fierce storm, kept it from ripping me apart. But he couldn't keep me from drinking it into me.

To the point of agony.

I struggled, desperate from the almost-knowing, the almost understanding. He wouldn't release me to it, wouldn't let me grasp that final ecstasy of comprehension. Instead, he drew me into his calm.

And, impossibly, I did calm. My frantic thrashing settled into a quiet awareness as the sensory immersion artist in me remembered how to switch off any emotion not pertinent to the scene, any outside thoughts skewing the sensations that would tie the audience to the character that housed them. Slowly, the cacophony became a storm's symphony—ecstatically beautiful to behold.

I became the observer, but I sensed the ancient clash with something other than the tools of my profession: my skin, my eyes, my ears, my tongue. I sensed it with the same senses I used to understand the peace in a dappled patch of shade in my beloved woods; the same senses I used to feel the lives that had gone before me as I wandered a forgotten cemetery. Those senses that knew there was something *more*.

Something more. Something more, if I could just reach out, just reach a little further into that bright darkness. Then I would know; I would understand and everything that had seemed so utterly senseless would reveal its meaning with blinding clarity—the death of my father; the loss of my life and my freedom to this disease; the violent indifference of this sunken city. All that awful, beautiful mystery taunting me, it could fill me. All I had to do was fling myself open to it, embrace it with fang and claw and an animal scream. It licked at the edges of me. With its touch, I felt powerful and terrifyingly whole.

The kiss broke.

A chill wind slapped at me. The tiny flicks of pain matched the scattered charges of fear sparking in my chest. Unsteadily, I drew back, looked up at him.

"What did you do?"

I shivered. I could feel residuals of that desperate pull in my arms, my legs, everywhere. It wasn't fading fast enough. It was fading too fast. I was missing something. Something important.

"What just happened to me? What was that?"

My shark god, he just rested his hands on my shoulders and looked down at me with his blank face, but warmth seeped into me from his cold body, warmth and a soft feeling...affection.

He wasn't going to answer me.

"No, you can't mess with me like that, take me apart like that, and then—"

He pressed on my shoulders, directing me to turn. I watched him, wary, but finally curiosity won out and I let him turn me back to face the waters.

My strange guardian kept his hands on my shoulders as we both looked out at the boiling, black clouds lit with lines of electric fire. What did he want me to see? I look down the length of the ruins, but there was little left. The encroaching sea was too powerful for a small island to stand against alone.

Mo, help me. What is that place?

San Michele, *the island of the dead.*

Island of the dead: a cemetery. I waited. My AI knew I needed more than just a mere place name.

San Michele once housed the workshops of the great cosmographer, Father Mauro. Working deep within his convent laboratory, this Camaldulian monk created the greatest piece of Late Medieval cartography known to historians, his mappamundi *or map of the world*. The famed detail and proportion of the map he humbly attributed to discussions with Venetian navigators, the masters of the sea.

But there were whispers. How could a man who had not traveled to these exotic locations have drawn them with such precision? How could conversation alone lead to mapmaking of so much mastery? Those whisperers looked to the skies above the island and found their answers there in the tearing lines of the lighting, in the fractured shapes of the storm clouds that hovered over the convent. They intimated that the good father had stolen into Lucifer's dreams and projected those dreams onto the dark clouds above the laboratory. They claimed that as Lucifer dreamed his chaos into the world, Father Mauro copied down the shapes of places still unknown even to the sea-faring Venetians. They warned that such manipulation would end in disaster. You see, Lucifer's maps, hidden in the terror of midnight storms, served their own purpose: they guided witches and other unholy beings to their wicked enclaves where they would plot how best to steal souls for their master.

And indeed tragedy struck. Father Mauro's life's work, the great mappamundi, *was sent to the man who commissioned it, King Alfonso V of Portugal...and was lost to the negligence of* time. *Only a mere copy was destined to survive, a copy displaying but a portion of the master's power. Father Mauro died in 1460 before completing the second work.*

I sighed in frustration. A map dreamed by the devil. That lingering fear of missing something vital sharpened. I stared ahead and saw only clouds.

But as I watched, the darkness cracked. The morning sun ripped through the split horizon, golden and illuminating below the ceiling of storm. The sea shimmered in the light and I felt the warmth brush my cheeks. I tilted my face up for more.

His cold hands slid from my shoulders. The marrow in the bones of my shark-bitten arm shot with pain: he was gone. My shark god had slipped back into the sea. But the sun was still with me, clearing my head, sharpening my senses, setting my heart to beating again.

And for the first time in twenty-four hours, I had a thought that wasn't about poor little ol' infected me:

If my shark god was real...

...then those psychotic feral carriers were real, too.

And I'd left Ryan and Ben alone.

Hands shaking, I turned to scramble back across the tile rooftop.

Tonya Macalino

lives in Hillsboro, Oregon with her husband and two children. When not working on her latest novel, she runs a handcrafted lotion, cosmetics, and bath company (www.rustlingsage.com). She is an avid collector of folklore and folk history, far too many to fit comfortably within the pages of any given book. To read more of the little gems she unearthed during her research, please visit: www.tonyamacalino.com. For appearances and publishing news, find her on Facebook at www.facebook.com/TonyaMacalino.

Made in the USA
Charleston, SC
02 October 2014